I WOULD
HAUNT YOU
IF I COULD

I WOULD HAUNT YOU IF I COULD

First Edition All Rights Reserved

ISBN: 978-1-988964-26-3

This book is a work of fiction. Any resemblance to actual events or persons—living, dead, or undead—is entirely coincidental.

Undertow Publications. Pickering, ON Canada

Publication history appears at the back of this book.

I WOULD
HAUNT YOU
IF I COULD

SEÁN PADRAIC BIRNIE

UNDERTOW
PUBLICATIONS

For Sarah

Contents

New to It All

My first girlfriend, Niamh, was a scratcher. Saoirse wasn't like that. The first time Niamh asked me to stay the night, she was testing me out. I can see that now, in retrospect. Nothing too scratchy to begin with. "I didn't want to scare you away," she said to me once, with a laugh. "Oh, you couldn't have," I replied, laughing too. At this Niamh tilted her head. "I think we both know that that's not the case," she replied, lowering her voice, which was already an implausibly low and husky voice. "I had to ease you in." I smiled. I didn't argue; I never did argue with Niamh. In retrospect I can see that I was always afraid of losing her, but what good did retrospect ever do for anyone? In retrospect, there's nothing left to do. Understanding always comes too late. In retrospect, I can hear Niamh repeating herself: "Yep, I had to ease you in. You were so… new to it all." Perhaps she wasn't wrong. The morning after that first night together, I noticed the scratches in the bathroom mirror as I brushed my teeth with my index finger. I had forgotten my toothbrush. The scratches were livid. Once, she had made me yell out in pain, a long fingernail catching in the large mole in the middle of my back. I only remembered that then, standing in the bathroom with an index finger smeared with spit and toothpaste. One thing I hadn't told her at that point was that I was, until that night at least, at the antique age of twenty-four, still a virgin. In retrospect, it's obvious that she knew, but she was too kind to say anything about it.

Studying the scratches, I saw that they really were livid. Only one, though, beside the mole, had actually broken the skin, and a little scab had subsequently formed overnight. (I would notice the blood on the sheets when I went back to the bedroom.) The rest were a complex, delicate latticework. There was a kind of precision and an order to them that astounded me. They seemed to glow.

This excited me more than I could say. It still excites me now, in retrospect, after everything.

Things quickly progressed; I developed an aptitude for pain.

A year to the day of the night Niamh had taken my virginity, she ended things.

I was a mess for weeks that became months that became the best part of a year, but I shan't go into that. This story isn't about Niamh. What I will say is this: for years since, I have found myself on occasion in the middle of the night brushing my teeth with an index finger smeared with toothpaste, with no memory of getting out of bed and crossing the landing to the bathroom. Then, awake, but still under the sway of sleep, the objects of the waking world still edged with the clarity and glamour of dreams, I will begin to study the scars on my back, and grow so aroused that my cock hurts and my gut and heart begin to sicken with nostalgia. And some nights, I swear, the scars still seem to glow.

But this is not about Niamh. Saoirse, unlike Niamh, was not a scratcher. She was a biter.

We met three years to the day on which Niamh had broken up with me. There had been others in the interim, but nothing serious; nothing exciting.

In truth, in that time I had thought about Niamh a lot.

In the years since the end of our relationship, she had

begun to get in the way. (As she is in the way now.) I think, in retrospect, that those others could see that, that they must have glimpsed Niamh there, getting in the way, even if they didn't quite know what it was that they were seeing, what the thing was that was getting in the way.

I never asked Saoirse if she could see Niamh's figure hanging around me, getting in the way of things, but I am certain that she could perceive it quite clearly. (She never mentioned it off her own bat; perhaps she was too kind to say.) But one thing I think Saoirse did do was this: she set about getting Niamh out of her way.

So Saoirse was a biter. We laughed about it later on, of course, but the first time Saoirse bit me—really bit me—it was quite a big shock. In those three years since Niamh had left, I suppose my aptitude for pain had declined.

So when Saoirse bit me, I tensed, pulled back, and gave a yelp in a pitch I previously would have considered outside of my vocal range, though I think perhaps it was the shock of it more than the pain itself.

I looked at her and saw the light of the bedside lamp catching in her eyes, little duplicate bulbs beneath worn duplicate shades, and those eyes were full of worry and concern.

"No?" said Saoirse. "Sorry. Oh God, sorry…"

"It's okay," I said. "You just startled me."

"God, I didn't mean to. I should have asked. I mean—"

I stroked her shoulder. "It's okay," I said. "Shh."

"Sorry," she said again, in a small voice, while craning her neck to nuzzle my hand.

"Don't be," I murmured. "I like it."

She looked up.

"You do?" she said, and when I nodded and smiled, she too began to smile.

After that, things quickly progressed, and I rediscovered my aptitude for pain.

Saoirse, too, tried to ease me in. But I was a different person now—Niamh had changed me. So it fell to me to encourage Saoirse, to move things along. Soon, that first bite, which had left deep toothmarks in the flesh of my neck but had not broken the skin, began to seem little more than a nibble. We would laugh about it—about the yelp, about her worry.

But now I knew what Saoirse wanted. I knew what I wanted, too.

Only I had to reassure her. Apparently, her last boyfriend had broken up with her over the issue. It had freaked him out. She had hurt him, by accident. She didn't want to hurt me.

"It's okay," I said. "I have... an aptitude for pain."

She had tried, since that last relationship, to suppress her desire. In the year between that relationship's end and our first encounter, she had seen other people, and had suppressed that desire, and perhaps as a consequence nothing of enduring value had developed with any of these others; nothing had excited her. And she had felt on edge all of the time, panicked, trying to keep the lid on something, on something that would become an unbearable build-up of pressure.

Her specific technique was remarkable. It made Niamh's scratching seem clumsy and unrefined. Because Saoirse never once broke the skin. She has explained it to me, how she does it, but the explanation only begs other questions. Soon enough, I gave up on understanding.

Whether it comes too late, whether it comes at all. Sometimes understanding only gets in the way.

When Saoirse bit me, really bit me, for the second time, it was on my chest, deep into the pectoral muscle. The shock of it this time was something different to the first, a sudden and unexpected flash of pain that made me yelp. It was a cold, numb kind of shock. It was almost an out-of-body thing: I stared, interested but somehow uninvested, as if the body bitten into was not my own. In that moment I had thought *Somehow she has sedated me,* and my thoughts too had acquired a peculiarly distant quality. An iciness seemed to radiate out from the point on my chest. It was not unpleasant.

Teeth clamped on my chest, she looked up at me, and when I smiled she closed her eyes again.

When she let go, I saw how she had left what looked at first like a kind of cavity in my chest, and I felt an overwhelming surge of what might have been elation and what might have been horror. It was a feeling unlike anything I had felt before: a heady, new sensation, as yet unnamed, likely unnameable.

A cavity, but her teeth had not broken the skin. I stared, dumbfounded and panting, as Saoirse smiled up at me. A cavity, a declivity, as if the body was so much putty that might be moulded, not a surface that might be broken but a pliable substance, to be reshaped at will. Then she kissed my chest again, then the taut flesh inside my pelvis, beneath my abdomen, where a scar from surgery I had had as a young teenager remained visible, and then the inside of my left thigh.

Then she said: "Close your eyes."

"It has to be clean," said Saoirse, thinking carefully, the following day. I had exhausted myself trying to make sense of what she had done to me. "You have to make the cut *just so.*"

I nodded as if I understood, as if I could understand.

"If you get it right, there's no blood. It's like nothing tears. It's smooth. If you make the cut just so, the flesh just gives, parting as if it wants to part."

She pursed her lips in thought, then added: "Most people, I don't think they realise how—plastic... how *pliable* they really are..."

"When did you first discover you could do this?" I asked.

She glanced at me, then looked quickly away. "I was twelve or thirteen," she said, frowning. "I don't know."

"How did you find out?"

She blushed suddenly, and I had laughed before I could contain the laughter.

"How?" I said, trying to rein in my desire to tease her. I wanted to know.

I ran my hand through her hair. I held her cheek, her neck.

"Mafubaying," she said, smothering the answer with her shoulder as she pulled back from me. Then finally she laughed, too.

"Sorry, what?"

She gave me a stare.

"Masturbating," she said again, and the stare was an accusation of deliberate obtusity.

"What's so embarrassing about that?"

"Well. Not the masturbating. But afterwards…"

"Afterwards?" It was becoming harder to contain that laughter. I felt a wave of giddiness beginning to build.

Suddenly Saoirse held her right hand up in front of me.

"Can you see this?" she asked, tilting her head, her gaze, which a moment before had flitted around, bouncing off anything that wasn't me, suddenly fixing on mine.

"What?" My laughter had taken on a puzzled, worried note I wished I could take back.

"Can you see the scars? By the knuckles."

I held her wrist and peered closely. Yes, at the base of her index and middle fingers, there were the faintest of scars, encircling the fingers as if they had been severed like clay cut with wire. Scars so faint I wouldn't have seen them had she not told me. Scars so faint I would doubt they were there at all later on. Which you had to want to see to see at all.

"Afterwards," said Saoirse, looking down, taking a breath, "I decided I wanted to taste myself. So I did. My fingers. And something… I don't know…"

"Something?" I said.

"I guess I just started to chew."

She was blushing again.

"And that was when I discovered it."

I turned back to take a sip from the glass of water at the bedside. Putting the glass back down, I pulled myself up into a sitting position and sat back against the headboard of the bed. As I did so, the quilt fell down my upper torso, and I noticed the wound—which was not the word for it, whatever it was—at my chest. Already it had healed. What remained was a weird paleness in the flesh there. Give it a day, I thought, and it might not even look like it had been there at all. Like Saoirse's scars.

Now Saoirse was pulling herself around to face me again. I felt her scrabbling about under the quilt, until her hand clasped my wrist. She pulled my arm out from beneath the quilt and extended my hand from the half-fist it had contracted into. She splayed out my fingers one by one and three of my knuckles clicked in succession as she did so. Then she pulled herself up so she was leaning on her elbow, holding my right hand up by the wrist, looking at me.

"Let me show you," she said, and began to nuzzle my hand.

"Close your eyes."

It has to be clean, she had said. You have to make the cut *just so.*

The motion was so quick, so sudden, so precise. I didn't have the time to be afraid.

I felt a surge of that elation that was not elation. It was a kind of joyous nausea. A kind of voluptuous terror. I felt myself unlatching from myself.

I stared at her in shock and when the shock passed a wave

of discombobulation washed through me with a force that made me think I was about to faint. I did not faint.

Curled up at my side, her body shaped against my own, Saoirse looked up at me. She wasn't smiling—her lips were sealed taut—but I could see a deep satisfaction in her expression. She looked flushed. She was glowing.

I held my hand up and gazed at the stump where my index finger had been. I felt its phantom there, twitching, itching, jerking around. There was no blood.

It has to be clean.

There was no pain. The flesh was smooth, sealed. It wasn't ragged. It didn't even look as though the wound of some years-old amputation had healed. It looked for all the world as if there had never been a finger there at all. And yet I felt it there, twitching.

You have to make the cut just so.

Saoirse laughed through pursed lips. Then she opened her mouth, and I saw the index finger formerly of my right hand bobbing lightly on her tongue. It twitched, as if an electrical current had passed through it. I thought of the legs of dead frogs. I thought of the foot kicking up under the tap of a hammer on a knee. I felt the phantom finger twitch and saw the actual finger twitch in her mouth, after the briefest delay. Perhaps I did faint.

The next thing I knew, she was gripping the tip of the rogue finger between her own thumb and index finger and was carefully withdrawing it from her mouth. She held it up to me and I watched with horrified fascination as it twitched and flopped about in the cup of her palm.

Saoirse closed her hand over it, and I closed my eyes. I couldn't speak.

"Are you okay?" she asked.

I swallowed. My throat was dry.

She stroked my arm. She stroked my hand. I opened my eyes and watched as she clasped my wrist and lifted up my arm. She extended my hand from the half-fist it had contracted into. She splayed out my thumb and three remaining fingers one by one. Then she pulled herself up so that she was leaning on her elbow, holding my right hand up by the wrist, looking at me.

"Close your eyes," said Saoirse.

I felt that iciness again. I felt the flicker of a tongue against a hand that was not my own. I felt her lapping at the wound, and knew that wound was not the word for it, whatever it was, though it was all I had.

When I opened my eyes, the wound was gone. My finger, reinstated, shivered and twitched. Above the knuckle at its base, a faint white scar. I knew it would fade.

"Thank you," said Saoirse. "I love you."

◎

Things quickly progressed. Small and temporary amputations were merely the beginning of our experiments.

Another finger, a thumb. An ear. Other things.

Saoirse could open her mouth very wide. She had a lot of small, sharp teeth. I had not really noticed them before, but now they captivated me. They were very clean. They seemed to shine. Sometimes they seemed to glow.

I felt the phantom twitching of that finger and that thumb and that ear.

Sometimes the things we did were a part of sex, other times they were not. It was always pleasurable, but it was not necessarily a sexual pleasure, at least not for me.

At first, in the beginning, I was worried that other people might find out about us. In spite of my excitement, in spite of my commitment, I felt a kind of hypothetical shame: the shame that I *would* feel, if others discovered what we were doing. But at some point that feeling ebbed away. Nothing else mattered. The shame did not return.

"Watch this," said Saoirse, in bed one morning. I couldn't

have told you what day it was.

She opened her mouth and began to move her lower jaw laterally, out one way and then back the other, out again and then back in a repeating circle. Then she let it fall right open. She resumed the sideways movements, and then after a moment she lifted a hand up and began to increase the force and speed of the movements manually. I heard a click. It was like the sound of a well-made lid unlatched, of something working *just so*. With the four fingers of her right hand clamped behind the front row teeth of her lower jaw, Saoirse pulled her jaw down. It came easily. She let go, and it flopped open, sprung like a trap door.

Fucking hell, I said, or maybe only thought.

Smiling, eyes bright, slack-jawed, Saoirse nodded at me, then nodded at my hand.

Already I could feel a tingling in my arm, a developing deadness, as of pins and needles.

She took my hand. One by one, my fingers disappeared into her mouth. She had to force my hand against one side of her mouth to fit the lower knuckle of my thumb through, but soon that was gone, too. She held my gaze as she worked on me. Slowly, centimetre by centimetre, my whole hand disappeared. Her mouth, I realised, was very cold. I could feel a numbness beginning to permeate my hand. I could feel my own thoughts becoming distant. I could feel myself beginning to unlatch. It was not unpleasurable.

Soon her lips had closed over the top of my ulna bone, over the small ganglion on the topside of my wrist. At last I realised I couldn't feel my hand or forearm at all.

The centimetres became millimetres, until she fell still and closed her eyes.

Close your eyes, said Saoirse, and I don't know how she said it.

Then I felt her make the cut just so.

Soon the amputations were only a part of it. "I want to show you something else," said Saoirse.

"What?" I asked. I felt groggy but not unpleasantly so. More and more our experiments left me feeling stoned. It was a gentle kind of high. Idly I had wondered if something in her saliva, in the way she restored me to myself, healing the wounds that were not really wounds, bore a certain potency, but it was a wondering without urgency. It didn't matter what explained it.

By this point, I think I must have been indoors all week. I had not gone to work, and if my manager had telephoned then my phone had not rung. If my housemates had telephoned, then my phone had not rung. If my mother had telephoned—an unlikely occurrence—then my phone had certainly not rung. Not that I knew where it was; perhaps it had fallen under the bed. It could stay there.

"Do you remember the first time?" she asked.

Somehow the first time now seemed a long time ago.

"Of course."

I waited. She kissed my cheek, my chin, my chest. She stroked my head and played with my hand, pressuring the muscles beneath my elbow so that my fingers danced, a puppeteer manipulating the strings of my body. Then she closed my hand into a fist and kissed the knuckles.

"It's kind of like that," she said.

"Go on."

She sat up beside me.

"Close your eyes."

With the dexterity of a surgeon, she opened me up.

"Thank you," said Saoirse, sometime later that day.

The striated pattern of scars on my chest, above my heart, reminded me of fat marbling beef.

"I love you. I love you so much."

◎

It was some time after this that we had the closest thing that we ever had to an argument. Later, I would worry that I had made too much of it. I had over-reacted. Had I not led her to believe that such things were okay? Later, afterwards, I would ruminate on this, and on other things, on everything, until the frenetic questions whirling in my head made me incapable of sleep. Still later on, I would wonder if that first bite, that nibble, had really been an accident after all. Perhaps it had been deliberate. Perhaps she had been testing me out.

One night, I couldn't tell you when, what time, what night of the week it was, what week of the month or month of the year, I awoke to the sense of that radiating coldness spreading through my lower leg.

I lay very still, motionless in that soothing stoner repose, until I realised what was happening, and with what survival instinct I retained undulled, pulled myself violently back.

Saoirse gave a groan in shock.

I pulled myself up into a sitting position, falling back against the headboard of the bed, dragging Saoirse up the mattress with me, grunting and then retching.

Shhh, she said, and I don't know how she said it, for her lips were clamped around the middle of my right calf, and I could not feel the foot.

Shhh.

"What the fuck are you doing?" I said. "What the fuck are you doing?"

Millimetre by millimetre, centimetre by centimetre, Saoirse withdrew.

She lay recovering at the foot of the bed, panting, scowling down at the sheets.

"You could have really hurt me," she said, and her voice was peculiarly flat and affectless.

I laughed suddenly. It was a jarring sound. "Excuse me?"

She looked up. For a moment her eyes seemed unfocused,

before her gaze fixed on me. I saw a coldness there, in that gaze, before it changed again, in what looked to me like a calculating way, suddenly filling with what looked like worry and concern, but somehow over-egged, an affectation of each.

Saoirse sighed; her head nodded forward and her shoulders slumped.

"I'm sorry," she said. "I thought—No. It doesn't matter what I thought." She looked up at me again. She tilted her head slightly and started to frown.

"I thought you liked it. I thought it was okay."

"I did like it. Do like it. But not like that."

She nodded, pursing her lips in thought. Then she grimaced. "Can you forgive me?" she asked, and if I had not glimpsed that coldness in her gaze a moment before I would have bought the worry and concern in her eyes hook, line, and sinker, and would have said anything to make things okay.

Saoirse pulled herself up the bed and then lay down at my side.

I didn't know what to say.

"I'm sorry," she said. "I love you. I didn't mean to hurt you. I'm such an idiot."

A moment later I realised she had started to cry.

Maybe the shock of that violation had brought me to my senses, because I began to worry about other things again. Reasonable things. My job, for one, though actually I didn't need to worry about that, because it wasn't my job anymore. The side effects of what we were doing. The scars did not bother me, but were there long-term effects? I had no idea. Saoirse didn't seem to understand the question.

"It's probably good for you," she said with a laugh. "Think of it as extreme osteopathy. I should charge by the hour."

Since our argument, I had tried very hard to make things okay. I think Saoirse was trying, too. But her laughter seemed somehow forced and inappropriate. It jarred.

There was something in the way.

Over the following weeks, we danced around it, but we both knew that something had changed. Once, drunk, Saoirse asked me if I trusted her. I said that I did. But I knew that she no longer trusted me in quite the same way.

"There's something else we haven't tried," said Saoirse, later that night, slurring a little.

We were drinking in bed, which is where we often wound up.

"Something else I haven't removed yet." She grinned. "Don't worry," she said. "I promise I'll give it back. Do you trust me?"

◎

Two years to the day of the first night she had bitten me, Saoirse ended things.

I was a mess for weeks that became months that became the best part of a year. It was only really after two years had passed that I began to gain any kind of perspective on what had gone on between us. By that time, I was seeing Kristen, who I had met a year into my new job at the county council, and who had spent more or less most of that year waiting for me to be ready for her.

"I could see there was something in the way," said Kristen, a few months in. Then she smiled. She has a beautiful smile, which reminds me of Niamh's a little. Most of the time I try not to think about it. "I guess I just had to move it out of the way."

We were drinking in bed. Kristen lay in the crook of my arm, her glass of wine on the bedside table, and she was trailing a fingertip over my chest.

She stopped at my heart.

"Is that a scar?" she said.

"I don't know," I lied. "I've always had it. And here too."
I raised my hand, to show the pale ring around my index finger.

"Weird!" she said, and laughed.

I realised I had been holding my breath. Kristen hadn't noticed.

Suddenly she moved, thinking of something.

"My little brother was such a terror, you know."

"I don't know."

"You wouldn't think it now, but he was. This just made me think of that. One time when he was off school sick, he went into my room. I was into Barbie dolls then, Sindy dolls, all that shite. I had quite a few of them."

"I don't believe you."

"I know, right. But I did. When I got home from school I found them out all over my room. He'd ripped the arms and legs and heads all off, anything that came off, and had put them back together again all mixed-up and the wrong way round."

I thought of something Saoirse had said to me once, and shivered.

Most people, I don't think they realise how—*pliable*... how plastic they really are...

I realised I was holding my breath again. Kristen sat up and turned to lift her glass of wine from the bedside table.

"Did you put them back the right way round?" I asked, just to say something.

"I did, but it didn't work. They wouldn't stick. They kept falling out. And that's how I grew out of Barbie dolls."

Last night I found myself standing in the bathroom under the flickering glow of faulty halogen bulbs, and I had no memory of getting out of bed and crossing the landing to the bathroom. It was the middle of the night. Awake, but still under the sway of sleep, the objects of the waking world still edged with the clarity and glamour of dreams, I began to study the scars on my back, and the scars that striated my joints and which showed, very faintly, over several of my organs, marbling my body like fat in beef, and not for the first time I felt as though Saoirse had never quite put everything back. Not for the first time I felt like something was missing, and I wondered about the time I had awoken to find her doing what she did to me, and whether there were other times, occasions on which I had not woken. By day most of the time the scars are too pale to see, but at night they acquire that clarity of dreams and seem to glow. I think of that coldness I saw in Saoirse's gaze and feel it radiating inside of me, its icy locus in my chest, its radial edges playing at my scalp and in my fingertips and my toes.

I have yet to see either Saoirse or Niamh again. The past is a dream. Sometimes I think I never knew them at all.

When I went back to bed, I found Kristen crying in her sleep, though when I woke her she could not tell me what the dream had been about.

Sometimes understanding doesn't come at all.

Out of the Blue

After the funeral, after the wake, after everything, Dad came home.

He just turned up one day out of the blue, wearing the old navy-blue suit in which we had buried him that April, waiting in the path for someone to answer the door. He hadn't rung the bell. He was just standing there with his eyes closed, hands hanging loosely at his sides. It was not like him. It was a sunny day.

"Dad," I said, after regaining control of my jaw, and already I felt overcome by an insidious unreality, a stiff and quite contained insanity. Displaced from myself, I saw myself as if from afar, and in the very far distance I could hear a person screaming, and that person was me.

I had recognised him through the translucent glass of what, until that April, had for forty years been his own front door: the shape of his shoulders, his silhouette. I had recognised the cut and colour of the suit in which we had buried him, even through the glass. I had known—*known*: in my bones, in my gut—that it was him, even though he seemed to be slumping a little, and in life he had never slumped, not even a little, not even at the end. He was the sort of man who pushed his chest out. Who kept his chin up. Who went to the gym once a week, even in his eighties. He still hadn't replied to me. "Jesus," I said.

I peered at him, expecting some trick or prank to reveal itself on that July morning, expecting him to unthread before me like an image in woven smoke. At the same time I felt the currency of my expectations depreciate. I expected any minute now to find myself rolling over in bed, waking up, but I did not wake up. Instead I laid my hand on his shoulder and felt the fabric of his jacket. It was the same jacket. My hand did not pass through him as if he were a hologram cast by concealed projectors, as I had expected it to. He was quite insistently tangible. But still he had not opened his eyes. For some reason it was this fact that bothered me most of all. Why wouldn't he open his eyes?

From down the street I heard the neighbour's cat give a pained *miaowww*, and a car clatter over the speed bump in the road beyond the unkempt front garden, and two teenagers amble past chatting and laughing, sharing the earbuds of a smartphone, but all of these sounds now belonged to another world. A circle had been drawn around me, around us, enclosing us in and keeping them out; I was here, in the doorway with my father, where time had congealed, and the teenagers and the cat and the traffic were over there, in a world in which things like this simply did not occur. A matter of yards had become a gulf.

I swallowed. I felt his cheek with my hand and was shocked by the coldness of his skin. I'm not sure what I expected. Maybe make-up, on warm flesh. Maybe silicon or finely sculpted wax. I narrowed my eyes further, tilting my head as I examined him, trying to discern traces of make-up, the subtle edges where prosthetics met skin, the line of the zip concealed in the fabric of the monster suit, but there was no make-up, no prosthetics, no zips, nor any monster suit. It was just Dad come home. Taking a step backwards, I stumbled on the doormat, nearly falling to the floor.

Regaining my balance, I looked at him again, and laughed.

"Hello," I said, for want of anything better to say, and again he didn't respond. Then I turned quickly and went inside.

I was talking to myself in the living room when I realised that he hadn't followed me through. I went back out into the hall to find him still standing there on the path with his eyes closed.

"Dad," I said. "Come in."

At that he came forward, moving slowly down the hall.

I wondered then was he a vampire, had he needed inviting in, was that how this thing would soon be working out, but then I considered the sunlight, bright and warm on that summer morning, twenty degrees already and sure to rise, and resolutely, insistently ordinary, falling on the long grass of the front lawn, and discounted the idea. He didn't look like a vampire, or at least he did not look to me how vampires are supposed to look. That person I had heard screaming in the distance began to chuckle.

"In here," I said, gesturing, and Dad followed me through, before stopping in the centre of the living room.

I watched him with a strange dissociated amusement, because there was an oddness to the way he moved, as if, instead of just walking down the hall, the complete action had first to be broken down into chunks, and these chunks in turn broken down into smaller chunks, and each chunk and every subsidiary chunk of which it was comprised carefully executed in its turn, one by one, step by step.

"Take a seat," I said, and he seemed to pause, caught between the various options of seat he might take, before moving to his old leather chair in the corner and sitting down when I pointed and said, "there." He sunk into the chair as if gravity pressed down on him with unusual force. It was not like him, to sit like that.

"Well," I said, trying to think of something to fill the silence, "this was unexpected. Can I... get you anything?"

He didn't reply.

Already, of course, I was thinking through the implications of his return. It would present certain logistical difficulties, such as explaining it to anyone, and to everyone, or trying to keep it a secret. Each of these options struck me as impossible. At the very least I would have to explain it to Annie, my partner. Annie was finally pregnant, and we had, after much discussion, made the decision to move into the house, something I had been reluctant to do for a whole host of reasons but which we had decided was the wisest course of action, at least in financial terms. It would get us out of our little flat and onto the housing ladder, even the lowest rungs of which had always seemed out of reach, and in any case it was a bad time to sell. In his last year or so, Dad, a fastidiously tidy man, had let the building fall into disrepair, and we had decided to overhaul the whole place, put in a new kitchen and bathroom, redesign the living room and redecorate both the master bedroom, the smaller bedroom, and the box room on the middle landing by the loo. There was an attic and I had plans to convert that into an office, a prospect that rather excited me, so I could work at home if I ever managed to go freelance. There was a shed, full of rusting tools shrouded in spiderwebs and cluttered, dusty work benches, which we would have to clear out in time, when we had the time, and I doubted we would ever have the time. There was a cellar, but I can't say I had the mental energy to even begin thinking about that. It had been a lot to take on but Annie hadn't wanted to wait: when we moved, she was twelve weeks pregnant, and things were going well, and she was the sort of person who always needs a project. If, after all of that, I still wasn't happy living there, then we could sell.

And now, it seemed, we would have to work around Dad. Perhaps we had been getting ahead of ourselves. I wondered what his return meant for our ownership of the property. I would have to talk to his bank and his solicitors. I would have to contact his GP. I would have to do all sorts of things, all of them absurd. Then my thoughts turned from what I had to do to what I had done, what I had seen. I remembered the shock of seeing him laid out in the funeral parlour for the first time after we had said goodbye, after the doctors had withdrawn support, after the grim monotone of the ECG machine had fallen silent, his body so utterly reduced, made waxen, like a very good effigy made from photographs by someone who had never met him in person and so had never seen how he would fill a room, command an audience, charm children and women and other men, never felt his force of personality, and so had made this thing, this bad facsimile of my father lying there in a suit that had belonged to my father, to be put in a grave under the name of my father, but which never could truly have *been* my father, not really—no: because, irrationally, I knew that my father had not died. It was a very calm, perfectly reasonable voice that told me this. That told me what I already knew, that my father had not and in some sense could not die. These were the stupid, secret things I thought at that time. That that voice, equanimous and insane, quietly insisted on. I never confessed them to anyone. Death is scandalous, absurd, and obscene. We manage it carefully, so as to ensure that its taint will not transfer on to us, the still-living and the not-yet-dead, even though it is always within us already, like an incubating virus, like planned obsolescence. I remembered the shock of seeing that waxen fake in the casket. His blank expression had borne the faintest trace of surprise, as if he was rather startled to have discovered himself dead, and of distaste. It was that thing that had arrived at his home that morning, out of the blue. He looked like he had been sucking on a lemon. That made me smile, because Dad hated lemons. Thinking of lemons, of banks and doctors and home renovations, my mind boggled at the things I would have to do.

I went through into the kitchen, poured a glass of water, downed it, poured another one and downed that too, then poured a third. Then I counted to ten with my eyes closed.

"Okay," I said, and went back into the living room, expecting this comforting nightmare, if it was a nightmare, to have segued back into the reasonable waking normal quotidian ordinary mundane regular sensical world I had blithely inhabited until five minutes before. Maybe I'd just had a moment, was all. It can happen.

But Dad was still sitting in his chair. His eyes were still closed. He was still wearing his suit jacket, although the tie, a darker blue just a shade or two shy of black, had come loose. His hands were lying limply on his thighs. He was expressionless, except for that faint hint of surprise and distaste.

"Okay," I said, and started to laugh, and I laughed until the laughter convulsed into tears, which startled me, because I hadn't cried at his funeral. Through tears, I saw the time on the clock above the mantelpiece, a clock my mother had chosen before she had left my father, a long time ago, and started to panic; any moment now, Annie was due.

◎

I remember that first, halting conversation with Annie like it was yesterday. Because the second you let another person into a situation like this, the second you begin to talk about it, it becomes real: it's a fateful moment, and it retains a crystalline presence in my memories of the early days of this thing. She had finished work early that afternoon and was removing her reflective trouser clips from her calves, her bicycle leant against the wall, when I saw her through the same glass I had first seen Dad. She was crouching down, rifling through her pannier and swearing under her breath, when she saw me opening the door.

"Oh," she said, standing. "You're in. I think I left my keys at work." She smiled and leant over to give me a kiss.

I tried to smile back at her as she pulled away but it didn't feel very convincing; a glimmer of something in her eyes suggested that she had noticed that something was amiss. I found myself acutely aware that she was on the other side of this thing, for now: that once I told her, she would cross to my side of it, and never go back.

"I'll take this," I said, and wheeled her bike through into the hall. I gripped the handlebars tightly, watching my knuckles turn white.

"Thanks."

"Good timing," I said, which was an outrageous lie. "I've just put the kettle on."

"Fab. I'm dying for the loo, but I'll be down in a sec."

I froze as she went up the stairs, only relaxing when I heard the bathroom door close and the lock slide into place behind her. The box room was next to the bathroom. The door was shut and Dad was in there, standing by the window with his eyes closed. From the back he looked as if he was gazing down into the garden, lost in a moment of contemplation, but he wasn't gazing down into anything. Nothing I had said to him had managed to persuade him to open his eyes. And there was something else I had noticed only belatedly, with horror, and on which leaning in I had listened closely to check, and the sense of infestation that had rippled through me then, as I had stood so close to him that ordinarily I would have felt the heat of his body on my cheek, was indescribable, but that thing that I had noticed was this: his silence. His utter, unfathomable silence.

Some time ago, I read about the composer John Cage, who had gone to the University of Chicago to see, or rather to hear, something called an anechoic chamber, a room made to absorb the reflection of all sound waves. In that silence, Cage, to his puzzlement, had heard two sounds, one of low pitch and one of high, and when he had asked the sound engineer from the University about the sounds, the engineer had replied that the low sound had been the circulation of his blood in his body, and the high sound the noise of his nervous system.

My cheek millimetres from my father's cheek, I heard neither high pitch or low, neither from my own body or from my father's, nor even the faintest weakest whisper of his breathing. In that moment the house too might have fallen silent, might have been holding its breath, might have become anechoic. I had stood up, gazing down into the untended garden that my father was not also gazing down into, and for a moment I remembered playing on that lawn as a child while Dad worked in the shed, and I closed my eyes. At that moment, in the box room, I felt supremely alone. Never mind that Annie was due. Never mind that my father was there. In the darkness behind my eyelids, I saw nothing, and heard nothing; I heard neither the circulation of my blood, nor the high pitch of my nervous system at work, nor the usual quiet creaking of the house. That circle around me, around my father and I, was drawing tighter.

I was so startled to find him still stood there beside me when I opened my eyes that I almost actually jumped.

I heard that chuckling.

Then I hurried from the room, closing the door behind me as I went. It seemed that this thing would not be going away.

◎

"Stephen was funny about it, of course, but fuck him. I mean, really, if he wants to…"

It was hard to tune into what she was saying to me.

"And then—"

"Annie," I said, more abruptly than I had intended to say it, halting the flow of her complaint. Stephen was her manager. Fuck him, I thought. She looked at me with wide eyes over the rim of her cup, waiting for me to speak. She slurped a little bit as she drank the tea.

I closed my eyes.

"What is it?"

I opened my eyes. "There's… something," I said, and those two words were absurdly difficult to expel from my mouth. "Something I need to tell you."

"…go on."

"Something I need to show you."

"Okay."

I realised I had stood up and started pacing around. I tried to stand still for a second, to get a grip of myself, but failed. For a moment I saw myself as she must have seen me: about to tell her that I had been to the GP and received a terrible and unexpected diagnosis; that I had been cheating on her; that I was in trouble with loan sharks or credit card companies, that I had been gambling again; that I was leaving her.

She put the cup down on the saucer, which was sitting precariously on the wooden arm of the sofa. She pursed her lips, waiting for me to explain.

"Upstairs," I said, then turned and walked out of the room.

After a moment, delayed by something or other, she followed me. She was still on the other side of this thing.

"In the box room," I said.

She was on the cusp.

No one ever reacts how you expect them to react. That's one thing I've learned.

Annie's mother died when Annie was seven years old. The year before, her pet rabbit, Victor, had been savaged by a fox or foxes that had broken into its hutch in the garden. Maybe she had left the hutch unlatched, she didn't know, but whatever had happened, Annie knew that Victor's death had been her fault. It was on *her*. That was something she had understood with frightening certainty. And a year later, more obscurely, but with that same awful certainty, her mother's death would also be on her, would also be her fault, would also feel like a savage rebuke for some unfathomable infraction. As if she had left her mother's hutch unlatched, and maybe, secretly, consciously or otherwise, had wanted the foxes to get her. Maybe her mother had done something to anger her. Maybe

she had even deserved it, according to the logic of some child-
ish grudge. Annie had known, aged seven years old, that she
wasn't innocent.

These early experiences had combined to form a height-
ened sensitivity to the facts and business of death, a peculiarly
intense horror in the face of its rituals and bureaucracy, as well
as its representation in books and films. She couldn't abide
violent movies. She couldn't stand going to funerals, and it
was only with my support that she had managed to attend
the funeral of her own father two years before the events I am
now describing. She had struggled to visit him in hospital.
She had struggled to deal with the paperwork and solicitors and funeral directors, those smooth professionals in the
business of mortality, in its orchestration and its handling, in
its packaging and despatch, in its sanitisation and its softly-
spoken commercial exploitation. She even struggled with
going to see the doctor on her own account, in case someone
died in the waiting room while she was there.

But beyond this she entertained no other phobias or
superstitions. She was normally such a calm, sensible person,
with vastly more common sense and practical know-how in
the business of life than I; no one ever would have guessed.
"It's like I thought I was normal for a while," she once said to
me. "And then I was so rudely awoken. Other people don't do
this, do they?"

So I was shocked, to say the least, when it was not that
other Annie who responded to what was waiting in the box
room, but the practical sensible reasonable competent woman
she appeared to be the rest of the time. Perhaps by that point
I was getting used to the feeling of shock: a distant thing, to
observe, rather than to be flooded by.

"Hello, John," she had said in wonder, peering closely at
my father's expression of surprise and distaste, as if somehow
she had expected this. As if it made sense to her.

◎

Later: "Okay, we need to work out how to deal with this."

"How are we supposed to deal with this?" I said, laughing, before cutting the laugh short because its strained high pitch carried an hysterical edge. I was pacing the living room again. I was pretty sure I would soon be scoring grooves in the carpet if I didn't stop, but I didn't care.

"Look, just think. So he hasn't opened his eyes."

"No."

"He hasn't said anything."

"Nope."

"He doesn't respond to anything you say, except to go where you tell him to."

"Nope. I mean yes. Exactly."

"Right."

"He doesn't..."

"He doesn't what?"

"He doesn't seem to smell..."

I hadn't thought of this, but she was right. "Nope. He doesn't smell of anything." It was one of the weird things I had noticed, among all the other weird things, along with his silence and his low body temperature, without really realising it: that he really didn't smell of anything. Not of morgues or funeral parlours or of a body gone cold. Not of coffins or of the earth, nor of his own smell in life: talcum powder, Dove soap, too much aftershave.

"If he was... he would..."

"Decomposing," I said, saying the word she did not want to say. "If he was decomposing, he would smell." I laughed at that, giving into the hysteria, feeling the carpet and the floorboards and the house as such give way a little beneath me, just a little, as if wood and masonry could suddenly vacillate. "He's been dead for four months," I said.

"Are you—"

"Yes, I'm sure he's dead. There's no pulse. I checked. And his face."

I had placed two fingers on his neck and felt nothing. I had rolled up his sleeve and placed them on his wrist and felt nothing. Then, and this had not been easy, I had lifted up his eyelids and peered into the empty colourless marbles of his eyes.

"Every time I go back into that room, I expect him to be gone. But he's always just there."

Annie was nodding, but she wasn't listening to me.

"Shall we… call an ambulance?"

I groaned, imagining the circus that would ensue, and imagining that circus I realised something with quite shocking force that I had not yet admitted to myself: that I did not want to call an ambulance. That I did not want to call his solicitors. That I did not want to tell anyone or involve anyone else in this strange business. In telling Annie, I had let someone else into the intimacy of a thing that should have remained between my father and I, and had felt a palpable, bodily wrongness in admitting her into it, but I could not see how I might have done otherwise. In the box room, I had pulled the blinds when it had occurred to me that the neighbours might see him standing at the window, gazing down into the garden through closed eyes.

I didn't want to tell anyone and I didn't want to do anything, and now I wished I could un-tell Annie, who had paused, frowning, before looking at me, and after a moment I think that she recognised this, too. And she knew how stubborn I could be.

For that first week, we kept him in the box room. We kept the blinds drawn. I would visit him now and then, which is how I thought of it, *visiting Dad*, but I never stayed for long. His body gave off no heat, and I found that if I spent too much time in the room with him an unpleasant chill would worm its way into my muscles and my bones: psychosomatic, no doubt, but no less insistent for that. Sometimes I would talk to him, and on those first few occasions I think I still somehow expected him to respond. Every time, as I had said to Annie, I expected to find the small room empty, and in a sense it was: he was like a void, an abscess in the house, a black hole sucking worlds and galaxies into its yawning maw, given the shape and likeness of a man.

Dad occupied that room and he occupied my thoughts. Wherever I went, I was thinking of him. I was distracted at work, would lose the thread of my thoughts, become lost in conversations, become suddenly disoriented in the performance of day-to-day activities, in supermarkets and newsagents, at the sink in the kitchen washing up, or down in the garden mowing the overgrown lawn, watched through drawn blinds and closed eyes by my father up in that room. Driving home one evening, I nearly ploughed into a car stopped at the roundabout off the A27 ahead. I don't know if the inhabitants of that vehicle actually noticed: the driver must have, but she did not signal to me, did not shout or gesture. There were children, I saw, two girls and a boy, in the three back seats. I could have killed them. I could have killed myself. Dad only seemed to respond to me, and to simple commands: go here, stand there. I wondered what he would do if I died. I wondered if I would come back, too. I wondered if those children would have come back.

One Saturday, three or four weeks after Dad's return, Annie called to me from the dining room, and when I came through, carrying a cup of coffee in my hand, she asked me to take a seat at the table with her, and I knew more or less what was coming my way.

She took a deep breath and then looked at me. She seemed to study me for a moment, a long moment, before beginning to frown as she cast around for the words of what she had to say. "This won't do," she said at last, and part of me wanted to say *what won't do?* with feigned and pointed innocence, but I bit my tongue.

"Okay," I said, taking a sip of the coffee, which I promptly spat back into the cup.

"What?" Annie asked, sitting back in surprise.

"It's cold." I wiped my mouth. "Stone cold. I mustn't have boiled the kettle. Shit." I must have filled the whole cafetière with cold water, having waited for a kettle switched off at the plug to boil, and then decided that it had boiled in any case.

She passed me a tissue from the box of tissues on the chest of drawers behind her, and I dabbed at my mouth, then the spillage on the table.

"This won't do," she said again, very carefully, while seeming to study the lifeline on her palm. Then she looked up at me. "I know how this is for you. But it won't."

I thought: You do not know how this is for me. You do not know how this is for me. You do not know how this is for me. You do not know how this is for me. I wasn't even sure that I knew how it was for me. "Well, what do you expect me to do?"

"My sister came over today."

"Oh?"

"I haven't seen her in weeks. She was wondering why. Apparently I've been very distant."

I nodded as if I agreed. I was happy for Jessica to be distant. I was happy for her to be tremendously distant.

"The whole time she was here," she continued, beginning to frown again, "I was terrified, I was terrified she would go into the box room."

"Did she?"

She gave me a sudden look, then looked away. "Of course not. But she could have, at any time. And anyone could, at any time. If we ever have any guests."

"I'll put a lock on the door."

"Well, I thought about that, but the thing is, she'll notice it. She'll try that door instead of the toilet door, being nosey, then she'd say she got the two confused, but really she would be snooping around, because that's what she's like. And a locked door—she wouldn't let a thing like that go. She'd want to know." She looked at me again. "She wouldn't let it go, believe me."

"Then tell her we locked it just to keep her out. Tell her to piss off."

Annie's expression concisely conveyed what she thought of this suggestion.

"Well, where?" I said. "What do you suggest?"

"I don't know. The shed?"

"The neighbours would see us. Mrs Wallace is always fucking watching everything from her window. She would see. And she'd call the police."

"What about the attic?"

I pursed my lips. "It's a tip."

"We could clear it out."

"Yes. I was going to turn it into an office."

"Oh for fuck's sake. We need to move him. Do you understand? We can't just have him there all the time. We need to move him. If you won't call... I don't know—if you won't call whoever the fuck it is who is supposed to deal with such things, then you need to move him. Because he cannot stay in there. Do you understand? You need to move him."

I was nodding again. "Okay," I said. "Okay. I'll begin clearing the attic tomorrow."

Annie smiled. "Thank you. But let's begin tonight. Jess is coming over tomorrow."

I groaned, cursing inwardly, but we started on the attic that evening.

◎

When someone close to you dies and the most private aspects of their life evaporate with the cessation of their minds, other parts spill out into the world, and it falls to you to gather those things, moving through the hidden spaces of their life, suddenly and rudely privy to some of their innermost mysteries.

Dad's mystery, the one that did not evaporate like morning dew as the new day progressed, was not especially interesting: it was not salacious or incriminating, nor, for anyone else, particularly outlandish. Nevertheless, its discovery came as a shock to me, the memory of which has an air of quaintness now, given the shocks—the word is scarcely adequate—then still to come.

Dad was a tidy-freak and the attic, I discovered late that April, had been his dirty secret. The precision and order of the way he had kept the rest of the house up until his sudden decline had hinged, somehow, on the chaos that flourished in secret above our heads. I had already been up there a couple of times, but Annie had not, and now she craned her neck as she peered around in wonder, her head poking through the hatch, and said "My *word...*" as she took it all in.

"You did want to start tonight," I said.

"Yep."

The room was full of cardboard boxes in teetering stacks and bin bags, suitcases and carry cases in barely ordered piles, some of which almost reached the rafters. Stood under the weak light of the bare bulb, I felt overcome. Annie's wonder at the sight of it all began to irritate me, so I said, "Could you go and get some bin bags?"

"Yep," she said again, and her head vanished from the hatch, and I was alone, surrounded by the overwhelming accumulated stuff of my father's life. By that point, the rest of the house had begun to feel like it belonged to us: enough had changed that it was on its way to becoming our own. But here, in the attic, above everything, was a space that remained resolutely my father's space, even if in all its clutter and mess it formed the perfect opposite of his public self.

Annie's head re-appeared through the hatch. She held a roll of bin bags up in one hand. "Here," she said, smiling, and for some reason her smile angered me.

"Change of plan," I said.

"Oh?"

"We can clear it another time. It'll take forever. He can come up here now. I'll make some room. Could you get me one of the dining table chairs, though?"

"Sure."

Alone again, I felt the tug of reverie as I surveyed my father's secret hoard, and realised that I was bothered by that sense that I was violating his privacy, because I knew that he would not want me here. He would not want me to see the chaos here, because in public he was always tidy, trim, poised and proud, and my presence in the attic would have felt like an invasion. That pride was always quick to anger, and the fact that I was allowing my partner to see it all would have brought him to the boil. Alone, I noticed the guilt in me, a dispassionate noticing, as if the feeling belonged to another person, and at the same time I felt the tension in me, as if I was braced for something, the pre-storm anticipation of an argument that would never break.

The top of a wooden chair poking through the hatch startled me out of what had become a trance.

"Great," I said, which seemed a daft thing to say. "Thanks." I took the chair in one hand and then, after a moment's thought, a moment's sudden hesitation, as if putting it down was somehow a fateful decision, placed it in the middle of the room under the dangling bulb.

I looked at the empty chair, at its hard shadow falling on the floorboards beneath it. Under the hard light the shadow looked heavy; I wondered were the beams capable of bearing the weight of a shadow such as that.

"Okay," I said.

Annie's voice came from the landing, though it seemed to reach me from a much greater distance away: "How," she said, "...are we going to do this?"

I shook myself, pulling myself free of that reverie, then clambered down through the hatch. Annie held the step ladder as I descended, and I did my best not to look over the banister down into the stairwell and the drop to the ground floor below.

"I don't know," I said. "We'll see. He just tends to go where I tell him to. I don't know if he can climb. We'll just have to try."

The notion of hauling the deadweight of his body up into the attic filled me with horror.

"We'll just have to try," I said again.

The next day, Jessica came, and I kept myself busy sorting things out. When they sat in the garden so Jess could smoke, I started sorting through the things in the attic in the company of my father sitting on the chair. I found myself apologising to him, but telling him that it had to be done: that I had to go through his things.

"I know what will cheer you up," I said, turning to look at him with a smile. "I'll bring your chair up here." Neither Annie or I had ever taken to it: it was positioned at a slightly odd angle for watching television, and always seemed slightly uncomfortable, slightly cramped, slightly awkward to sit in for any length of time, but it had been Dad's chair, its old leather worn through, and maybe that was the point. "I reckon I could get it through the hatch," I said. When I lifted it to test its weight, I was surprised by how light it was.

Progress was slow. I needed to clear out the mess, but unpacking anything only seemed to expand it. Moving one object dislodged a dozen others: photo albums in shoe boxes, correspondence with banks and solicitors going back decades, darts trophies, snooker trophies, biographies of sportsman whose names and faces I only dimly recognised, piles of old clothes, white shirts and brown trousers and a pink Fred Perry, the first and only computer Dad had owned, an Amiga, the dust cover still wrapped around the monitor, with a box of pristine floppy disks; and a plastic bag full of unidentifiable cables, Christmas decorations, old certificates from his job, boxes of rum, a box of two dozen vinyl LPs, a box of my mother's jewellery. That last thing brought me up short.

When Annie and her sister came back indoors, I went outside, and started poking through the junk in the shed.

The weeks went by. Annie grew big. My father's house, all of it except the attic, was soon overwritten with the detail of our own lives, becoming our own home, day by day. I was surprised to find myself realising that Annie had been right, that this had been a good idea. We decorated the box room, painting the walls a pastel yellow before changing our minds and repainting it green, replacing the old blinds with newer, better blinds, and installed a cot, the assembly of which had flummoxed me until Annie had taken over, glanced at the instructions, and then gotten on with it.

Jessica's visits, once rare, increased in frequency. I finished emptying the shed as the late summer gave way to autumn. I got a man in to repair the door and a section of the roof. I removed the old work benches, disassembling them in the garden, a process I found rather more enjoyable than my attempted assembly of the cot, then drove their splintered carcasses to the tip on Wilson Avenue.

It began to feel as if Jess had moved in with us. She never, so far as I was aware, actually stayed the night, but sometimes I could have sworn that she was there after I went to bed and again in the morning when I got up for work. I kept my resentment in check. Annie liked having her around, I knew, and Jess knew that I knew that, and weaponised it. I told myself that after the birth, after a week or two, she would be on her way. But if Annie needed her there, for now, then I could accept that. I didn't have much choice.

It made for a slow winter.

Annie went into labour one morning in January: seven hours later, at 15:04, our daughter, still nameless, arrived in the world, changing everything, as children do. Nothing prepares you for that upheaval.

But this isn't the story of Hannah, as we would eventually name her, or the new life her arrival would make for us in the house that had for so long been my father's home. A life that had started with the smoothest of births soon encountered the difficulties that would define its earliest years. As that life progressed, through sleepless nights and health visitor visits, doctor's appointments, hospital appointments, medical tests and the awful waiting for test results, Dad remained in the attic, sitting in his chair, unchanged through everything, oblivious to the lives unfolding below him. But to say that, I realise, to say that he was sitting there, is to misconstrue the truth of it. He was not sitting there: he was seated there. He was not the active subject of a sentence, but its object, even if it remained impossible for me to think of him as such.

Now and then I still visited him. I still talked to him. When Jess came over, or when I needed some time alone, I would climb back up into the attic and continue tidying. For a long time I did not know what it was that I was doing.

Hannah stabilised. Her condition improved. The months went by.

Hannah thrived.

Now and then, Annie would gently try to raise the topic of my father. "We should do something," she would say, and I would find a way of gently shutting the conversation down, agreeing in principle and then growing vague on the specifics.

One day in April, three months after Hannah's second birthday and a week before the anniversary of my father's death, I realised that I had finished the job: all the junk, the tat, the crap and stuff, the boxes and cases and bin bags, the hoarded treasure and trash of my father's life was gone. Several journeys by car out to the tip over that last year had seen to the bulk of it, and then bin bags for the rubbish collection and charity shops had seen to the rest. A few things I kept. There are always a few things.

Dad sat in his chair, in the empty attic, under the harsh light of that bare bulb.

I had finished hoovering around him, and as I unplugged the hoover I surveyed the space, and thought the thought I had convinced myself I was not truly thinking, picturing that room above our house as I wanted it to look: with a desk where I could work, and softer lighting, and rugs, and bookshelves, and my own chair in which to read and doze as the radio murmured to itself, and maybe a sideboard with a kettle and a small fridge containing milk and other essential supplies.

I looked at my watch. It was ten past two. Annie didn't know I was home: I had called in sick especially, having to all appearances departed for work as usual, before doubling back to the house once I knew partner and daughter would be gone. Ten past two. That gave me a couple of hours, which would be plenty of time.

I had seen the ambulance take Mrs Wallace to hospital the day before: a fall, her son had told me over the garden wall—painful—a broken hip—she was beside herself...

If she goes, I had thought, with a cruelty that had startled me, *I hope she doesn't come back.*

"Dad," I said, "I need you to stand up for me."

My father stood. If only in life he had been so biddable.

"Come to the hatch. Over here."

He stepped toward the edge. I had clambered down onto the top rungs of the ladder, and was standing up through the opening, doing my best not to look down into the stairwell below: heights have never delighted me.

Earlier that day, I had tried lifting him, to make sure that I could do it if I needed to. I am not especially strong. I run, but I don't work out. And lifting a dead person is like lifting a sleeping person: they do nothing to help. But I had built myself up to the challenge, and in the centre of the attic, I had lifted my father up from his seated position on the chair, and he was heavier than I could have imagined. "I thought you were supposed to get lighter when you died," I said to him. "What, have you got rocks in your pockets?" There was no chance I would be carrying him down, like a drowsy child given a fireman's lift to bed, and maybe it was just as well. I found myself laughing as I imagined the tenor of his complaints at being carried so.

"He just seems to go where I tell him to," I had said to Annie, two or so years before.

"Dad, I need you to come down on to the ladder. Hold on to the ladder. Can you do that for me?"

It seemed that he could.

"Good," I said. "Good." I realised I had broken out into a sweat. He was standing in front of me on the ladder now, his eyes, as ever, closed, a few rungs up from where I was positioned ready to try and catch him if he toppled back. Below, I had laid out quilts and blankets and pillows, just in case. Clammy hands make steel ladders slippery.

"Good," I said, taking the last steps down to the landing, and for a moment stumbling on the tangle of bedding. "Now all the way."

"Great," I said. "Well done."

Which, on reflection, seemed like a daft thing to say.

In the distance I heard that chuckling.

◎

If I had feared another massive clear-out job, I needn't have worried: the cellar was all but empty. A few bin bags of loose bricks and tiles, a rusting band saw blade lying in a coil, a pile of old newspapers returned half to pulp by years in the darkness, the remains of some unfortunate rodent, and other, less identifiable things: it had only taken an hour or so, three bags instead of dozens, and only the single journey to the tip on Wilson Avenue. I had taken the hoover down with me, and passed the plug up through the dining room window, where I could plug it into the socket beside the radiator. The cable was easily long enough. I gave the uneven stone floor a quick going over, working by torchlight, in an awkward crouch under the low ceiling, but it was more for me than it was for my father: Dad wouldn't mind. After banging my head for the fourth time, I decided that that would do.

The door, which had not been locked, had nevertheless taken some serious dislodging: I had shoulder barged it four times before eventually pushing through into the darkness. Closing it again now, it seemed to stick fast, and required the application of an almost similar level of force to re-open it. I had found a small padlock, in any case.

"Dad," I said, peering out through the little door. "Come in here."

He crouched down, then began to crawl forward into the space with that weird piecemeal way he had of moving, each motion a discrete and clunking step.

"I'm sorry about your chair," I said. "It doesn't fit." That was a lie: I had broken it up and taken it to the dump. "But I got you the basket chair, okay? I got that through."

He stopped halfway into the dank space, blocking the light behind him, and for a moment I felt a chill run through me that had nothing to do with the temperature underneath the house: I felt it worming into my muscles, into my bones.

In that moment, the thought of that rotten old door coming shut behind him gripped me, and I felt the slosh of nauseous dread in my stomach at the prospect of finding myself trapped down here, alone with my father in the cellar, because I knew that that door wouldn't want to be opening the other way. And Annie, I thought, would have no idea that I was here: as far as she was concerned, I had gone to work. And I was willing to bet that no one would hear me shouting for help. And time would pass, and life, eventually, would go on, as lives tend to, in the house above my father and I, and Hannah would only know of me from photographs and the stories her mother would tell; but the strangest story, I was sure, she would never tell. Annie would never come down here. Eventually, and sooner, not later, she and Hannah would move. The house would sell. A new family would move in. Maybe one day an adult or adolescent in that family would find me here, thoroughly decomposed, and my father still seated on the basket chair, an old blanket laid across his lap.

Not for the first time, I realised that I hadn't issued sufficiently explicit instructions. Dad had come in, as I had told him to, but I had not told him to take a seat in the chair.

"Come on," I said, as if this was his fault. "Take a seat."

He crawled past me to the chair, then stood up into the space.

"Go on," I said. "Sit. I brought you a blanket."

I laid it over his lap, as if he would need such a thing.

"I'll be back soon," I said.

Once I had crawled back outside, I made sure to padlock the door behind me. I didn't want some neighbour's cat or adventurous child or anyone else finding their way into the cellar. At least Mrs Wallace wouldn't have seen me.

Back in the kitchen, I made a cup of tea, then brought it through into the dining room, where I took a seat at the table and tried to come up with the lies I would tell when Annie and Hannah came home.

◎

In time we can grow accustomed to the most extraordinary things. The outrageous and outlandish become inconveniences you soon find ways to work around. Given time, our sense of the world might expand to accommodate things that by rights make a travesty of all accommodations, all proprieties, all rightfulness.

And children, well, children will accept almost anything you tell them.

Hannah turned five years old exactly one month ago.

When she was four and a half, she asked me why she didn't have Grandmas and Grandpas like her friends Tessa and Holly.

We all have secrets.

I had tried hard to come up with a decent lie to tell to Annie, but my faculties of invention had failed me. In the event it didn't matter. Two months after I had moved Dad down from the attic, Annie had broached the subject again, quietly and almost in passing, attempting a different tack this time, and I simply told her that I had sorted it.

She was startled, of course. "Okay," she had replied, nodding. "What did you do?"

"It doesn't matter," I said. I rubbed her shoulder. "I sorted it."

"He's gone?"

I didn't answer, but I let her construe my silence in the way that she wanted to construe it. The easiest lies to tell are the ones that people want to believe. And I had become skilled in telling them.

"It's sorted," I said. "I thought maybe it was time to turn it into an office. I've always wanted an office."

The bet was that she would not want to pry into the details, and the bet came off.

"You have," she said, beginning to smile.

At some point I had lost the key to the little padlock on the cellar door, but I had managed to break it off with a wrench from the tools remaining in the shed, twisting hard against the metal. It was a feeble thing, really, but it had done its job for a couple of months. The new one I had purchased that morning was rather sturdier, and I wouldn't be losing the key, because it had a combination lock, the six digits of which I had set to my father's month and year of birth.

"Dad?" I said, after I had opened the door. I shone the torch light into the cellar. The beam bounced back off his pallid face, and even after everything the sight of him just sitting there surprised me still, but only for a second. For a moment I thought that his eyes were open at last, but only for a moment.

No one ever reacts how you expect them to react.

"Dad," I said, "there's someone I would like you to meet."

Now Hannah, shy and curious, five years old and seven days in age, holding her dolly close to her chest behind me, was on the cusp.

The Turn

She was a fool to be driving, two drinks down and in a desolate mood, and the narrow lanes of the weald given to sharp, capricious turns. She wasn't used to roads without streetlamps, nor to skies without the glow of light pollution. She had set out without thought, without destination in mind, and at some point she had left the A roads behind her. At least it isn't raining, Marie thought, or murmured: small mercies.

Under the bouncing headlights, the hedgerows loomed over the roof of her car, and at the foot of each row on either side of the lane Marie could have sworn she could see eyes gleaming under the light like cat's eyes, steady and unblinking. She drove slowly because she didn't know the way. Because it was dark. Because she was tired. The last few days had taken everything out of her. Anna had been in. Marie knew she had been in. But she had not answered the door.

The engine cut out and the car grumbled to a halt as she crawled out of a dogleg turn. Swearing, she hit the wheel, then sat back in her seat and rubbed her eyes. At least, she thought, she had noticed the turn in time. A word came to her lips, unbidden: *proprioception*. She had corrected course before she had known what she was doing, as if some other hand had adjusted the wheel. As if her body had sensed it before her eyes had seen it through the dirty windscreen of the car. Now she slipped her phone from her pocket and swore again, misfortune piling on misfortune: the battery was dead. She had a torch in the boot, she remembered. If she could have pulled over anywhere else she might have kicked back here to sleep off her stupor, but she was in the middle of the road. Groggy, she remembered the emergency lights. It seemed the battery was fine, the car's electrics still worked; and she swore for a third time, upon realising that she didn't have the charger for her phone, which she might have plugged into the socket of the cigarette lighter. The attachment was in the glove compartment but the frayed cable was gone. Thinking of the emergency lights, she wondered would anyone see them in time. She would have to rely on the emptiness of the night—she had not, so far as she could recall, passed another car since Lewes. Even here, it seemed, in Sussex, at night, it did not take very long to disappear.

She cursed herself for not just booking a room somewhere in Lewes. She had wanted to give Anna her space. Well, she had it now.

Peering around, Marie marvelled at the turn, and wondered how many accidents had occurred at this spot over the years. The thought spurred her into motion, visions of another vehicle careering round the bend and into the back of her own car filling her mind with atrocious images.

With the bonnet open, Marie confessed to herself that she really didn't know very much about the insides of a car—or of anything. Not for the first time she thought of how the world was a system of black boxes nested within black boxes like Matryoshka dolls and of how powerless she was when things broke down. Unlike Anna, she was not practically-minded. Dumbfounded by the array of mechanisms and components, of caps and cables and other unidentifiable things, she remembered the manual in the glove compartment. Opening the passenger door, she dug it out. She thought to sit down and read it in the passenger seat, then saw again the vision of another vehicle smashing into her own, and so walked what seemed in the dark a decent distance away and where, standing awkwardly, her breath steaming in the late autumn air, air that tasted more of winter than the summer gone, the manual in one hand and the torch in the other, she tried for a while to wring sense from the text and graphics it contained.

Ten minutes later she decided that the fault was not mechanical: instead, to her surprise, the petrol tank was simply empty. She had no idea how that could be: had it not been near-full that morning? The only good fortune, she reflected, on this ill-starred, starless night, was that another vehicle had yet to collide with her own, though it was the kind of good fortune that might at any moment be transformed into disaster, and in her thoughts the night ahead stretched out toward eternity, a horrible prospect: she did not want to spend the night alone, and here, on the weald, in the middle of nowhere, or at least of Sussex, a county she scarcely knew. She was too far from any town now to walk back for help, and she did not feel she could simply abandon the car stopped dead in the road. But she feared trying to sleep in it. If there had been two of them, they might have released the handbrake and tried to push it forward. But there were not two of them. She was one, Marie thought. Just one. The idea bore a harsh chill. Sometimes the world seemed a callous place. Could she try to sleep at the side of the road, against the hedgerows? She had nothing in the car that she might use for bedding, unless a spare tire would suffice for a pillow. And the night was cold. It was nine o'clock, though it felt like midnight. It would only get colder. It was a long time until dawn.

Marie wondered how a competent person would deal with this, a person who was not an idiot, who was not driving half cut in the dark in a strange county. She tried to picture what that person would do. What, for example, a person like Anna would do.

In the first instance, Marie thought, Anna would not have sat behind the wheel with a heart rate raised by wine and grief, her brown eyes full of tears. She would not have been so reckless.

Stepping up to the edge of the hedgerow on one side of the lane, Marie leant on tiptoes to peer over at the countryside beyond. Blank colourless fields stretched out a way before the darkness cancelled the view. The night was quiet–she did not think she had ever heard such silence before: no birds to sing, no dogs to bark, no crickets chirping, hardly a breeze to stir the hedgerows; only her breathing, which in the dark might have come from someone else's lips, breaths drawn from a stranger's lungs. Looking down at the foot of the hedge, she saw no little eyes staring out, and smiled despite it all at the way exhaustion had made her hallucinate. She was tired still, but could feel herself waking in spite of it, in mind at least if not in body too. Sometimes the lonely nights brought a cold lucidity. She thought about her life. She thought about Anna. The situation revealed itself with a clarity unavailable to her in the waking hours. Sitting down at the foot of the hedgerow, she almost laughed. Instead she coughed into her hand.

She could, Marie realised, turn the fog lights on. Fog lights on top of headlights: it was something. That would give another driver a greater chance of seeing her, of course, if indeed another driver came along. Either way she doubted the flicker of the emergency lights would do much good. The only problem would be if the car's battery died, and she wondered if bad luck did not come in threes, like buses or events in fairy tales: the empty tank, the phone dead, and then the battery. At least the torch had juice, though how much she could not say; she had forgotten she had even had it in the car, and only Christ knew when she had put the batteries in. It was probably Anna's. Maybe Anna, unwitting, could light the way for her. Come on now, Anna, she thought. Don't abandon me here.

Frustrated, cold to the bone, she settled on a plan, or at least a thing she could do. And surely, she thought, in a situation such as this, something, whatever thing it was, was better than naught. Looking over the hedge, she had seen no houses, but that did not mean there was not a house nearby. She would walk one way down the road for ten minutes, then return if in that time no house appeared; then she would walk the other way. She would leave the headlights on for that duration: half an hour at most. She would have to hope that no one thundered round the bend. The walk at least would go some way to warming her. A plan, however threadbare, would loosen the knot of tension in her gut. Something, she thought. Better than nothing.

The lane snaked. The hedgerows loomed. The sky, over-cast in the day, was untouched by star or moonlight. Around the second turn in the lane and the sudden total darkness shocked her still: now Marie was sealed in. She felt abruptly, irredeemably alone. As if she could have closed her eyes and disappeared. She walked close to the hedge on one side in case another vehicle suddenly bore down on her. She felt the darkness as a physical thing, less an absence of light than an object itself, endowed with heft and density. She ran her hand lightly along the leaves of the hedge as she went, before wincing when something sharp—a thorn?—caught the tip of a finger.

Please be a house, she said aloud, sucking her finger. Her voice then in the silence and the dark sounded so strange to her own ears that she paused: it sounded scared, Marie thought, and not quite her own. She thought of her own voice played back on answering machines, always a discomfiting sound, and then thought of the messages she had left for Anna. Had she listened to them?

After five minutes, losing any sense of herself in space, as if her head might have painlessly separated from her body and her limbs drifted off like objects gently detaching in water, she began to panic. The darkness and the silence were asphyxiating. She was trapped. She might, she thought, be stuck here forever, wandering these country lanes, no longer quite in Sussex but neither somewhere else, slipped between places, between something and nothing, lost somewhere in the gaps of the world. The morning would never come. There would be no house, and she would not find her way back to the car.

Scant use in that. She turned back. A crook in the road brought the headlights of the car, its emergency lights still flashing merrily away, like Christmas lights, she thought, come early, and relief that almost winded her. Thank you, she said, to no one, to the night, to the darkness which might by some caprice have not brought her here again, and her voice was a strange and hesitant thing.

Marie was trying in vain to switch on her phone again, to trick the battery into mistaking its emptiness for charge, when the vehicle came round the bend.

Blinded by its lights, she leapt back, and for what might have been an eternity waited for the hideous smash as the moving car crashed into her own. She saw shuddering metal and breaking glass and felt the whoosh of air as the flames went up. But the crash did not come: belatedly, miraculously, Marie realised that the car had stopped in time. She shielded her eyes against the fog lights with a hand, waiting for the driver to dim them, but whoever it was seated behind the wheel did not do so. She waited for a long time. The pace of her heartbeat took a long time to slow. If the other driver had not been driving so cautiously—it didn't bear thinking about. She thought of rent metal, saw spilt petrol ignite, saw herself, from afar, as in a dream, in the resulting inferno. Eventually the driver's door opened.

Then, after a small delay, a silhouette appeared against the light. It was a woman, Marie saw. For a moment, full of irrational hope, she thought it was Anna come to rescue her, Anna returning her calls, Anna in the night with a changed mind and a changed heart, before the driver's figure registered as slimmer, straighter, more wiry and compact. Why hadn't she dimmed the lights? Marie wondered, annoyance already overwriting her relief. They were blinding her.

The stranger stood there in the light unmoving, unspeaking.

Hello? Marie said, and thought again how her voice was not her own. In the night it seemed what belonged to you might so very easily be taken away. In a darkness such as this Marie understood how the normal fixtures of your life might come unfixed. There was a tremble in her voice she didn't recognise. She did not know why she sounded so afraid.

Are you okay? the driver replied at last, or seemed to, because somehow Marie thought she had imagined it, a voice heard in dreams, and her voice like Marie's own hoarse and choking voice had an oddness to it, like a voice on an answering machine, from a bad line, from a distant place. Perhaps, Marie wondered, in the void of the nighttime, any human voice would sound strange.

I think I'm out of petrol, Marie replied. And my phone is dead.

The stranger seemed to wait, her silhouette in the light so still Marie thought for a moment that she might have been replaced by a cardboard cut-out of a person placed there in her stead. But then she turned and with peculiar speed vanished in the light.

Blinking, baffled, after a lag, after a small delay, Marie heard the boot open, then slam shut. A moment later the fog lights went off and the engine died.

She waited.

Here.

The driver appeared suddenly, and Marie started back.

She was a small woman, with cropped brown hair and freckles spread across a pale face, a small hooked nose, deep bags beneath large brown eyes. She looked uncomfortable. She was worried too, Marie realised, and she thought how frightening it must have been for her: to stop just in time; to be alone, then to see a stranger there in the night. She was holding a plastic can. Marie frowned, her reaction delayed, stuttering, as if she did not know what it was; then her stalling brain caught up. Unleaded, said the driver, with only half a question mark.

Thanks, said Marie, lagging, stuttering again, before her stalling brain caught up. Thank you. Yes.

She took the can and walked to the side of her car. She unscrewed the fuel cap and poured the blessed liquid in. What a stroke of luck, she thought. At last. She wouldn't have to spend the night out here in the chill dark after all. The other woman did not speak as she filled the tank. Marie wondered what to say. Should she introduce herself. Make small talk. Pass the time of day. That made her smile. She wondered why the stranger kept extra petrol in her car, before deciding it was best not to look a gift horse in the mouth. Surely she hadn't siphoned it off her own—

I can't thank you enough, she began at last, turning around with the empty can to hand it back, but the woman was gone, and her car was gone, and Marie was alone again.

She chewed her lip, baffled again. She had not heard the vehicle reversing round the bend. She climbed back into her own car and put the plastic can in the passenger seat, then started the engine. The dashboard display now registered twenty miles in the tank, but that was inexact. It was an old car. She glanced in the rear-view mirror, expecting lights.

Nothing.

She drove.

On the edge of town, the engine died for the second time. With the momentum of the hill Marie eased the vehicle to a stop at the side of the road. Twenty miles, she thought, with a small laugh of despair. It could not have been three.

She looked at the plastic can in the passenger seat. She thought of that woman in the fog lights. She thought of the dogleg bend of the lane. Had she recognised the driver when she had appeared then, so suddenly, shocking her backwards, when she had returned from the boot with the can?

She got out of the car and took the plastic can and locked the car and walked.

She thought of rent metal, of spilt petrol igniting.

On the forecourt of a BP station she sniffed the can on a whim and stopped. It didn't smell of anything: stagnant water, maybe some dead leaves in the bottom of it. She thought of that woman in the darkness, a silhouette against fog lights. She tilted the can and put her finger to the remaining liquid as it spilt onto the floor, lifted her finger to her nose and sniffed. Water. She sniffed the can again. Licked the water from her fingers. Water. Then, tasting copper, she noticed the blood, re-membered the thorn, if it had been a thorn, as she had trailed a hand along the hedgerow in the dark.

When she looked up, the automatic doors of the station had opened before her. The lights of the shop might have been a vision of an alien world. They dazzled her. She closed her eyes and held her breath. She waited. She exhaled slowly through her teeth. Then she went into the shop, where electric chillers hummed like pylons in the empty night, to request some measure of fuel in an empty can, a kindness, a small mercy, a little help. Then she would drive back and park up by one of the pumps and fill the tank to the brim and pay. Something. It was a plan. It was better than nothing.

By the time she left the station it had started to rain.

Like a Zip

Her finger had been sore and red and swollen for a while. It was the index finger, for pointing things out. With the finger extended, accusatory, indicative, Alice examined the wound. The hangnail was the longest she had ever seen. It reminded her of the freakish stray hair that always grew out longer than the surrounding soft hair of her left forearm, and which inevitably regrew not long after she had plucked it, and which was what she had thought the hangnail was, for a moment, before she had realised the peculiar truth of it.

Upon noticing it, she had sat stock still and stared at the hangnail for a full minute, filled with horror and wonder, forgetful of what she had been doing before it had arrested her attention, as everything in the world that was not the tip of the index finger of her right hand receded into the uninteresting background gloom. Then, refocussing, she had walked into the bathroom to get a plaster from the cabinet. Later she would need to soak and clip it, Alice knew, but beneath the knowledge of this, of what she knew that one should do, Alice was already dimly aware of what she knew that she would do. In an instant she had seen what possibility the hangnail offered, and she could not unsee it.

It was like a zip.

Alice had always wondered what lay inside of her. Not the things that one knew resided inside of every body, the organs

and the viscera and the skeleton, the bile and the blood and
the snot and the brains, not the ordinary contents of the of-
ficial inside, but of another, stranger interior. All her life Alice
had known that she harboured such a secret.

As a child, she had wondered at others, did they possess
such recessed chambers, and if they did—perhaps they did
not—did any intimation of that secret place ever reach their
conscious minds? Was it a lie that all the adults of the world
conspired to maintain? Was something terrible and profound
staked on the maintenance of that lie? Or—and this thought
filled her with despair—was she the only one? A hollow girl.
Like a painted egg, drained of white and yolk, full of air.
Perhaps that explained why she never got sick: not a thing
inside for any sickness to work on, to cling to. Until this, she
supposed. An infection of the exterior.

Later, her father had made her put away such thoughts,
deploying all manner of threats and inducements, employ-
ing a richly diverse company of doctors and therapists and
teachers and friends, until she too, quite overwhelmed by it
all, had acquiesced in the deception. Then, later, in a moment
of wholly uncharacteristic recklessness out on the motorway,
he had died, thrown through the windscreen of his car, and
standing on the hard shoulder in the rain, under flashing
lights, unscathed, Alice had seen what was inside of him.
Nothing much.

Did she know then, in the moment in which she had
first noticed it, that the hangnail offered confirmation of the
obscene *idée fixe* of her childhood? Later, briefly, she would
think that she had. She would wonder, only briefly, for just
a moment, how such a mundane trivial unpleasant thing
as a hangnail could exert such fantastical allure. And then,
abruptly, all wondering would cease.

Alice decided she would begin that night. The excitement
of anticipation made the afternoon grind slowly. Finally, after
ten o'clock, she could get away. Her husband, slumped dozing

in front of a film he had said he was watching, would sleep in the spare room downstairs. He always did. She didn't need to lock the door.

Her husband, her bedroom, her life, their house, her job as a secretary in a primary school, his debt, her savings, their daughter gone off to university—everything beyond the tip of her index finger began to recede into a background from which not a thing would re-emerge. Alice tapped the swollen root and felt a sharp hot soreness. In the middle of the swelling, a little crack. It leaked a pale fluid. And then the hangnail, half an inch long, dangling. She gripped it with tweezers. A gentle exploratory tug set off a sharp hot flare of pain. Alice closed her eyes.

One, she said.

Two, she said, steeling herself.

Three, she said, and with decisive force Alice pulled it back.

The pain was exquisite and extraordinary, but greater than the pain, clearer than the pain, was a relief such as she had never known.

It came down, down her finger, down along her hand, down along the back of her wrist, a thin translucent fibrous strip peeled back like a tag to remove the packaging of some newly purchased household appliance. For a moment Alice stared in amazement at the injury, panting and exhilarated, as she caught her breath. Her nerves sang. Her finger burned.

Like a zip, thought Alice, standing naked in her bedroom, the curtains of the windows drawn and a single bedside lamp throwing her huge and stooping shadow up onto a wardrobe within which hung clothes she would not wear again.

Do it.

She dug the tips of the tweezer into the open swelling, searching blindly for purchase within the sickly wound, and tugged. Another strip. It came clean and smooth, like cello-tape pulled back. It reached her elbow, adjacent to the first, then with the *oomph* of one final yank crossed the joint, before running to ground on the underside of her arm.

Again.

As she worked, methodically, with great concentration, Alice heard faint laughter, and it was a while before she recognised the laughter as her own. She realised her cheeks were wet, and that the wetness was from crying. That she was crying. That these were her tears, tears of laughter and relief.

Like an orange, she thought. Like a banana skin. Like an onion. Like the skin shod of a eucalyptus tree and no trunk beneath it. Like a zip.

She thought of her father gone through the windscreen. Of her father, going through the windscreen. Of her father undone.

When the relief threatened to overwhelm her, Alice forced herself on. She could not stop halfway. She would see it through.

The similes, a distant part of her thought, were quite inadequate. In truth it was like nothing else.

Gone midnight, alone, as her husband dreamed his dullard dreams downstairs, she unpeeled herself, pale fibrous strip by pale strip, until there was nothing left, nothing at all, except faint and fading laughter in an empty room. A pile of clothes lay discarded at the bedside; empty dresses hung in the darkness of the wardrobe, swaying gently with some fugitive draught.

Hand-Me-Down

The monitor only allowed one-way communication, so although Danni could listen to her child if she needed to, she could not respond, like a one-way mirror, she thought, in a police interrogation room, but then the baby couldn't respond anyway, not yet, and her brother had given her the device. It was the first, she imagined, of many hand-me-downs, and she was glad of the savings. She didn't need all the bells and whistles, and they weren't cheap, and she wasn't rich.

At first the little image had proved a source of fascination: Sophie's cot, even when empty—the little view into the back bedroom, into her baby daughter's world, which on the monitor always looked a little different, a different cot, in a different room, and a different baby under the blankets. She hadn't been sure she really needed it, because even in those first few weeks, with all the disruption, Sophie had slept like an angel, as Danni's mother had informed her several times, whilst cooing, and had asked Sophie herself, *just like a little angel, aren't you dear?* but her brother Jack had really recommended it—he was the sort of person who always liked some new device to fiddle with, and seemed keen to pass it on, get some more use out of it, he said, having purchased an unnecessary upgrade, slow its momentum towards it final destination as landfill—and, well, free was free. You couldn't argue. And she found she liked it. Or at least that it interested

her in an idle kind of way. Just looking at it sometimes. The
different cot in the different room, a different baby under
the blankets. Through its poor resolution it was like seeing
through a gauze. In those days, as she felt herself going slowly
mad, it provided some measure of distraction from the torpor
that had claimed her since the birth.

Sometimes it was like looking through the screen as
through a window into the baby's room; other times, as if the
monitor, hoarding secret depth, contained its own room, its
own world, beneath the plastic of the screen. She wondered
why she found it so peculiar. Her mother, to whom such
things were deeply alien (we never had anything like this
when you were a child!), and who hated phones, had never
owned one, immediately took to it. It's better than telly! she
said, on several occasions, as she spied on her granddaughter
in the back bedroom.

Those first two months of her life, Sophie was the calmest
child. Danni's mother was shocked: neither of her two children, she pointed out repeatedly, had let her get much rest.
She made it sound like an injustice. But it was an injustice
that would soon receive some small redress, because it was
around that time, when Danni would find herself staring idly
at the little low-res image of the different cot in that different
room, that Sophie's angelic period came to an end. Danni had
not known it was just a period: it became a period in retrospect, she saw, through its elapsing; and, as she would see, it
really had elapsed, for good. And for worse.

One October evening, having finally settled her daughter
down, as she tried to relax, to loosen the tension in her shoulders, sipping a cold beer, the television on but muted, she
glanced at the monitor and stiffened suddenly, all the tension
ratcheting up her spine, through her shoulders and neck, and
it was a moment before she understood what she was seeing,

her shock causing thought to lag.

Buffering, she thought, and heard a hollow laugh, her own laughter become a stranger laughing, as she hurried through to the little room at the other end of the flat. She was used to this kind of dissociation: it was not unfamiliar, was not uncomfortable. Behind her, cold lager foamed out of the bottle of beer, pooling on the coffee table, adding a new landmass to the archipelago of beverage stains adorning its unlacquered surface.

Later, returned to the living room, she picked up the monitor again and studied the image of her sleeping daughter. In a trick of the light or the lack of it, of snugly layered fabrics and the camera's low resolution, the cot had appeared empty. Only appeared, she thought. Only *appeared.* But then even appearances were more than mere appearances.

It had appeared empty.

That, she would think, in the weeks ahead, had been the very first time, had been the start of it all.

Sometimes I think I'm going mad, Danni said to Roisin, whom she had known since primary school and with whom she stayed in intermittent touch. As children they had bonded over a shared love of horses, and Roisin's parents had been rich enough to buy her one, later, once she was in secondary school, by which time Danni had learned that they inhabited very different worlds. The ferocity of Danni's jealousy, of which she had felt acutely embarrassed at the time, had been a long time fading, though in retrospect she supposed that the horse had been a cypher for other jealousies; and now they were the always-meaning-to-meet-up kind of friends, seldom meeting up; but this time, it appeared, they had actually meant it, or Roisin had meant, for it had been at Roisin's instigation and insistence.

I haven't seen you in months! Come on! How's baby?

Danni had found herself caught between two undesir-
able options: to have Roisin over to visit, or to venture out.
And her own mother had not been shy of commenting on her
appearance: you look pasty, dear. You'll never attract another
man looking quite so pasty. Well, unless he's pasty too. And
who wants a pasty man?

Men were lower down her list of priorities than her mother
might have liked.

Going mad? Roisin asked, sipping tea in the living room.
She was pregnant herself, with her second child, a month to
go. Some people, Danni thought, looking at her, are good at
pregnancy. Some people are good at motherhood, and some
are not.

Now Danni was staring at the coffee table. It looks like an
atlas, she thought idly. Then she glanced up, realised that she
was lagging.

I guess I'm just tired, she said.

Roisin nodded. It's a lot, isn't it. And for you—especially—

Roisin pursed her lips, halting mid-sentence, afraid of the
indelicacy on the tip of her tongue.

My mum helps, said Danni. Then she laughed. Sometimes
too much.

She's worried about you.

Danni nodded.

So why 'mad'?

As if on cue a tinny gurgle gargled through the speakers
of the monitor.

I keep going into rooms and then forgetting why I'm there.
The other day, I was halfway to the shops before I realised I
had no idea what I'd gone to get. Almost had a panic attack.

Good to get out. Get some air.

Danni nodded again. The other evening, I was sitting here,
and I glanced at this thing, and her cot was empty.

Her cot was empty?

Looked it. Seemed to be.

Had she escaped? Once, my mother found me wedged upside down between the cot and the chimney breast. Dad called me Houdini.

Apparently not, said Danni, wondering what Sophie would grow up to make of her own father. I don't know why I'd thought that, except that when I looked at the screen she wasn't there. I nearly had a fit. I can remember it clearly, you know? She wasn't there. Then when I went through into her bedroom there she was.

Roisin touched her hand. It's hard work, she said. You were tired. That's all.

I know.

Roisin smiled, setting her cup down on its saucer.

Danni wondered did she still have the horse.

It's good to see you, Roisin said, and touched Danni's hand again, at which Danni flinched. Then sighed.

She would have to get better at this, she told herself, at appearing okay.

Sorry, she said.

It's fine. Really. I should be getting going.

As Roisin stood to her feet, she picked up the monitor. Maybe I should get one of these things this time around, she said.

Danni was relieved when Roisin was gone, glad of the empty flat. Empty except for herself and the baby in the cot.

◎

Now, the next day, her brother would not answer his phone.

Danni missed him. He had been stressed a lot lately, had seemed distracted when she had seen him last. When he had given her the monitor, among other things. Which was how long ago? She left him a message:

I haven't seen you in weeks! Aren't you going to come round and see Sophie?

I get lonely here, she didn't say.

Maybe you could take mum off my hands, she said.

Call me when you get this.

What was the word? On the tip of her tongue. She could taste it, the word for the way he had seemed before. Furtive. No. Secretive. No. Distracted. Sort of.

Evasive, she said, to the empty flat.

She had been listening to the dial tone on the landline for a full minute when she put down the phone.

He didn't call.

That night she didn't sleep.

◎

The next evening, watching television, she glanced at the monitor, not for the first time, and felt the world go silent and cold.

Reaching over, she picked it up from the arm of the sofa and peered at the screen.

Sophie? she said, tilting her head.

That's not Sophie, she said to herself.

Released from the vice of shock she scrambled up from the sofa and hurried through to Sophie's room at the back of the flat, thinking: that's not Sophie. That's not Sophie. That's not Sophie.

She lifted the baby from the cot and held her up for scrutiny.

Sophie, she said, rocking her daughter in her arms, and standing in the darkness of the baby's room she wondered if it was possible to die of relief.

Disturbed, Sophie started to cry.

◎

It was after this that Sophie's sleeping got really bad, as if the disturbance of that night had never passed. It's my fault, Danni thought repeatedly, a thought that became a refrain, a loop, a negative mantra: it's my fault—I disturbed her, put my own stupid fears on her—I woke her up that time and now she never sleeps, now she'll never sleep.

Exhaustion made the world grow thin. The fabric of the world, Danni thought, has become threadbare. The world is wearing through. Or I am. Like an old dress I am wearing through. Gauzy. The world is an old dress and it is wearing through.

The monitor wasn't much use through those nights, each night become a small eternity, a capsule prison universe she doubted she would ever leave. It wasn't much use because she was in Sophie's room half the time and the other half of the time Sophie was in with her. But still sometimes she found herself looking at its little screen.

It nagged at her.

Nag nag nag, she thought, picturing horses.

Her phone lit up and Danni frowned. She never kept her phone on silent but apparently she had muted it. There were three missed calls. Shapes on the screen. They were letters, she realised, lagging into sense: Mum. With a jerk she caught up. Her mother had called. She had found herself doing this a lot lately: zoning out. A ping and a new message appeared, announcing voicemail. Idly Danni wondered if you could mail a voice. Seal it in an envelope and slip it in a postbox. She realised she was smiling. As she listened to the message that smile stiffened into a grimace.

Darling would you please answer your phone? I called round today and you didn't answer. Were you in? I thought you were in. You are making me worry. This isn't like you. And Jack—Lord, why have I been cursed with such difficult children? I don't know what's got into that brother of yours. Or into you. Just give me a call, okay. Okay. Bye.

Evasive, thought Danni, tasting the word. That was the word. Jack was being evasive.

Why was Jack being evasive?

◎

Danni had always wanted to be an actress, once she had given up on her initial dream of owning a stable, a whole stable of horses and the land around, before the grey disappointments of life had set in. But now Danni was an actress. I am an actress, she said aloud. Leave the horses to Roisin. I am acting. This was what she told herself, a new refrain, a positive mantra. She was an actress, playing a part. Unshowy, no protagonist, part of the supporting cast, part of the scenery. The sort who never looked like she was acting. It took tremendous effort. She let the Health Visitor into her flat. She smiled and made small talk as if it were a language in which she was fluent, and tried to detect if the Health Visitor had detected anything beneath the surface of her smile.

Sophie is a good weight. She looks healthy. How's she sleeping?

Danni delivered her lines.

He had a long, thin face and a lantern jaw, and there was a greyness to him, as if he lived in monochrome, and a gentleness, and under the caring gaze of his grey gentle eyes she felt scrutinised and exposed.

She delivered her lines.

She had read something the other day, about fake Health Visitors, strangers who posed as Health Visitors and called in at the houses of new parents to spy on the children. Why? Were they pedophiles? Maybe. Sometimes they were afraid of pedophiles, were vigilantes checking up on children they deemed to be at risk from pedophiles. Pedophiles everywhere. No one seemed to know.

Danni smiled, wondered if the man here in her flat—was his name Jack? John? James?—was a stranger acting a role, and here she was in turn, delivering her own lines with great elan, two actors acting at the intersection of two different plays, each unaware of the other's duplicity.

But she didn't think so. She had seen him at the Children's

Centre on Ivory Place.

Thank you, she said, smiling, as he stood to leave. He said something or other about future dates and she agreed, nodding, smiling, smiling, and then closed the front door behind him. Slowly her smile stiffened into a grimace, and then the grimace began to fade.

All the effort of acting took its toll.

She felt herself give way, fell asleep on her bed as Sophie, an actress too, deep in role, sleeping for the first time in what might have been forever, lay quiet in her cot. Exhaustion made the world seem thin. She is wearing through.

The world is wearing through. Sometimes she finds herself dozing unawares as dreams slip through from the other side like shapes passing through a gauze. There was the grey Health Visitor who wanted to take her baby away, the baby that was a fake, a doll of exquisite wailing shitting realism, fitted, it amused her to think, with a one-way listening device, deployed by the Health Visitor to spy on her. And there were others, too, other strangers, creeping about; the peopled shadows teemed.

She had seen her brother in town, across the road, carried downhill by the flow of the Saturday crowd. He hadn't seen her, or at least he hadn't appeared to see her, before the river of people took him away.

Appeared, she thought.

Her mother would not stop ringing. She wondered what she could do about that.

At night she looked out of the window and saw a shape sitting on the bench across the way, under the canopy of an elm tree, a tall thin man in a raincoat, she realised, his long face shadowed beneath the raincoat's hood. He gazed up at the window of her flat with eyes that caught the light of a streetlamp and catching it appeared to glow.

Danni, she said, to the empty flat, which wasn't empty, Danni is evasive. Then hoarse laughter filled the empty flat which wasn't empty, through lips that did not move.

◎

The question was, in whose employ were they? Was it the grey Health Visitor, her brother, who was always up to something, or her mother meddling, sending someone to keep a watch on her? Or someone else?

Danni pulled the curtains closed.

Exhaustion had set an aching in her bones. She swung her foot, turned her leg at the knee, dug her toes into the mattress. Sciatica.

She dreams.

◎

She is in the flat that isn't the flat, its colour gone, the edges of things grown jaggedy like the image on the screen. In her dream she is inside the screen, in the screen flat, in the secret hoarded depth of the monitor, and she is not alone. No one ever was in an empty flat, she thinks. There was always herself for company, that ghostly companion. There was her baby and the baby was crying and its cry was like the ringing of a telephone that she dared not answer. There was something else, too, somewhere, someone, a tall thin shape, a shadow moving carefully, always at the edges of her vision. Then the shape turns—

◎

and for a moment steps toward the centre of her vision, and she sees a long thin face, looking at her, regarding her, a man who wears a rictus mask of longing and despair, a smile stiffened to a grimace, and a face she recognises but cannot place, a name upon the tip of her tongue—she can taste it—

◎

but then she woke, to the ringing of her phone.

◎

Her neck was stiff. She was on the sofa, but could not remember falling asleep. It was morning. It felt like morning. The ringing of the phone cut out.

The flat was silent except for the churn of her own body, the beat of her own heart, the surge of blood through veins.

As she sat up the monitor fell off her lap and to the floor. She hadn't realised she had been holding it. On the coffee table her phone began to dance with the poltergeist force of its vibrations, ringing again. Irritated—why wasn't it mute?—she picked it up and powered it down before the shapes on the screen could lag into letters and sense.

Nag nag nag, thought Danni, picturing horses.

She slumped back on the sofa, sighing, began to yawn. To sleep so deeply and to dream such fevered nonsense, and then to wake even more tired than you were before—what was the point?

The flat was silent.

Sophie is being evasive, she thought.

She looked at the monitor, screen-down on the carpet, and the urge to pick it up and smash it up and disperse the pieces far and wide seized her suddenly.

No, she told herself, and held herself. Her arms around her knees, her knees pulled to her chin, she held herself.

I need to talk to Jack, she thought. Jack is being evasive. I need to talk to *Jack*.

The call clicked straight to voicemail.

◎

Danni settled Sophie in the pram, the pram that Jack and his wife had given her, among other things, and within minutes

Sophie was sleeping. Why now, she thought, why not at night? Why now, why not at night. Why now?

Jack lived on Ewat Street, off Southover Street, up the hill. It wasn't far, but Sophie knew that fear could elongate the shortest distances, could expand brief moments into capsule prison universes without end. It took an hour to work up the courage to go out.

I am okay, she told herself. I am okay. I appear okay. Through appearing okay she would become okay, convince the world and through convincing the world convince herself that she was okay, and so be okay.

Okay, she thought, let's go.

It was cold outside. The autumn, hasty for winter, was closing in, and by six o'clock the evening had darkened into night. The night brought rain, fine pellets of rain that bore an icy edge, and Danni realised she had not dressed for the rain, nor for the cold, but it was too late now: she was on her way.

Through small streets that began to twist and elongate, she passed between lonely islands of light beneath the street-lamps, pushing the pram with Sophie sleeping through the oceans of shadow between. There wasn't much traffic on the roads and the pavements were all but empty. Everyone was tucked up indoors, in the warmth. Why now? thought Danni. Why not at night? Why now, why not at night. The question repeating in her thoughts like the clip-clop of hooves.

Nag nag nag, thought Danni, picturing horses. I shall nag my brother into answering.

But the little house on Ewat Street, when she reached it, was silent and dark. The curtains were drawn and the house seemed in a cagey mood, as if the windows were narrowed eyes, as if masonry could scowl.

Parking the pram to the left of her brother's front door, its pedal brake pushed down, she crouched to peer through the letterbox, and in what light reached the hallway carpet from the streetlamp behind her she saw a pile of letters, bills, ads for fast food restaurants, estate agents, a local chiropractor.

Jack? she called through the letterbox.

Voice mail, she thought. You've got mail.

Jack?

Jack is being evasive.

Why is Jack being evasive? thought Danni, who might also have said it aloud.

I could call mum, she thought, or said aloud, but the thought filled her with immediate dread. I can't be dealing with that right now.

Or Sandra: Jack's wife.

Yes.

She pulled her phone from her pocket to find it dead, and swore.

Glancing round, her heart lurched into her throat: the pram was gone.

She spun on her heel, ready to scream, then stopped immediately, shuddering still. To the right of the house where she had parked it, the pram stood waiting.

She moved to release the brake but it wasn't down. Through empty streets that lengthened and turned, through lonely islands of light and the shadows in-between, she hurried home.

That night she saw him on the monitor as the world went cold and still, the grey thin shape. She must have knocked the camera when she had settled Sophie down an hour before, for in its purview now was only half the cot, a stretch of carpet, and the old green chair opposite; and sitting in the chair there was a man.

She couldn't move. She held herself, staring at the screen, through the screen as if it were a window, into the little room at the other end of the flat, and could not move though she willed to move.

Sometimes when Sophie couldn't sleep she would work herself into some position whereby it seemed that she was looking up at the camera's lens. Under that infrared gaze her eyes would glow like cat's eyes, like the eyes of a devil; and now that shape, so tall that even while seated its head appeared to brush the ceiling, turned its face to look at the camera, at the camera and through it, to Danni on the other side, at Danni gone rigid on the sofa, and its eyes glowed like a devil's eyes, and the sounds of its breathing and of the crying of her daughter seeped through into the living room, as Danni felt her own uncertain self give way.

◎

She awoke exhausted, stiff and sore, unable to recall ever falling asleep, and when she rushed through into the back bedroom she found her daughter lying happily awake in the cot. If relief could kill. Sciatica played a nervous trill through tired legs.

Danni ran her hands through her hair and paced the room, circling the cot. She drew the nails of her right hand down the side of her face, drawing blood.

This can't go on, she said. This can't go on.

In her pocket, her phone, dead the last time she had looked at it, began to ring.

This can't go on.

She declined her mother's call and thumbed through to her brother's name in the list of contacts, then stabbed the screen with her index finger until it made the call.

He answered.

◎

Jack?

Jack?

Danni.

She listened closely. There was a strange sound on the line.

Oh Danni, he said.

Was he weeping?

It was not like Jack to cry. A strange sound.

Jack—

I know why you're calling. I'm sorry. I'm so sorry.

Did you—she paused, unable to comprehend for a moment what he had done to her—did you know?

The crackling line made his sobbing strange.

I'm sorry.

Why?

Because—

How could you do this to me?

There's only one thing you can do.

He sniffed.

Where are you?

There's only one thing you can do, he said.

What?

Silence.

What can I do?

Pass it on, he said. Give it away. Give it to someone new. I don't know why. But it—I don't know. It seems to work. You have to pass it on. I'm sorry—I was desperate, and you were—I'm sorry…

Pass it on, thought Danni.

Another call came through and her phone asked if she would like to place her brother on hold. She saw the shapes of letters, lagging into sense, become a name: Roisin.

Yes, thought Danni, picturing horses, as she pressed the screen to answer.

Pass it on.

Yes.

After all, Roisin was surely due.

Holes

I've got a new rash, he said.

Show me, she said.

He lifted the hem of his shirt, his toothbrush held between his teeth, turning his hip so that she could see.

Weird, she said.

Wasn't there last night, he said. At least I don't think so.

She crouched down to peer at the rash. Upon closer inspection, she wasn't sure that it was a rash after all.

Can I touch it? she asked.

Do you want to? he said. He took the toothbrush from his teeth and coughed into his hand.

Actually, no.

She stood up straight. Does it hurt? she said. Is it sore?

Nope.

He resumed the brushing of his teeth. She stepped out of the bathroom, crossed the small hall back into the bedroom, and took the pot of moisturiser from the glass table in front of the mirror. She unscrewed the lid and dipped her finger into the cream, then began to apply it to her face. Then she paused and looked at her hand as if it had betrayed her.

She heard him spit into the sink.

Had she touched it? Had she now smeared it, whatever it was, a rash or something else, possibly catching, all over her face? The thought made the skin of her face itch. It made her scalp itch. No, she thought, I didn't touch it. But the skin of her face and the skin of her scalp continued to itch.

With the thick Nivea forming a pale mask, she stepped back into the hall. He had finished brushing his teeth and for a moment looked like he was pulling faces at himself in the mirror. When he saw her reflected in the mirror looking in at him, he stopped like a boy caught doing something he shouldn't have been doing by a ghost.

You should get it checked out, she said. Make an appointment.

He groaned. I'm sure it'll go away. He coughed into his hand.

Maybe, she said.

Skin is weird, he said, sounding throaty. And the older you get, the weirder it gets.

They swapped places, squeezing past each other in the bathroom doorway. He gave her a look as they did so. Was she shrinking back from him?

She squeezed some toothpaste onto her brush, trying not to think about the rash, if it was a rash. Her scalp itched.

She heard the hairdryer from the bedroom. A moment later he emerged, hair half-dry, uncombed, his shirt untucked, ready for work inasmuch as he ever was. She was pulling her lower eyelid down, examining the redness in the white of her eye below the iris. She had washed her hands before doing so. She turned to him, leant back when he leant in to give her a kiss. He gave her a look and then smiled. She kissed him on the cheek.

See you later, he said, still smiling. I'll get it checked, okay?

She heard him coughing in the stairwell.

She set the toothbrush back down on its charging stand. Her scalp continued to itch.

◎

If it was a rash, it was an odd kind of rash, he thought: a patch of something or other under the fuzz of hair halfway between his crotch and hip, a small variation on the surface of the skin. It was almost nothing, almost unnoticeable. But the affected area seemed peculiarly smooth. It seemed peculiarly delicate. He had felt the trill of a shiver when his fingers had first touched it that morning in the shower, and when the oddness of it had first properly struck him he had begun to probe at it a little. There was a slight discolouration.

Seated at the desk in his cubicle, he coughed into his hand. All week he'd felt under the weather, a latent cold coming on that had never quite come on. It had lingered on the threshold of his immune system, an itching in his throat, a little cough, a slightly underwater feeling in his sinuses, a little swell of pressure behind his eyes. And now the rash, if it was a rash.

He felt peculiar.

Four times at work he went to the toilet, locked himself in the cubicle, and looked at the rash. When he had finished, he flushed the toilet in case anyone outside the cubicle wondered what was he up to. Then he buckled his belt and decided if he couldn't see it, it wasn't there, it would go away. It didn't go away. Immediately that morning he had regretted telling her. The look of—what was it?—combined revulsion and attraction on her face when she had crouched down to peer at it. The wanting to touch it, and then the not wanting to touch it, and the leaning away. If he hadn't told her, maybe it would have gone away. Talk had made it real. Now thinking about it made it realer still, and stranger, and more worrying. He'd always been a worrier, doubts always boring through the surface of his confidence like woodworm. Better to have kept it to himself.

He returned to his desk. His scalp had started to itch.

How was your day?

Okay, he said. You?

Urghh, she said. I don't think I ever quite woke up.

He nodded. He'd been coughing all night.

Something in the air pressure maybe. I don't know. Did you—

No.

Are you going to?

It's probably nothing.

She looked at him. Okay, she said. If it changes.

Yes, he said. If it changes.

The timer on the cooker trilled.

Pizza. He looked at the melted cheese and felt no appetite. In school, he remembered, about to tell her before thinking better of it, he had once had a case of impetigo so bad that one of the other boys had named him Pizzaface. Not that his dad had let him go in: he'd been kept home for days. Nevertheless that boy had seen him peering down from his bedroom window, watching the other kids kicking up the autumn leaves on the walk to school, and had begun to cackle and taunt and point. The impetigo so bad that the kid had seen it from the street. It had been like a mask. He had felt the shame burning in his face. Humiliation. Now he moved the slices around on the plate, feeling nauseous, feeling peculiar, pondering that old shame.

I'm not hungry, he said.

You need to eat something, she said.

Hmm.

He tried a bite. It wasn't pleasant.

Pizzaface, he thought.

Steam rose in tendrils from the surface of the slice.

He traced a finger along the peculiarly smooth patch of skin halfway between his crotch and hip. If anything, it seemed smoother now, like polished marble with the give of flesh. It was discoloured, a swatch of pale grey on the skin. Had the colour changed? The shape? It looked desaturated. It felt wrong. He didn't feel right. He pressed down and felt a surge of nauseous wrongness in his gut, felt his stomach turn. He thought of hernias, and stopped pressing when the sense that the pressure of his finger might break the surface seized him. He pictured himself continuing to press and saw the skin break, saw the flesh give, saw his hand disappearing into the wet warm meat of his body.

Had it changed? Was it different? It felt strange to the touch. Too smooth. Airbrushed. And cooler than the surrounding flesh.

He flushed the toilet, washed and dried his hands, and opened the door. She was stood outside, pursing her lips. He hadn't expected her to be there.

Jesus, he said. You made me jump.

She looked at him.

Has it changed?

What? No. Why?

I don't know. She bit her lip.

It's nothing, he said, trying to reassure her, trying to reassure himself through doing so.

It's just a rash, he said, and tried to laugh. It struck the wrong note. Awkward. It hung in the air.

It's been bothering me, she said. Then she laughed, too. I don't know.

He patted her shoulder, squeezing past her into the living room. Did she lean back? Flinch? A momentary clench of anger stoppered his thoughts.

You didn't go to the toilet, did you, she said quietly, without a question mark.

What? No. I mean, yes. Of course I did. What do you mean?

You were looking at it.

It, he thought, as if she couldn't bring herself to say it.

At the rash, she said, to finish the statement, and to fill the silence as he stared at her with an expression of bewildered hurt. Sometimes when he looked like that he seemed impossibly young.

I'm not sure it's a rash, he said, sitting down on the sofa.

No?

No.

Then what.

He gave a shrug. I don't know. Skin's weird. I've had rashes before.

Christ, have I had rashes, he thought.

Did I tell you about the time I had impetigo?

I don't think so.

It wasn't good.

Is that a rash?

Well, he said, and paused to think. Girl lived next door to us, in our first house, nearly died of measles.

Did you catch it?

No, I'd been immunised. Her parents had refused.

Christ.

I had acne as a teenager. Insect bites that had erupted into—what's the word?

What word?

Pustules, he said. The word had a horrible taste that wasn't entirely unpleasant. He laughed. I even had ringworm once.

Jesus, she said.

I've always had bad luck.

She nodded.

What's your point?

My point? He looked at her.

She nodded.

My point is, this isn't like any of that.

She crossed the room, stood by the arm of the sofa. She put a hand on his shoulder.

Did you make an appointment?

He frowned. Then he shook his head. No.

You should. If anything, just to stop worrying about it. You always worry. It's probably fine.

Yes, he said. He looked up at her. Are you worried about it?

She laughed, looking away. I don't know. She looked back at him.

Might be catching, she said.

He awoke himself coughing, itching all over. His skin teemed. She turned over beside him, grunting in her sleep.

He stood under the halogen light in the bathroom, naked, squinting.

He closed his eyes in dismay, hoping when he opened them that what he had seen would be gone.

It was not.

It had spread.

Perhaps two and a half centimetres by one, the new patch began just above the line of his jaw and finished just below. The skin was smooth and discoloured. It felt soft: pushing against it, he felt that weird give again, as if were he to press hard enough he might just push right the way through. Never mind the bone of his jaw. Under the surface of that patch of weird discolouration he imagined the bone too would part like thick smooth porridge or half-dried glue, like the seared top of a creme brûlée tapped with a spoon.

Stepping backwards, he raised his foot and placed it on the corner of the bath, tilting at the hip to examine the first patch in the mirror.

Oh God, he said, feeling a fresh churn of nausea at the reflection held in the glass.

He stared agog at the image, before lowering his gaze to look at the thing direct.

The pale marble smoothness had become a shiny jet-black spot, jewel-like, an obsidian depression.

He looked down at the depression between his hip and groin, and a sense of rippling infestation passed through him, bringing his skin out in goose bumps, making his skin itch from the top of his head to the tips of his toes, making him sniff, making his eyes itch, too, his ears, making his scrotum tighten and his anus clench and his toes claw at the rug beneath the sink.

Slowly, slowly, he moved his hand toward it. Slowly he extended an index finger; slowly he brought it closer to the surface of the thing.

But there was no surface. Instead his finger passed through, disappearing up to the first knuckle and then the second before sickened panic made him withdraw. He'd felt nothing there. Nothing at all.

He felt the room turn, felt his mind slide with sudden vertigo.

There was a hole in his body.

◎

There is a hole in my body, he said.

Panic had knocked his focus out, had stoppered his thoughts, stoppered his ears with white noise. He gripped the sink. He needed something to do.

He flushed the toilet, washed and dried his hands, took the towel from the radiator and fastened it around his waist, and opened the door. She was stood outside in her nightie, pursing her lips. He hadn't expected her to be there.

Jesus, he said. You made me jump.

She looked at him.

Has it changed?

What?

Squinting against the light, she saw him. She saw it.

Your face, she said, raising a hand to point. He

remembered the pointing of a schoolboy down in the street below his window. Pizzaface. The ripple of old shame. He was full of an old fear. He felt infested, infectious, pestilential. She tilted her head. For a moment her gaze fixed him in the doorway, helpless and confused, and then he brushed past her into the hall. He walked to the side of his bed, saw the pint glass of water on the bedside table, and drank.

You have to ring the doctor in the morning, she said. Okay?

Morning brought the third patch, beneath an armpit. He couldn't decide if the patches were itchy or if it was the thought of the patches that had him scratching. Once, as a child, he had fallen in dogshit whilst playing football out on the playing fields, and after running home he had spent an hour in the shower, furiously scrubbing himself, convinced the taint of filth would never go, was in his mouth, his eyes, had seeped into his pores. He had passed the rest of the day and a portion of that night scratching himself, chasing phantom itches as they danced from arm to chest to back to neck to foot to eyelids to the interiors of his ears. Now he wondered if the sense of it had ever really left him. This time it wasn't just the patches he had scratched. His chest in the night had become crisscrossed with red lines as if some furious editor had scrawled out a torso of unworthy sentences. But he didn't care about that. He studied the third patch. It was faint—fainter than the first, at least at the time he had noticed it—but it was there.

There. Its thereness, bluntly insistent, a matte fact, dumbly, dully true, appalled him.

She spoke through the door.

Ring the doctor, she said. Is there anything I can get you?

No, he said. It's fine. He glanced at his phone, placed on the corner of the bath, a message to his manager half-composed on the screen. Thanks, he said.

How are you feeling? she said.

He opened the door a crack. He felt the pulsation of the obsidian hole beneath the towel and worried that she knew, that it was obvious. Knew what exactly? He didn't know. But obviously it was obvious. There was a hole in his body. That was it. It made no sense. Suddenly he felt shy of callous scrutiny. He felt a dozen gazes poring over him, prodding him with fingers sheathed in latex gloves, examining the morbid symptoms of a strange disease. Holes. Or a hole. One, for now, but surely more to come. What if the holes were only like the pus of some infection, he thought, outward symbols of an obscure disorder? Had the patch on his chin begun to darken? He had studied it. Looking at it had made him think it had. Prolonged scrutiny deepened extant fear. It was hard to say.

Tired, he said.

Get some rest, she said. But make sure you ring the surgery. Okay?

He nodded.

A pause as she thought to kiss him. Instead she patted his shoulder, then looked at her hand in mild disgust at the limpness of the gesture.

I'll call you later, she said.

Okay, he said. See you soon.

He heard her coughing in the stairwell. He waited, listening, for the shutting of the door.

◎

He was studying the black cavity of the first patch when he noticed the fourth.

Seated against the arm rest of the sofa, his legs stretched out in front of him, he held a little pocket torch in one hand and his phone in the other, directing the camera towards the inexplicable aperture between his hip and groin.

The edges were smooth, still marble-like, though soft. He

prodded them gently, afraid to push too hard. It was quite unlike any other wound he had suffered, any wound he had seen. The flesh was not gashed, was not sutured or cauterised, was not ragged and raw as if the meat had been scooped out like so much ice cream from a tub or hacked out like plaster from a wall. It wasn't painful. It was easier to describe by the things it was not than by the things that it was.

He fumbled with the camera app on the phone.

The flash flashed.

Blurred. His trembling hand. He tried again, tried to steady himself, surprised himself by succeeding.

Flash.

Nothing. Less. The surrounding flesh in focus now, bleached and made sickly by the LED, and the edges of what he had taken for a rash now seemed smoother than ever, but within their perimeter there was only a void, a little pocket of nothingness. With the detonation of the flash the lens had caught no detail, no surface texture, no bodily mess, no blood, no fat or sinew, no anything.

Easier to describe by the things it was not than the things that it was.

Dropping the phone down on the floor, feeling a fresh swell of nausea, he noticed the back of his hand, and began to laugh with a despair that sounded to his ears like someone else's forced and insincere amusement. His own laughter did not sound like that at all. It was like someone else was laughing through him, he thought, an alien convulsion of his body, unbidden and uncontrolled. He thought of that laughing boy, pointing up at his window.

The smoothness. As if airbrushed. Marble, with the give of flesh. The slight discolouration.

He realised he had started to cry, in fear and in confusion.

Down on the carpet, the phone lit up. He squinted to read the notification, wiping his eyes.

How are you feeling? he read.

I have no idea, he said.

Have you rung the surgery? he read.

About that, he said, as if she could have heard him.

Now the second and third patches had gone black, become little holes. He thought about timing the duration of the process, watching from the first pale hint of discolouration until the skin went dark and then, somehow, by some bad, impossible magic, became those impossible cavities; but, restless with panic, he could not settle long enough to do so.

She had told him to ring the surgery. Better to go to the hospital, he thought. He heard her saying this and for a moment thought that she was there, saying it, insisting he go, over and over. He knew he should do so but could not bring himself to venture out; his shame—for that was what it was, was it not? he had thought, if you really interrogate it, surely shame—confined him to the flat. Showing her had made it worse. It stood to reason. He laughed at the phrase. If showing her had made it worse, what might showing a parade of nurses and doctors, strangers all, achieve? It stood to reason. And what, reasonably speaking, might they do?

His hand, his arm, his arm pit, his chin.

My point is, this isn't like any of that.

Had he known from the start, from the first moment he had touched it in the shower?

He paced the living room, disappearing in patches, swatches of grey on his body darkening like photographic emulsion exposed to an excoriating light, a body riddled with voids.

It continued.

In a way he was not surprised. It was a nonsense that made a kind of terrible sense. He was always unlucky. He wondered all his life had he been waiting for it. For something to happen to him. The boy pointing from the street below, marking him out. Taunts and laughter. Aged twenty, he had told a doctor he felt marked. At the time it had struck him as an odd turn of phrase, unexpectedly deposited in his mouth. He had always catastrophised. He had always expected the worst, and expectations carried weight. Unreal, they exercised a certain force. Now the obscure disaster was here. Patch by darkening patch, it was spreading, faster than any rash, any virus.

He saw the phone light up on the floor.

He nudged it with his foot, setting off the flash. It blinded him. When his vision returned he wished the blindness had stayed.

He stood under the halogen light in the windowless bathroom and watched the little patches of nothingness bloom across his person.

◎

The worry wormed through her all day.

She did not know what she was worrying about. The rash? If it was a rash. It wasn't anything, wasn't anything much. Then why did it worry her?

She had seen a kind of panicked understanding in his eyes as he'd stood there, holding the door to the bathroom open a crack, or, she thought now, holding it closed, keeping her out, earlier that day.

He was always keeping her out.

Where have you been? she had thought. Where did you catch it?

Through the door she had heard him talking. He had always been a talker in his sleep and in that moment she had thought that he sounded like he was talking in his sleep.

My point is, he had said, *this isn't like any of that.*

He had not replied to any of her text messages.

Where are you? she had said to the screen of her phone. As if he could have heard her.

She had tried not to think about the rash. In trying not to think about it, she had found herself thinking about it constantly. That weird discolouration. That fading. It had spread to his chin.

This wasn't like any of that.

He wasn't wrong.

She wondered had he gone to the surgery and knew that he had not. Anything bad, he always put his head in the ground. Never did him any good. Never helped.

She thought about the rash.

She coughed into her hand.

Her scalp itched.

She left work early, made her excuses, too distracted to think.

Why had he not replied to her texts?

For a moment—a brief, comfortable moment she would have liked to have extended indefinitely, and to which, later, briefly and unsuccessfully, she would try very hard to return—she assumed he had done as she had asked.

The flat was empty. He had gone to the doctor's.

But something nagged at her. Was it like him? When had he ever taken her advice? When did he ever do the sensible thing?

The empty flat felt peculiar.

A note. Might he have left a note?

The dining table in the living room was empty except for the usual mess of bills, receipts, bus tickets, books. There was nothing on the side in the open-plan kitchen. Nothing on the bed in the bedroom. She checked the mantelpiece. Nothing. On the TV stand—nothing.

Why couldn't you have left a note? she said, thumbing clumsily through the apps on her phone until she had found the messages.

Read receipts. Unreceived. Last Seen: 14:07.

It was 17:05 now. For fuck's sake, she said. Where are you?

In the middle of the small living room she trod on some-thing, nearly slipped and fell. Looking down, swearing, she saw his phone.

His phone.

Now the cold knowledge that something terrible had hap-pened took a hold of her. For him to go out without his phone. His phone? Him? No. Never. Unless—

She looked back at the door. Unless by some unlucky coincidence he had only just left. He would come back. She stood, listening for footsteps on the narrow staircase outside their door, the creak of the building, for his coughing in the stairwell. If he had left without his phone, he would return at once. It wouldn't take him long to realise. He would always return, would rather be late to wherever it was that he was going than go there without his phone.

She listened.

She coughed and looked at the device down on the floor.

Where are you? she said.

Did she know? she would wonder afterwards. Did she know then? She hadn't wanted to touch it.

She forced herself to crouch.

A wash of nausea as she moved. Her knees cracked as they flexed, let off little flares of pain as she rose.

The device recognised her fingerprint, the lock screen opening after the stutter of a small delay.

She swiped through the apps most recently used. Mes-sages. Photos. Camera.

She saw the little thumbnails of the camera roll. Was it then that she knew? She told herself she could not be seeing what it was that she was seeing. She could not.

She closed her eyes, hoping when she opened them that the world would have come to its senses.

It stood to reason.

She opened her eyes. She opened the Photos app. She gasped, dropped the phone onto the floor, and walked into the bedroom, as if she could get away from what she had seen, could unsee it, could cancel it out.

Hyperventilating, eyes full of tears, she stood in paralysed panic by the mirror in their bedroom.

She saw it.

She lifted a hand to touch it.

A slight discolouration. A little patch. Smooth. Soft. An inch below her collarbone.

She stood for a while in the bedroom, in the empty flat, and watched it slowly darkening.

I Would Haunt
You if I Could

1. INVENTORY

I live in a fourth floor flat on Wick Road. It's an old Regency townhouse, divvied into one-beds; I believe it used to be a private school for young gentlemen. Lined with elm trees, the street runs perpendicular to the sea. I'm up in the attic, in what must have been the servant's rooms, at the top of a flight of steep and narrow, twisting stairs, lit by weak bulbs hooked to motion sensors that only grudgingly detect your presence. If you stick your face out of the kitchen window, and angle your head so that you're looking south, you'll see the channel. Awkward but possible, though not for me; I'm scared of heights. Jack liked to do that, like a Labrador sticking its head out a car window, stupid and winsome, tongue lolling in the wind, and he'd call for me to join him, but I never would. Nevertheless I like to keep a window open so I can smell the sea. Last month, during the storm, the waves laid out a thick carpet of pebbles over the promenade and lawns. Some reached the Kingsway, which runs east to west, and I even found a few at the bottom of my road. Someone must have carried them there in their shoes, lodged in the lugs or slipped inside to bother tender soles, but I like to think the storm managed it; I would love to wake up one day and find that I'm living on the beach, and the sea outside my door.

My mother makes a habit of inviting herself round.

At first it was only my name on the tenancy, but when the landlord, Bryan, found out there were two of us living here, he put the rent up another fifty quid pcm. He thought that was reasonable—it is important to his self-image that he be considered a reasonable man—but when Jack moved out, of the flat and of my life, he didn't bring it down again; and so the rent is what it is, which is two thirds of my income.

(Sixty-six point six percent of my working day, I think, I am working for Bryan. Sixty-six point six percent of the food I eat to get through the day, I eat for Bryan. Sixty-six point six percent of the calories I burn between the hours of 9am and 5.30pm, I burn for Bryan. 666, I think: the number of the Beast.)

Since Jack left, my mother's visits have increased in frequency. *Honey, I was in the area, so I thought I'd pop by, on the off chance you were in…* she'll say, though I don't know who else she knows who lives round here.

A sweet old lady inhabits the ground floor flat. She owns two black kittens who have the run of the stairs. One is shy and scared of strangers; the other is bold and curious. It is too late now to say anything. On the first floor, a man named Simon, surely too tall for the low ceilings of our building, lives with his Italian wife, a lady who when we first moved in was often seen struggling about on crutches, as Simon had run her over by mistake. The couple on the third floor are rarely in: they live someplace else, and come to town for occasional weekend breaks. (It boggles the mind—the thought of owning a place like mine for just occasional use. I'm sure it would make me *furious* were it not for my natural equanimity.)

This close to the sea, everything gets damp; I'm forever on at Bryan about it. He always says there's not much he can do. *This close to the sea,* he'll say, quite reasonably, *everything gets damp. So there's not much I can do.* After all, water is insidious. It gets behind the cupboard in the bedroom where it blooms like dank pressed flowers above the skirting board and through cracks in the walls and at the window frames. The colour of tea stains the ceiling in a splotch above my bed—even Jack couldn't have spilt tea on the ceiling. A dehumidifier tries in vain to keep the condensation from the windows, which in the winter light becomes thick crystalline beads, refracting sunsets, spotted with black mould. It gets into your lungs and in your bones and dreams.

When I was a child, I was afraid of three things, in descending order: one, of drowning; two, of heights, at which I would always hear *the call of the void*, a term I never heard until much later on, but which struck me, when I learned of it, with the force of an epiphany: *yes*, I thought, *that is the thing that calls to me*; three, of other children. So: drowning, heights, and other children. Now I live in a fourth floor flat by the sea, alone.

I have always possessed a talent for solitude.

But voices travel—other people are never far away. In the bathroom, through the ventilation shaft, you'll hear Ethel on the ground floor talking to her kittens, or gulls and pigeons calling and cooing near the outlet on the roof, which makes it sound as though they've made their nests within the metallic echoing heart of the building. Sometimes I'll hear Simon murmur something to his wife. For such a big man he has a gentle voice. It will feel like he's in the room with me, which isn't ideal when I'm trying to have a bath. Next door sometimes a door will slam, and I'll think a door has slammed somewhere in my own flat, which can be quite alarming when you live alone in a flat with only four doors. (Bedroom, bathroom, living room, and front, arranged around the square metre-and-a-half of the 'hall.') Sometimes, as I heat food in the kitchen/living room, I'll hear a muffled cough, and turn around, but of course there's no one there. In the evenings I'll listen to the television on the other side of the wall in the apartment on the south side. I do not know who lives there, nor who lives on the north side, nor in the basement flat four floors below.

The ceilings are very low. Jack used to crouch. Sometimes I picture him, stood there by the window, his face lit by the sunset, crouching still.

When my mother visits, she never fails to enthuse about the place. It sets my nerves on edge. It would suit her well enough, liberated as she has been by the unexpected death of my father: with ample space for one (so she thinks), well-located, so close to the sea and various conveniences, and in a lovely old Regency building, it is a ready screen onto which she can project her fantasies of return. Because, as she never fails to tell me, she was young here once, and had such a blast; and she worries—she *worries*—that I cannot permit myself the freedom to have fun.

Thank you, mother.

I thought about installing a witch ball, to keep her out. They're quite fashionable nowadays. Wikipedia informs me that they were used for float fishing, and became connected with witchcraft in the 17th Century, but that doesn't interest me. The coloured glass would look pretty in the light here, hung above the sash windows or perhaps the flat's front door, as the building faces west. The windows are the flat's best feature: the light is wonderful. I like to lie in it. I would like to float on it, as on gentle waves. Can one drown in light?

I am prone to nightmares, small compulsions, and problems with my skin. Dry skin, eczema, etc. I spend a fortune at the chemist on Western Road—my bathroom cabinet stuffed with ineffective creams and witches' potions. Last summer, after a muddy, humid walk on the downs, a plague of tiny spots rippled across my shoulders. I felt grotesque, ashamed, bizarrely marked out. Jack was aghast but curious, simultaneously wanting and not wanting to touch the rash. *Prickly heat! Like a baby*, exclaimed my mother. Later, grown maudlin on wine, she said: *When are you going to have a baby, Genni? You know I don't want to be an elderly grandmother...* Since Jack left she has mostly moved on to other lines of enquiry.

Something else she said to me the other day:

I think you're depressed, Genni. (Thank you, mother.) You radiate sadness. (Depression is a cold sun.) You know I have the number of an excellent therapist. (I know she's been sleeping with her therapist, and she knows I know, and I know she knows I know, but for the sake of decency we maintain the fiction of my ignorance.)

He's over in Seven Dials. Not far at all. He's a lovely man.

I don't want to see your therapist, mum, I say, sighing, then quickly correct myself: *A* therapist. I don't want to see *any* therapist. In case she takes it personally; she's a master at making impersonal things personal. Perhaps she's testing me, daring me to breach our mutual silence on the question of her relationship with this man. I picture him: tall, tanned, all sonorous and gentle, masculine authority, the sort she likes.

She purses her lips.

Perhaps if you *write* about it, darling, she says, speaking softly now. Do you still keep a diary? (I do not.) You always used to write, scribbling in your *note books*. (I did. The way she says note books, as if it is two words instead of one, makes me bristle.) It can be very therapeutic, you know. (Yes, mother.) It might help you make sense of your feelings. Help you bring them under control. Impose some order. Wouldn't it be nice— not to be so upset all the time?

But I'm not upset, I want to say. That's not the problem. There's not a problem. Or the problem is I don't feel anything.

I'm not upset, I say.

Oh, darling, she replies. You don't have to lie to me.

And so I write. I book two weeks off work, and I write. About where I live, about my neighbours, about the mould on the windowsill. I describe it. Nonsense accumulates. Does it make sense of things? Perhaps. Does it help—is it therapeutic? Unlikely. But there's something else, I'm certain now:

something somewhere between description and—how best to put this?

Something between description and *production*.

2. POWERS

Something strange.

I bought the witch's ball. It is pretty, in the light, as I knew it would be. When I saw it, hanging blue and alone from a coat stand pushed awkwardly into a dusty corner of the Help the Aged branch on Church Road, I knew that it was mine, that it was meant for me. Standing on the pavement as the traffic splashed through pools of dirty water on that grey day, it seemed the prettiest thing in all the world. I screwed a hook into the ceiling above the door—Bryan be damned—and then lay down in the light to drift and stare and just quite mindlessly enjoy the sight of it. And I thought to myself: I wrote about you, and now you are here. Yes.

My mother is insidious.

When I was seven years old, I went through a phase of telling anyone who'd listen that I had psychic powers. I had discovered the topic of such abilities in a rather dry and academic book not intended for seven year olds that I had found on a school trip to Moulsecoomb library, near where the viaduct crosses the Lewes Road, after eluding the sight of Miss Lutrario to browse the aisles of the adult section. I was sniffy about all of the books in the children's section: I've always been a terrible snob, as my mother likes to remind me. I remember drifting through the library in something of a daze, as if time had been cancelled, all the pushing and shoving of life suspended. I have been prone to such episodes ever since: this was the first that I recall. In that floating mood, I came upon the book I know not how, found a cozy, cushioned corner where motes of dust hung like tiny lazy angels in the shafts of daylight falling through the window, and I read. It was a slow and dreamy afternoon. Later that day, after finally locating me, Miss Lutrario delivered one of the stern telling offs that were her stock-in-trade, but they let me take the book, loaned out on my new account with my new white library card that bore the green logo of the county council on one side and my immaculate signature on the other. (I have always prided myself on my handwriting. It is neat; I am neat.) I read of telepathy, pyrokinesis, telekinesis, automatic writing, spirit photographs, and telephone calls from the dead. Eventually I convinced myself that it was true, I had psychic powers, and I would become fiercely defensive in the face of anyone who tried to question me. It tickled my father. I spent long afternoons practicing. For a short while my mother tolerated the obsession, which spilled out in diaries and drawings and objects crafted of paper and card, string and PVA glue, wire and pipe cleaners and glitter and ink, but once it had endured so long that she could no longer comfortably rationalise it as a *phase* when discussing me with her friends, her tolerance ran dry. I remember her tilting her head, frowning, pursing her lips as she studied me, and I felt like a problem down *here* where I was, for her over *there*, on the other side of some *thing* I sensed but did not fully understand.

(I live my life, I think, in the shadow of things I sense but do not understand.)

Then she found the library book under my bed, months beyond its due date; I had become terrified of the scale of the fine that must have accrued, a terrible, growing, malignant claim of the past weighing on my present and my future, and so had hidden it, in the hope the library would forget. Would neglect to keep count. (Someone, I think, is always keeping count.) And perhaps they did—forget, I mean. Either way, I never went back. I never saw the book again. I still recall its title: *PSI: An Investigation into Psychical Abilities*. The author was some kind of a Baron from Germany.

I ring Bryan about the damp. The splotch above the bed

is getting worse. From tea it has darkened into the maroon of dried bloodstains. It is peculiarly symmetrical. I wonder is it a face. I squint, and it becomes a butterfly.

Two men come round, geezerish, friendly, fortyish but young in the face. I wonder if they're brothers: there's a likeness. And I quite like them. I make them cups of tea as they position a ladder in the stairwell outside my door, at the top of which is the attic hatch. The last flight of steps is the steepest. When I moved in, the delivery men, helped by Jack, got a bookcase lodged in that narrowing space. At the time I feared they'd never extract it, and we would have to negotiate our way around it every day as we came and went. Eventually it would become a mere fact of life. They tried their best; now the bookcase stands in my mother's house and the cream walls of the stairwell still bear the imprints of its corners. For a moment I wonder if these are the same men, then dismiss the thought. Bryan's guys prop the front door open, and once the ladder is in place they clamber up into the attic. I watch on nervously, worried the ladder might slip and one of them fall. I really don't like heights. And I hear it, though it's not me up there: the call of the void. Some movement downstairs makes me lean round the door to take a look. The shadow of a cat at the foot of the stairs, a swoosh of its tail, turns and is gone. The carpet where the ladder stands is rucked and scuffed by years of neglect. (I have never seen anyone from the managing agent, only Bryan and the guys he sends.) I stand in the flat and listen to the careful tread of work boots in the ceiling above my head.

I go into the bathroom and stare at myself in the mirror. From the air vent I hear Simon murmur something. I pick out a name: Ethel. Then—I think—a second name.

Can blood run cold? It's a phrase we use, a cliché, of course (of course), but I think it might be true.

ma

    ree

       an

No, I think, willing it not to be. I stop to listen, willing Simon to speak again. Did I hear that name? Or did I hear some other sound that these tired ears construed into those three diabolic syllables?

Suddenly I am aware of my own breathing, which has grown heavy, and I force myself to relax, which never works. When I was a teenager, I used to use mantras to get through the panic attacks that afflicted my secondary school and sixth form years. Strings of magic words I'd recite while I hid in toilet cubicles. Affirmations. I try to recall them but cannot. I sit down on top of the toilet lid and close my eyes. There's a pulse above one eye. The beginnings of a migraine fissure behind my temple. I open my eyes, and suddenly the bathroom light pulsates with awful brightness. Nauseous, I reach and tug the light cord, which entirely blacks the small room out.

Did I hear that name?

And if I did—a coincidence. It is someone else.

(I have long been susceptible to coincidence.)

What does it mean? It doesn't have to *mean* anything, I try to tell myself. (Meaning is terrible, a veritable trap.) But what does it *mean*?

(My mother's name is *ma-ree-an....*)

I feel pressure building behind my temple. I scrunch my eyes shut. Go away, I think.

Go *away*, a little louder now.

AWAY, I scream, and a sudden crash-bang-scream follows on the heels of the word, and I fear I've screeched it aloud. It is some time before I realise that the crash and bang occurred outside my head, outside the darkness of the bathroom, on the other side of the door.

(Later, I will tell myself that correlation is not causation.

Like a mantra: *correlationisnotcausation—correlationisnotcausation—correlationis*not*causati....*)

I step outside; the light assails me. The flat appears to tilt. The ladder has fallen. A man groans from round the corner, down the stairs.

Gary? a voice calls from above. Are you alright, mate? Gary? *Fuck.*

The shuffle of boots.

(Coincidences.)

Later, before the paramedics take Gary away, the one not called Gary, flustered, half dazed, remembers what had brought him here, and makes conversation in what might be an effort to assert some kind of normality.

What we thought, he says. Storm damaged some of the tiles and there's a leak. We've put a bucket in for the time being, but Bryan and the others will have to get it seen to. I mean, you can see the hole.

I nod. Thanks, I say, with the appropriate level of solemnity.

He reaches into his pocket, remembering something. There was this, he says, with a wan smile, and for a moment I think—and how I *cringe* to think of this, from my arsehole to my scalp—that he's about to offer me his number.

Instead he shows me a pebble, of a cool grey hue that ghosts with blue, almost a perfect circle, but flat, one that would be ideal, say, for skimming off the surface of a lake.

Are you brothers, I think.

No. He laughs weakly.

(Did I say that aloud? I didn't mean to.)

People always say that. But no—not unless our mothers lied to us.

I laugh a little too forcefully, and he glances at me, then away.

For a moment he looks as if he's about to weep. I suppose we're both in shock.

Looking back, I think he sowed a seed.

I replay the conversation. In memory, I think, one recalls conversations like voices heard through water.

We've put a bucket in for the time being, but Bryan and the others will have to get it seen to.

Bryan, I think. And the *others*.

And for the first time I realise that it's only me who is renting here: Bryan and Simon and Ethel and the retiree ghosts on the third floor, they're a gang. There's an association of freeholders, and I'm not invited.

Is that unreasonable?

I don't know why it bothers me so much.

I picture covens and sects and secret societies. The pomp of strange rituals, rhythmic chanting and the banging of drums, and a sacrifice.

When he leaves, I sit down on the sofa, exhausted, and feel something in my jeans press against my leg. Next door a door slams hard. A TV gibbers. I shift my weight around and fumble the object from my pocket.

The pebble, perfectly round. I don't remember him giving it to me. Grey, ghosted with blue. No, I think, recalling the storm: that can't be it.

Then, with fleeting concern: I hope Gary didn't break his neck.

3. MAGICAL THINKING

The sound of a hoover in the flat awakens me. Why is someone hoovering my flat? I should sit up in bed but my exhaustion is a dead weight pinning me down. There might be some small malignant person sitting on my chest. He or she feeds on me: every day they grow fatter off the bounty of my life. I hear someone cough. A man. Simon. I hear the hoover bump into the wall. I want to scream GET OUT OF MY FLAT but before I am able to do so I realise that he's out in the hall, hoovering the stairs. He does this sometimes. I forget that he does occasional jobs for the management company.

In the bathroom as I pee I hear Ethel talking to her cats.

Oh, *Fuchsia*, she says. What have you brought me this time?

When I return to my bedroom, I notice that the damp's got worse. Now the dank patches bloom out from behind the tall boy against the external wall, beside the boiler cupboard. I don't have enough energy to swear. The maroon stain above the bed seems larger, but perhaps I'm imagining that. It isn't a butterfly, I think—that's a face, and no lie. I wonder should I message Bryan. Would that be unreasonable, not 24 hours after the accident? It is Sunday morning. I can leave it 'til the Monday.

Instead Bryan messages me. I don't know why. I suppose because it happened here.

Thought you might appreciate an update. Terrible news. Gary died last night in hospital. Viv and I hope you're okay. Take care.

Is this numbness shock? I wonder if I'm a psychopath. I wonder what he hoped to achieve in telling me. What am I supposed to *do* with this information?

Poor Gary, I think, and the thought sounds fake.

I take some paracetamol for what might be the beginnings of a headache.

When we first moved in, the walls of the flat were a horrible yellow. If you had painted a small patch that colour, just to test it, I suppose you might have thought it could look quite nice, but the total effect when all the walls bore that hue was subtly horrible. It seemed to pulsate very slightly. I could see it when I closed my eyes. It's the colour of suicide, said Jack. It seemed to seep from the walls, staining the light in the rooms, tainting the objects inside them. The first thing I did was paint them white. It took three coats, and even then I doubted my eyes. Squinting, I'd say: I can still see it. It's fine, Jack would reply. So you don't want to kill yourself anymore?

I asked. No, he replied. But now, on this Sunday a little more than a year on from that conversation, I squint and think I see it again. A subtle wrongness. A slight pulsation.

That wasn't right, I think to Jack. Not suicide. It was the colour of murder. Because after fourteen months in this flat already two people are dead: Gary and, nine months ago, my dad.

I'm washing up a few plates in the sink when my mother texts me.

Lunch?

I groan. It would be good to go out. I wonder how I've reached a point in my life when only my mother and my landlord ever contact me, then quickly bracket the thought, box it up, toss it up into the attic of my head or down into the cellar of my soul. Whatever, wherever: *away.*

Warm light streams in through the window though the day is cold. I peer outside, squinting.

Sure, I text, feeling a mixture of relief and defeat.

Café Rescue?

I hate that place, but at least it's near.

Sure, I say, and congratulate myself on how positive I sound today. Perhaps I need a new approach to life, a studied, focused Positivity. Today I shall lean into positivity. Today, everything I say and do shall be a *positive* thing. Positivity is a kind of magic, one in which I have never been adept. Good things come to those who are positive, I think, and chuckle positively at the thought.

I feel lighter already. I open all the blinds in the bedroom and the living room. Let the light stream in.

I don't know why I'm feeling good today.

1 pm, my mother replies.

The Rescue Café is a little place off Palmeira Square where the roads clog with buses around the lawns of the round-about and seagulls and pigeons defecate in flowerbeds. Jack and I used to meet on the Square sometimes after work, before going for a drink in a pub down in one of the mews. I shouldn't hold that against it, though: I'm being positive. The cafe's one redeeming feature is that its sandwiches are excellent, albeit over-priced. In fact, it's not really a little place, but the low-watt bulbs that hang bare and low on long wires in some over-thought decorative arrangement throughout its interior ensure that it's so gloomy it might as well be. There are dead roses pinned to little planks of wood, hanging too—you have to dodge both the roses and the bulbs. And there are too many tables—creaking, ill-balanced, salvage-chic—for the space. You worry about elbowing other people in the waist and so hold your elbows close to your sides. You worry about spilling your coffee so keep a finger resting lightly on the saucer. At the front, blocking the space by the till so that when you wait to pay you have to stand awkward-ly, not really knowing where to put yourself, there's a table of bare untreated timber on repurposed cast iron legs on top of which some turntables sit unattended. I have never seen them in use. I can't think of a worse place to listen to music. A panoply of telephones and typewriters cling to the walls like weird creatures in the deep-sea gloom. Everything, it seems, has been retrieved somehow, rescued from landfill, salvaged from scrap. I once had a nightmare that I was due to meet Jack here for lunch: I was terribly late and feared what he would say to me; when I arrived, all of the seats were taken by very attractive people with easy smiles and good teeth and skin, and so I stood, not knowing where to put myself, then one by one by one each of the telephones started to ring. I rushed to answer, first one and then the other, expecting Jack, but each time I picked up a receiver the ringing would flit to one of the other models.

Shush, Genni, I tell myself. Be *positive*.

Luckily a table's free, room enough for two but in the draught of the door when it opens, which my mother won't like.

I sit and the waitress, with terrifying, silent efficiency, has appeared and placed the menu down in front of me before I've settled in the chair. I smile and say thank you; she regards me with the wry boredom of someone infinitely cooler than I could ever be.

I frown and pretend to study the menu. When I look up, she's still there. A single perfect eyebrow rises on a face that doesn't otherwise move.

Erm, just a latte please. Thank you.

Food?

I'm waiting for someone. I gesture at the other chair. The waitress looks sceptical, then somehow nods without moving at all, before retreating gracefully into the deeper gloom at the back of the cafe.

Be positive, I think. A mantra: positivePositive posItiVePoSiTiVepOSITiVe—

Genevieve! Wakey-wakey!

My mother materialises onto the chair in front of me and rudely breaks the spell of comfort I had cast for myself. I look around at the other customers, louchely wrapped in the comfort blankets of their phones, suddenly self-conscious. My mother fills the space in a way I could not: her elbows do not press defensively into her waist from either side. She spreads out, bag and coat and scarf over two chairs, then sighs contentedly to herself as she looks around. I see her flash a smile in greeting at the waitress, who emerges with my latte.

Almond milk decaf latte for me, thanks.

She takes the menu and tilting her head holds it close to her face. She needs glasses but couldn't possibly wear some. She tried contacts once but they made her howl in agony. Do you know what you want? she asks me.

I'll have the tuna melt, I say, and try to smile at the waitress, who is smiling at my mother, but whose smile fades when she turns to look at me. I wonder what it's like to be so pretty and so cool. Not in a negative way, though: not with resentment or jealousy, but with a positive, outward-facing, empathetic curiosity.

My mother frowns. Quite a *lot* of cheese, I would have thought, she says, and my positivity takes a little dent. She almost *tuts*; by some tremendous effort of self-discipline she manages not to. Never mind: I have decided my positivity is more durable than that. Two weeks ago I undertook Resilience Training at work and so now I have it in my Resilience Toolkit to deal with minor knocks such as this.

I'll have the quinoa salad, my mother says, and beams up at the waitress with a high-watt smile that could light the trendy gloom of the Café Rescue all by itself, and the waitress nods and smiles and takes the menu away.

So! my mother begins, and I brace myself and reach down into my Toolkit to rummage through its imaginary contents, which I picture as implements of torture jangling in a sack.

I've been *thinking*, my mother says, after a pause. She leans across the table and gazes at me meaningfully.

I realise I'm nodding as if she's said something I agree with; it's an effort to make myself stop.

Yes, she continues. *Thinking*. Please hear me out, Genni.

When have I ever *not*? I think but do not say, clinging tight to my positivity and the implements in my Toolkit.

My mother takes a deep breath.

Now, these last few months, you've been through a lot. First your father, of course. And now this poor, poor man.

Gary, I say.

Gerry, says my mother, nodding, staring down at the bare wood of the table and pursing her lips. Her eyes have filled with tears. The table might have been rigged together from the wreckage of sunken galleons. Or perhaps its wood was cut from one of the diseased elm trees down my road.

So, I've been thinking, it would be good—*good*—for you to get out of the flat for a while. I'm not saying—hear me out—I'm not saying take a holiday. I know you haven't the money. And you know I'd help out if I could, but after all the *debts* your father left…

Then what? I say flatly.

My mother gazes at me sadly.

We could swap flats for a time. A fortnight, say. A flat swap! Isn't that a nice idea?

I'm shaking my head.

Hear me out, Genni.

No, I say. No.

Hear me out.

I'm hearing you out.

The waitress appears with our food and I sit back to give her room as she places the plates on the little table.

My mother frowns, shakes her head, rubs her brow as if she can feel a headache coming on. Me, I think: I'm the headache coming on. Haven't I always been?

(I do not say these things.)

My mother thanks the waitress.

No need to *hiss*, she murmurs, pointing her chin at me like the tip of a weapon. It's just an idea.

I nod.

You don't have to make a decision now.

I continue to nod.

But give it some thought, okay? Take some time to think it over. Don't just dismiss it out of hand.

I nod some more. I look down at the tuna melt, which isn't a tuna melt. I lift an edge of the panini and discover what I assume is some kind of pesto chicken thing.

Quite a lot of cheese, I would have thought, I think, and wonder if the waitress and my mother are in cahoots.

My mother picks at her salad.

Okay, I say. I haven't the energy to complain, so I take a bite of the panini, which is difficult to chew.

My mother looks at me and smiles.

I have one other suggestion. I know how you tire of my

suggestions, Genni, but only one more, I promise.

I try to smile back at her.

She reaches to her coat, draped over the chair beside her, and removes her purse from its pocket. From out of a pocket in the purse she draws a business card, which she slides across the table in my direction.

Something I've suggested before, she says. I know you've said no before but I just thought, after everything with that poor man Gerry, that you might reconsider. That's all.

I purse my lips and think: I didn't know therapists had *business cards.*

I find myself nodding. Be positive! I think.

Thanks, I hear myself say.

Later, as I turn to follow my mother back out into the glare of sunlight outside Café Rescue, I hear a telephone begin to ring somewhere behind me. Confused, I turn, and for a moment think that it's one of the decorative phones hanging from the walls. Frowning, I try to see, but my eyes have already adjusted to the sunlight and the interior of the cafe has been plunged back into darkness. Behind me, my mother is studying her watch. I find myself turning the business card over in my hand. Something nags at me, but I can't think what.

4. WISHLIST

I like to browse houses for sale on the internet and imagine which I would buy. I have certain criteria: ticking boxes narrows the search. I will own the freehold. You can get thousand-year leases, but even my mother won't live that long. I want to own the earth on which it stands. Forgive me. I know it's a conservative fantasy, but there it is. I want a house: not a flat, not a maisonette. No neighbours above or below. I would like it detached, frankly, if not located on its own island faraway, but in this fantasy that seems a step too far. It is important to be reasonable. In this fantasy I won't ask too much. I assemble mood boards for interior design projects, colour themes, house plants, items of mid-century furniture. I would like to be near a train station, perhaps Portslade, or Hove, or maybe Southwick. That puts the price up, of course, but I think it's necessary. I don't drive, and it's important to be able to get away. I would like to be relatively close to the sea. A modest garden or at least a yard. I would like an attic with a desk at which I might write about things other than myself. An attic with a hole in the roof through which you can glimpse the colour of the sky. Or a window through which you might, if you stick your head out of it, glimpse the sea. I picture Jack there, looking out. Perhaps an attic room is a step too far. Perhaps a two-bed will suffice. Yes. That would do for me—yes. I lose track of time. An idle fantasy becomes a reverie, becomes a fugue of Google searches and browsed galleries and bookmarked URLs. It feels close. Another world, just like this one in all other respects, beyond the thinnest membrane. I could poke my fingers through. I could will it into being. If I had half a million quid.

What brings you here? he asks at last, and I can't quite believe I've done it.

I shift in the chair. It's not very comfortable. I wonder what did I expect: a chaise-longue? Some kind of velvet fainting couch?

My mother suggested I come, I reply. It was my mother's idea.

Did you want to come, yourself? For yourself?

No. Maybe. I don't know.

I nod, though I don't know at what, before looking up, expecting this tall, leathery, handsome man to speak, but he does not. The silence hangs in the air. The room begins to tilt. I shut my eyes.

Do you not want to be here?

I've been here ten minutes and at last he's twigged.

Isn't that a leading question? I ask him.

Your answer to the previous question implied you might not want to be here.

(This is infuriating.)

We can change the subject.

(Did I say that aloud?)

Yes.

What do you want to talk about?

Nothing.

You don't want to talk? Or you want to talk about nothing?

I suppose that's the heart of it. My mother asked me what upsets me. But nothing upsets me. That's the problem. I don't feel anything. Just a flatness.

Okay. In the last few years, would you say anything particularly upsetting has happened to you? Not did anything *upset* you, but did anything that others would consider let's say objectively upsetting happen to you.

I shrug. Something about the dynamics of this encounter are making me feel like a teenager: it's unpleasant, but weirdly comfortable.

My dad died. My boyfriend left me. A guy died in the stairwell of my flat.

That's quite a lot. Did these things upset you?

Yes. Dad dying upset me.

And your boyfriend?

Yes and no. Mainly it was just such a shock.

And this guy?

Gary? Gary dying, yes.

So Gerry dying upset you?

No and yes.

Okay.

He nods, looking off to the left.

In the silence I imagine him rising from the chair to stand over me. I am paralysed, as one sometimes is paralysed in dreams, or perhaps someone has tied my hands behind my back with rope. The room is a field somewhere and the bright sun behind him sets his face in hard shadow, through which his blue eyes gleam. As he looms he lays a hand atop my head with a kind of tenderness. He murmurs something. A prayer, I think. A string of incantations. I feel something writhe inside of me, a second self that lives somewhere beneath the skin, and I realise that I am only its carrier, and it is as this man's murmuring becomes a shouted chant that my second self begins to thrash in pain, and he draws it out, out, out—

You can't blame your mother for everything, Genni.

I look up suddenly. Did he really say that?

Excuse me? I rub my eyes against a headache coming on.

Why did your boyfriend leave you?

(Where does he *get* these questions?!)

Do you need *qualifications*, to be a therapist? I ask, because I want to change the subject, but the vehemence of the question surprises even me.

The therapist isn't surprised. Nothing surprises him.

Why do you ask that? he asks me. His voice is sonorous, gentle, and infuriating. His eyes are quite remarkably blue. *Piercing blue eyes*, my mother would say. But I don't want to be pierced.

I shrug. Maybe I fancy a career change.

Do you?

I don't have a *career*. Well, maybe I do. In admin. Is it a career if you've been stuck in it for the last eight years and can't see a way out and never wanted to get into it anyway?

He nods and looks off to the left again. I wonder what he's nodding at. Something in that field. Does he see it, too?

How long have you been sleeping with my mother? I think, but do not say. Do you fuck your other clients, or just her? I think but do not say.

Instead I say: I'm sorry. I don't think this is my cup of tea, after all.

Did you mean to kill that man? he asks, but his lips do not move as he says it.

He's still looking off to the left as I leave the room. I wonder what he's looking at. Before the door closes, he says:

You can't blame your mother for everything, Genni, and I swear to God, he starts to laugh. Through sealed lips he starts to laugh.

As I walk home from Seven Dials, I spin my rejection of therapy as a positive thing: I tried it, but it wasn't for me.

Back indoors I can hear Simon hoovering the stairs. *Again*, I think. Is it really necessary? As I take the steps I dread having to squeeze past him along one of the narrow corridors, but by the time I reach the final flight it's clear he isn't out in the stairwell at all; and it appears that someone is hoovering my flat. I feel my muscles tense and my stomach turn just a little bit.

I take the steps one at a time, trying to get a hold of myself, to stave off the panic I can feel starting to build. I stand outside the front door on the tiny landing for a moment and try to calm myself.

The hoover stops as my key turns in the lock.

Bryan? I think.

This cannot be.

I step into the flat and there she is, wrapping the power cable back into place.

Genni! she says. How are you?

I make straight for my bedroom and shut the door.

Genni? I hear her call.

I have to gather myself. I take my coat off and toss it on the bed and study my face in the mirror.

Be positive, I think, but I can feel it failing. My bottle of water from last night is sat on the bedside table, on the side I still consider *my side* as opposed to *Jack's side*. I grab it and drink. Then I steel myself.

I open the bedroom door.

What are you doing here? I say.

I thought I'd visit!

Mum—

I was in the area.

I nod. In the area, I say. Mum, I saw you two days ago.

Yes. And?

Her smile deteriorates, then quickly reconstitutes.

Mum, I say, why do you have a key to my flat?

Faint puzzlement flits through her expression. Genni, you gave me the key. When you moved in. In case you ever got *locked out?*

No I didn't.

Yes you did.

No I did not. I did no such thing.

I can feel my nostrils flare. My eyes are wide. I repeat myself, then add: And am I locked out? Do I look locked out?

Her smile fades and she emits a sigh of wearied concern.

Genevieve, she says. You've just forgotten.

She places the hoover neatly in the corner of the room as if that's where it belongs. For a second I think she's going to pat it and say *there's a good boy*.

Well, I'm sorry, she says instead. I didn't mean to upset you.

I walk to the sink and pour myself a fresh glass of water. I down it and immediately feel the need to pee. Is that physically possible? Whatever. I try to readjust. I turn back to face my mother.

I have things to do, I say.

She nods slowly.

I need you to leave, I say, when she doesn't move.

Very well. Did you consider my suggestion?

The flat swap? Sure. No, I don't think I'll take you up on the offer. Thanks, though.

And my other suggestion?

I laugh.

Actually, I say, beginning to relax for the first time since entering the flat, I did consider your other suggestion. In fact I've just been to see him. He'd had a cancellation.

Something like happiness fills her eyes. Oh *good*, she says. He's wonderful, isn't he?

I shrug.

Genni, I'm so proud of you, she says, looking down at the floor, as if the thought of pride in me makes it hard for her to look at me at all. This could be a big step for you.

Mum? I say.

She looks up at me.

It's not my *cup of tea.*

She flinches.

Now I need you to go, I say, and I practically frog-march her out.

When she is gone, I turn back into the flat, having double-locked the door, and in the living room collapse onto the sofa. On opening my eyes I'm assailed by the sensation that change of some sort has been at work in the room, and that there is something unfamiliar in its aspect, and I don't know how I had not noticed it before.

At first I can't tell what it is, what has changed. Something in the atmospheric pressure, perhaps. Something in the quality of the air or of the light.

I gaze around the room, trying to work it out. I stand then cross into the bedroom and try to work it out. I stand in the bathroom and hear Ethel say: *Fuchsia! Really, again?* in a tone of mild to moderate despair.

Then I realise what it is. Above the front door.

There's a tiny hole in the plaster from the hook. The hook has gone, too.

I drag one of the chairs from the dining table and position it in front of the door. I check its stability first: wouldn't want to fall! Hahahahaha. Then, with creaking knee, I step up onto the chair and feel a sudden dizziness spill across my vision.

Once I'm steady, I bring my attention to the plaster, to study the hole left by the hook, but now the hole has gone, too, which cannot be.

This cannot be.

I feel that dizziness slosh through me, and so, sensibly, I step down from the chair, wondering if plaster like puckered flesh might heal itself.

Unnerved, I retreat to my safe space—the bathroom—and close the door. The instant black-out darkness startles me, and for a moment I have to fumble for the cord.

This cannot be.

I stare at myself in the mirror and wonder do I recognise the woman staring back.

You look old, Genni, I think.

(My positivity is lapsing.)

No, I think, in my own defence: just tired.

Now something else is bothering me, but I can't think what.

I sit down on the toilet seat and close my eyes and try to recall the mantras I used to have.

When I open my eyes the yellow light of the bulb startles me. The yellow gleams from all the surfaces, and I see now what it is, the thing that bothers me: the bathroom is aglow with cleanliness. *Someone has cleaned the bathroom.*

Someone?

I exhale through my nostrils. Blinking, I leave the bathroom and cross into the bedroom, and notice the same thing again: the windows have been cleaned. The carpet has been hoovered. My bedside tidied up, my bed remade, my desk newly, strangely organised.

I look into the chest of drawers to see if she's organised my underwear, and am relieved to find that no, she has not.

Out in the living room I kick the hoover as if it's betrayed me. I guess it came with the flat. *Bad boy!* Bryan's hoover.

The hoover topples and falls. I sit down on the sofa, which also came with the flat, and then immediately leap back up and practically tear the bag out of the vacuum. In my fury it's quite a struggle, but when it comes free it does so with a satisfying explosion of dust, dirt, crap, all the shit my bitch mother hoovered up without my permission, and it billows in clouds as I shake the bag and laughing as it spills I start to cough and rack and so drop the bag and spin away, delirious.

There's skin in that bag, I think, in the dust that stings my eyes and irritates my throat: my skin and Jack's skin and my mother's skin, and dad's.

Giggling, staring through watering eyes, I turn back to give the bag a kick, then fall onto Bryan's sofa instead, where I struggle round onto my side and curl up in a foetal position, push my face down between the cushions and close my eyes.

My rage is a dam that is bursting, I think, and feel my squashed old tired face begin to smile.

Now *rage* is my cup of tea—yes.

And all the things that cannot be: all the things that cannot be—yet *are*.

5. SOMEONE IS TYPING A MESSAGE

Yes.

My mother has this amazing ability to misbehave quite terribly and then immediately draw a line under it. While I, if I fuck up, will ruminate for days, half mad with guilt, my mother will not: she'll just call a few days later, back to her breezy self, judgmental and relaxed and amused, as if she had done nothing wrong, and sometimes it would make me wonder had I imagined it, the thing she'd done, the thing I'd thought she'd done. And each outrage, of course, always also serves to shift the threshold by which other outrages might be judged.

Now, from the way she let me march her out of the flat, I think she knows that she overstepped the mark: she would never have acquiesced to such a show of force if she had not. So I know she knows, and she knows I know she knows, and still she draws the line.

I'm having a coffee in Café Rescue when she calls. I don't usually come here alone, but I needed to get out of the flat. When things begin to get to me, its walls draw in; its low ceilings press down; the old yellow pulsates through the coats of trade white that I put down just over a year ago. I'll find myself turning to say something to Jack, only to realise with a jolt that he is gone.

Perhaps another coat will do it, I think, and am delighted by this green shoot of positivity, and by the thought of having something practical to do.

Are you going to answer that? a man on one of the fashionably rusty metal stools by the window says, scowling, jarring me out of my reverie, and I notice that my phone is skittering across the table, creature-like.

For a moment, goofy and delirious, I want to yell *Sure, isn't that what it's for?* and leap up and take one of the phones clinging to the wall and pretend to answer that instead with daft theatrical aggression, but instead I say: Oh. Sorry.

Genni, my mother says.

Her voice is soft. This means she's drawn the line but still sees the need to deploy some small measure of tact. I wonder what she wants, because it's her wanting-something voice: wanting me to do something for her, that is, rather than the sterner wanting-me-to-do-something-for-my-own-good voice.

I let her wait a moment. A power move.

Genni?

Yes. Hi, I say. Sorry.

Where are you? she asks, and I picture her pressing her ear

into her phone, trying to lean into my world as if the device were a little portal through which she might pass bodily.

I'm in Starbucks, I say, and the waitress, passing my table, looks at me as if I've just broken wind.

Starbucks? My mother is startled. Oh, she says.

Silence. I let her wait. She expects me to speak. I bite my lip. Another power move. A minor flex.

I wanted to ask, she starts to say, then stops to clear her throat. I wanted to ask for a favour. Might you be able to pop by mine sometime this weekend? Only I need to get some things down from the attic and I don't trust my knees.

I don't trust every bit of you, I think but do not say.

Genni?

Oh, God, I think, did I think but also say? Bad Genni.

Sorry, yes?

Genni, did you hear me?

Yes, I say, sighing, thinking *haven't you got someone else to do that sort of thing for you?* Because my mother always has men fussing around: surely there's some bloke who could do it?

Yes, I say. Sure.

Great! Thank you. I'm going on a little *holiday*, you see.

Suddenly, I beam. The dim hanging bulbs seem to flicker on a little surge of power. She's pissing off for a week: yes! Perhaps I'll get a week of peace, a week of no little comments, no suggestions, no demands.

Okay, sure, I say. Mum, I need to go.

Tomorrow, darling?

Yes, sure.

The morning, if you can.

Of course.

By ten?

Yes. No problem.

Thank you, Genni.

I hang up the phone before she can say anymore. She'll think that's an insult, which it is, but she'll quickly rationalise it as something else.

I drain my cup. As I walk to the door, the guy on the stool smirks at me and says *Starbucks?*

Fuck off, I reply, smiling cheerfully, as I step back out into the light.

◎

I'm walking back past the Starbucks on Church Road when I see them.

They are sitting in the window, which is fogged on the inside, rendering them into impressions, but not so imprecise as to fail to resolve into the terrible certainty that yes, yes, that is *they*, that is them: there they are. Just two people having a coffee. They look like they're enjoying each other's company: they look so *normal*.

This cannot be.

Because it's Bryan and my *mother*; a tall almond milk latte for her, I expect, some kind of massive monstrous coffee-flavoured lactate bucket for him.

She reaches across the table and touches his hand.

I am staring. I mustn't stare. I hurry on, and already I am doubting that it was they I saw, but in my heart I know the cold truth, and my brain begins to whir as it seeks out explanations, joining dots, connecting discrete bits of uncertain information, forming awful new certainties.

Had they ever even met before? Do they know each other?

How? Since when? In what capacity? Why was she reaching across to touch his hand? Are you kidding me??

At least no one's hoovering the stairs when I get home.

That cannot be, I tell myself. It cannot be.

It wasn't them.

They.

No.

Except, yes—*yes*.

Stray dots connect. Three dots dance. *Someone is typing*

a message. Then they settle. Someone isn't typing anymore. The yellow walls press in; the ceiling pushes down. Dank flowers bloom. The shape above my bed seems to smile benignly down at me. I know that cannot be, yet there it is. It's definitely a face now. It's getting worse, but it seems wrong to pester Bryan about it after Gerry's death. And if I call him, will it even be he who answers, and not my witch mother, *ma-ree-an?*

I might be losing it, but I'm not stupid, I know what this is: a patch of damp is smiling at me; my *mother* and my *landlord* are friends, lovers, co-conspirators; and I, by force of will, caused a fatal accident. I'm not stupid, but knowing better cannot save me. In a glass of water a knife looks crooked: knowing better cannot correct for that. But what if the knife is really crooked, and the water is crooked, and the glass is crooked too: what then? Yes, perhaps the knife is crooked after all.

Guilt is an infestation, a subdermal pestilence. You feel your skin ripple and itch, your nose wrinkle and twitch; there's a coppery taste in your mouth and you feel as if your heart has slowed and time has slowed and all the world beyond the central fact of your shame has receded into meaninglessness. Only guilt: the central meaning.

I can't bear this, I need a thing to do.

I take the bus to the B&Q out on Lewes Road, buy two tubs of paint, return to the flat, and all the while I feel the eyes of strangers assessing me, on the bus, on Western Road, as I fumble with the keys to get back into the building as the darkening heavens open above me. Fuchsia watches me from the second flight of stairs, and her eyes are bright and full of judgement. It's dark in the hallways. The sensors are slow to recognise my presence, slow to illuminate the stairwell. Where's your friend? I think. Have you killed her, too, Fuchsia? Whatsername. Lavender?

I don't bother to cover the furniture, or to change my clothes.

I paint. I paint until I'm exhausted, until my arm is dead. I sit on the edge of the bed and hear Jack say *it's the colour of suicide,* and suddenly my happy mindless meaningless peace breaks, and I realise what I've done.

That's not white paint I've bought, oh no.

I start to laugh, because there's nothing else to do.

I look at the tub and *cackle* like some cartoon witch.

Very good, Genni. Very good. Your best effort yet.

It is a pungent hue.

No, Jack, I think, *you're wrong.*

It's the colour of murder.

The motion sensors don't notice me and so the hall is dark, dark enough to make the slit of yellow light beneath the door of the flat below mine glow brightly. Usually I would hear them in, the ghosts of the third floor, moving about, murmuring to themselves, the retirees who spend most of the year in New Zealand but keep the flat for occasional stays, but this time I do not. What's their role, I think. What's their part to play? What's their position in this bizarre company? I stand outside the door a moment, listening. I expect to hear my mother's voice.

Instead I hear footsteps approach the door and in a sudden panic I jolt myself away.

Fuchsia, I think, seeing the bloody gift deposited outside Ethel's front door, *it's just what I've always wanted!*

Too late I realise I'm not dressed for rain but out I go, into the wind, into horizontal rain that stings my eyes and face. Was it raining before? I don't recall. I try hard not to think, replaying a mantra

correlationisnotcausation, correlationisnotcausation

or

ihateyouihateyouihateyou

as I walk down to the beach. By the time I reach the

Kingsway I'm sodden, but I don't let that stop me. I stamp across the boggy Lawns then kick pebbles out in front of me as I march along the promenade. Aside from a handful of daft joggers I am alone. Through the gust and bluster, I walk, head down. Calves burning, I walk and walk.

I'm on the groyne by the statue of a Torus, which—I googled it—represents the universe, watching the mad rise and crash of waves as the sun sets. I wonder do I want to drown, to die. Is that what I want? Is that why I have brought myself here? It would be a good night for it. The storm's just getting started.

Even from this low vantage I hear it: the call of the void.

I walk again, to stay these thoughts. Suicide is a focal point. It exerts a centrifugal force. Turned away from it, other thoughts circulate like water in a plug that never drains: of my dad and of my mother, of Jack and Gerry and Bryan, of myself as a child in a library reading of strange and terrible powers and of the hope that I too might one day wield strange and terrible powers, if I am a good student, if I apply myself, if I practice.

Sheet lightning shivers over dark water. As the waves crest the water glows.

All throughout my childhood I practiced.

I remember Jack, during another storm, hunched over his phone delightedly watching the registration of lightning strikes on a little map.

That was practically right on us! he says, and it isn't hard to believe him. *I think it hit the Starbucks.*

I've gotten to Saltdean before exhaustion brings me to a halt. I realise how drenched I am. With each step my trainers squelch. The cold eats into my bones and abruptly I am aware of the lightning and of the danger it presents. I suppose this implies I want to live. All strength departs. Once all strength has gone, beneath all that, some final somatic back-up reserve carries me to a bus stop where cashless I fumble with my

phone, touch input scrambled by rain, and try to purchase a
bus ticket on the ticket app, on which I note with weird clarity
that the price has risen, for prices always rise, and wonder
what will that work out per annum for me, as someone who
goes to work by bus, but just as the purchase finally completes
the bright screen of the device becomes a dark mirror reflecting a haggard face and some inexplicable flex of self-restraint
prevents me chucking it into the road, as if the phone's to
blame. An empty bus draws up. One moment it wasn't there
and the next it is, as if it has slipped through some cut or seam
in the nighttime. I try to smile as the doors rattle open.

My phone's died, I say, desperate, waving the device,
feeling pitiful. Look at the state of me! I think but do not say.
I don't have any cash, I say. I'm sorry.

The driver, a middle-aged woman with a very square face
and remarkably bushy eyebrows over pale blue eyes, smiles
and nods me on. I could collapse in thanks. Instead, unsteady,
I make my way down the aisle, where I take a seat in the row
second from the back.

I close my eyes and feel the rhythm of the vehicle work
through me. I feel every divot in the road, every pothole,
every speedbump. Surely my head exceeds the load my neck
can bear. I shall sleep, I think, and it will be good. I will get
dry and then I shall sleep for a long time, and then I can forget
all this.

The dead phone in my pocket begins to ring. *Jack*, reads
the screen. Panic and longing flood my system. Instead of
answering, I power it down. Shifting on the seat, I feel something dig into my thigh. I fumble in the pocket and pull out
a little pebble, which is perfectly smooth. I turn it over in my
hand. By the light of the bus it ghosts with blue. I remember
other storms. Storm Francis. I wonder what name they'll give
this one. Storm Genevieve?

With a lurch I realise I'm not alone on the bus. From the
row behind me a tall man leans forward; in the act of leaning

forward he appears. He could rest his chin on my shoulder if he wanted to. I think he might, because I can smell him, aftershave and sweat and Listerine and liquor, and from the corner of my eye I see the leather of his face wrinkle into some strange facsimile of a smile. His eyes are blue and piercing.

You can't blame your mother for everything, Genni, he says, through lips that do not move.

6. MUSEUM

A strange ringtone wakes me. I don't remember setting that. It is sharp and penetrative. It has a diabolical insistent melody. Woodpeckers, I think, have been known to tap the skulls of baby birds; *peck-peck-peck-peck!* and then they eat the brains. I've not heard this one before, but I shall name it Woodpecker.

I'm still soaking wet. My throat is sore and my sinuses congested. I feel like I've been dragged backwards underwater. Perhaps I jumped in off the groyne after all. I turn and reach to stop the phone but in fumbling accidentally answer it. My phone is too old to be waterproof. My mother's voice leaks out, tinny and full of interference like some melancholy robot expiring in a scrap yard.

Genni? she says, and I think *you're a woodpecker too.*

Genni?

Peck peck peck!

I fumble the device to my ear. For a moment the sound is scrambled. I should put it in a tub of rice.

Hi, I say, trying to sound awake. Hi, mum. How are you?

Genni, are you ill? she asks, because my voice is thick with cold.

Just under the weather a bit, I say.

My mother used to be a germaphobe but lately she's been working on that. She won't want me round, though. I could stay in bed. I could get dry and change the bedding and just stay in bed. I could work on that.

If you're not feeling well, we could—

No, it's fine, I say suddenly, suddenly fine. It's fine. What time is it?

9 AM.

Okay. We said 10, right?

Yes. Well, 9.30. But 10 is fine.

Okay, I say, and I don't know why I'm saying this. I'll be with you soon.

Okay, says my mother, and either the water in the phone or the quality of the signal or else some quality in her own voice makes her sound uncharacteristically uncertain.

Okay, I say, and hang up the phone, by which I mean I end the call and toss it on the floor.

The number 49 takes me to North Street, then from the stop just down from Princes Place, which clogs with people, the Coastliner takes me further east. From the window of the coach the sea looks calm. Sunshine diffused by clouds buffs its surface to a metallic sheen. In the daytime now last night might not have happened at all, but the damp in my trainers belies that.

My mother's flat is freakishly tidy, but that's nothing new. It's less than a year since dad died and she has reconfigured the place several times already. She knows builders, painters and decorators, handymen, and they'll never charge full whack. Colour schemes have come and gone like some animated gradient. Teal. For a while everything was grey and teal. Then came a flourishing of autumnal hues: oranges, auburns, browns, some faded red in careful accenting. Within a month of his death every trace of dad had gone. It was as if she had been waiting for it. It's a lovely flat, the second two floors of a maisonette, of which the websites would say *it's like living in a house!*, which it is, but my mother insists on calling it a flat on the basis of some grudge against my father. It has two thirds of the garden and the attic, and the guy downstairs is quiet and a pushover. My parents, downsizing after I left home, moved here ten years ago. The only thing wrong with the place is that it's in Saltdean. That was my father's influence. Mum has never forgiven him.

Later, much later on, I think: should I have noticed anything? Was that freakish tidiness not a little more freakish than usual? It's hard to say. I don't visit very often; since dad died, maybe twice.

But I should, I think, have noticed the boxes. Because no one packs like this for a *holiday*.

Stupid Genni.

It occurs me that this is my second trip to Saltdean in two days.

Genevieve! She sings my name with something resembling human warmth. I receive a forceful hug in the doorway, then she leads me inside and up the stairs as if I've not been here before. The shared stairwell is darker than Café Rescue, but the rest of the building fills with coastal light. The hug startled me: I wasn't expecting contact. Perhaps her therapist is really helping with her fear of germs.

Could I interest you in a *cup of tea?* she asks.

The weird emphasis jars. I glance at her and from her eyes can tell her mood is strange. Whatever, it doesn't matter: I'm just here to do the one thing for her, to get something down from the loft. Of course, that was just her pretext, but I can stick to it. I curse myself, knowing that she gave me the opportunity to stay in bed, and I refused it.

No thank you, I say. A glass of water, though. Thanks.

Glass of *water,* she says, looking round, as if the words are new to her, then fetches a glass from a cabinet and fills it from the filter jug.

I'm standing on the steps gazing down into the garden when she passes it to me. At the back of the garden, beside the shed, there's a swing chair my mother got my dad to install soon after they moved in. She's probably embarrassed by it now: it doesn't fit her current style themes. There's a rustic cheesiness to it, all romanticised childhood, that I'm sure she regrets. But the garden is lovely. And it's a garden! I wish I had a garden. I wonder who does her gardening.

She says something, which startles me.

You've always been such a daydreamer, Genni, she murmurs, standing behind me.

The proximity is suddenly uncomfortable. I turn and flinch, making room for myself, and she steps back. A flash of something in her eyes. I'm the headache coming on. As I turn away from the garden, I see, out of the corner of my eye, the shed door open, and a man step out. Glancing back I hold a scream. Blue eyes gaze up at me. Piercing eyes: a woodpecker gaze. That man is too tall for the shed. In his hand he holds a pair of secateurs. He waves, waving the secateurs, and I think of Leatherface from *The Texas Chainsaw Massacre*. My mum waves back, blind to this connotation. I push past her, out of the kitchen, and walk back into the living room.

So, I say, trying to focus, suddenly brusque, what was it you wanted from the attic?

Oh, you don't have to get it now, she says. Adrian can do it for me—I wasn't expecting him today. But it's nice to have you round. Are you sure you don't want a cup of tea?

I need to focus, I need a thing to do. No, it's okay, I say. I'll get it.

About that cup of tea?

The water is fine, I say, and try to smile.

My mother studies me.

Okay, she says at last, then follows when I head up the stairs. The attic hatch is directly above the stairwell. A metal pole, a hook at one end, is leant beside the cupboard on the landing. With a struggle I get the hook through the eyelet on the hatch, and turn the latch, and the hatch comes down. Fumbling, I hook the eyelet on the built-in ladder, and with a struggle I pull it down. I slide the bolts to free the legs in sections. Its feet clatter to the floor.

I feel my mother's sceptical gaze on the back of my head. Like a woodpecker, I think. Peck peck peck; and then it siphons off your brains.

I'm at the top of the steps when I realise she's not told me what she wants, and I look back and see the stairwell, see the drop, and the stairwell tilts and I feel a flush of warmth and something spill across my vision. Did I mention that I'm scared of heights? It appears that I forgot. And I hear it: the call of the void. I could fling myself down the stairs. I wonder how that would feel. The rush and then the pain, then nothingness. Unless I'm unlucky. I think of Gerry. Gary. I grip the ladder.

Genni!

I'm okay, I say.

You never did like heights, she says, once she's decided I've righted myself. Honestly, it's okay, Adrian can get it. Come down.

No, I say.

My mother sighs.

What did you want me to get? I ask.

She stares a moment. A little flex. There are two cases somewhere at the back.

I remember she mentioned a holiday, and nod.

Careful on the beams. Your dad put his foot through the ceiling once.

And you never forgave him, I think but do not say.

Anyone for a cup of tea? a voice calls up the stairs.

I don't want a fucking cup of tea, I murmur, as I pull myself up into the loft.

A light switch attached to one of the rafters turns a bare bulb on. For a moment it blinds me, but then my eyes adjust. It hums. Finally, I think, looking round, into the shadows of the eaves, a little peace. Up here my mother suddenly seems quite far away. There's something reassuring about the dusty, musty coolness of the air. I feel removed from things; I would like to be removed from things. The attic is full of familiar smells.

My mother might have reconfigured the rooms below three times in nine months, but it's clear she hasn't touched this space. A couple of small plastic storage boxes placed near the edge of the hatch, doubtless pushed into the gloom from one of the lower rungs of the ladder, is all. Everything else, from the boxes labelled by hand with a Sharpie to the miscellaneous crap sitting on a unit of shelves to a small row of old suitcases, is redolent of my father; suddenly, I think, I am in his presence.

Dad, it's been a while.

I find boxes of my own things and give a little squeal of delight.

I can't imagine my mother doing this: she would have just chucked stuff out. *Just get rid!* she would say to me. If it doesn't *spark joy;* and I suppose I have never *sparked joy.* Once, I came home from university to discover that she had binned a box containing some of my oldest diaries. I was stunned by the thoughtless cruelty of this, and of her surprise at my response, as if *I* were the unreasonable one. In the end I apologised for saying hurtful things.

So this was clearly dad, because so many things I haven't seen in *years* I find neatly set into three medium-sized boxes. There are CDs—Nirvana, Joy Division, Kenickie, Hole, Pulp— but I was never a serious audiophile. There are necklaces and bracelets and earrings, cheap and pretty and colourful, and I find myself vertiginous with the realisation of how much I've changed. There are envelopes of photographs bearing the logos of Boots and Fujifilm and Kodak, and little undeveloped rolls of film from instant cameras. Here I am, I think, in the museum of myself. I feel myself growing faint. I find old diaries, which I sit down to read, and in spite of the discomfort of a seat of chipboard, time passes and I hear my mother calling to me but I do not reply. I hear that man talking to her down on the landing below the hatch and I do not reply.

Because time is cancelled, finally; all the pushing and shoving of life has been suspended, at last. In this floating mood I sit and read and at some point stand again to continue idly browsing the museum of myself. Motes of dust hang like tiny lazy angels in the orange light of the humming bulb and I no longer know whether the bulb is humming or if it's just my ears or the background radiation of the universe as atoms and quanta and memories and dreams churn in the void of all that is and all that is not and must never be.

I come to books: a coffee table edition of Frida Kahlo's paintings, a copy of *A Room of One's Own* become the colour of tea, the collected Emily Dickinson, and, with strange, dreamlike certainty, as if I had always known I was about to find it here, as if I had known it was here in this box all along, the essential manual of my childhood: *PSI: An Investigation into Psychical Abilities*. It hasn't visibly changed; the paper hasn't aged or browned. I might have put it down just yesterday. Somehow its unchangedness astounds me.

Later I wonder did she mean for me to find it. Was this all meant to be?

My mother calls my name, breaking the peace in the loft; I find myself covering the book as if I do not want her to see it.

Genni, you've been up there over an *hour*. Adrian and I need to go out. Can you come *down* now, *please*?

Okay, I call, telling myself that I can and will return, and I take the book and gather a few bits and pieces into one of the boxes, its previous contents decanted onto a shelf, and then shift the suitcases for my mother and, stepping carefully, pushing the cases ahead of me, make my way back towards the hatch.

Anyone for a cup of tea? asks the strange man standing in my mother's kitchen as I come downstairs.

I'm okay, thanks, I say sunnily, floating on some new wave of positivity, and I take my leave of my mother's house.

◎

Bryan calls when I'm on the bus. I do not answer.

He sends a text: *Please call me.*

Panic begins to simmer, becomes a rolling boil, as I wonder what he wants.

7. ACTION FROM A DISTANCE

Maybe this is a good thing, Genni, my mother says, and I would strangle her were she here with me on Bryan's sofa, but she's not, lucky woman, because she's out in Saltdean and I am in Hove and I suppose that constitutes a safe distance.

(But I practice, oh yes. I am a good pupil. I apply myself. And all distances, I think, contain a certain propensity for collapse.)

The phone burns against my ear. A cooked meal. When they siphon my brains, they'll be piping hot.

A clean break, she continues, and for a moment the signal gargles down the line. I mean, after the way things ended with Jack. And everything.

Ah, yes, I think. Everything.

The sheer unthinkable totality. The vast immensity of things.

I read back through all I've written since I resumed writing and am surprised to count nearly 14,000 words! Amazing. Well, imaginary reader, I can only apologise. Who would have thought that in talking to myself I would grow so verbose? My mother, bless her heart, thought that I might find *writing* therapeutic.

Maybe if you write about it, darling. Do you still keep a journal?

You always used to write, *scribbling in your notebooks. It can be a very therapeutic thing, you know. It might help you make sense of your feelings. Help you bring them under control. Impose some order. Wouldn't it be nice—not to be so* upset *all the time?*

But now I wonder: if the talking cure is premised on the notion that one might *talk* oneself out of one's neuroses, does it not follow that one might also *write* oneself deeper into sickness, into neurosis, into despair?

Hahahaha!

Bryan calls again. Looking up from my book, I watch the phone gibber and twitch on the coffee table, creature-like.

He left another voicemail yesterday.

I turn the page of my book. A new chapter: Action From A Distance.

On Bryan's sofa, in Bryan's flat, on borrowed time, I make myself comfortable.

Time is cancelled; sleepless, timeless, I apply myself.

And all around me close walls throb, yellow with intent.

◎

Later, I play the voicemail back again, again, as if expecting it to change. And change it must, for the universe abhors all duplication: in the universe every bastard thing is singularly, wretchedly unique.

I pick up slight variations in tone each time, changes of emphasis, previously undetected inflections, new diabolic resonances. Nothing is ever the same again: its againness tells, eventually.

Hi, Genni, I trust you're okay, he says again. I've tried to call several times now but for whatever reason you've not answered. I guess that's your business, he says again.

He clears his throat.

Um, well, I was calling to say... Viv and I have made some decisions that have considerable implications for you. They've not been, erm, easy decisions, and in many ways you've been a model tenant.

(A model tenant! He actually says this.)

But for various reasons, we have decided to exit the rental market.

(Like some kind of malign vehicle performing some neat manoeuvre, I think but do not say.)

Like some kind of malign vehicle! I bellow into the mic of my phone, as if he could hear. Perhaps if I shout it loud enough. Because voices travel.

Erm, he continues, obviously we appreciate this isn't news that you would want to hear.

(No, Bryan, I suppose that's fair.)

But I wanted to let you know in, erm, person, before putting it in writing.

(This is *in person?* Okay.)

I didn't just want you to get it in the post and for it to, you know, come as a shock.

(Of course, of course.)

Now as per the tenancy agreement we have to give you three months' notice. And that's fine, it really is.

(It's fine.)

But if, erm, and sorry—if we might be able to arrange something sooner, that would be great. But, you know, no pressure.

When Jack and I moved in, we thought we'd had a stroke of luck: renting direct, without all the fibrous layers of additional parasitic agencies between us and our landlord. Now I wonder if agents are quite so bad: do they *talk to you like this?*

No pressure, he continues.

It is important, I think, to his self-image that he be considered a reasonable man.

The phone is baking my brain.

Give me a call if you need anything.

I need a roof, I think.

Anyway. Erm, yes. Speak soon. Bye now.

Bye!

I live in a fourth floor flat on Wick Road, I think. *It's an old Regency townhouse, divvied into one-beds…*

Except I don't live here anymore.

Children are natural philosophers. As a child, I would skip down the street, turning sharply, hoping somehow to startle fate. Was my every movement predetermined, or could I with some knee-imperilling *jerk* force myself out of the groove in which I travelled like a coin down a penny spiral?

When you die, I thought, everyone becomes a God of their own world, fashioning a new earth and a new sea, bringing new life among new stars.

A born introvert, solipsism seemed to me a more or less plausible hypothesis.

Once, it occurred to me that past, present and future existed simultaneously.

Or: if an event was inevitable, then in some sense it was already true, had already happened, already exists. Our deaths are real, our ends as sure as our beginnings.

My death, I thought, was a creature, already at large in the world. Perhaps that creature came first; perhaps our deaths precede us. It must track you down. Life is a hunt.

Perhaps.

I am *here,* I think, and I am *going.* I am here and I am not.

I sleep and wake to that weight again on my chest, pinning me down. In the dull dawn I lie choking. My jaw is open; something is lodged deep in my throat. It is not uncomfortable. Half-waking, half-asleep, I see its massive twitching proboscis withdraw, dripping spit and blood.

Perched upon me, it looks around, and gives a contented, sated sigh.

I study its face, its leathered skin, its white eyes, and in the centre of each eye is lodged some cold shard of blue, and it studies me in turn with abstract interest.

When next I turn over, that strange insectile beast has gone.

I search Gumtree, Rightmove, Zoopla. I untick my usual filters.

Oh *god*, I think, overcome with horror: I don't want to live with *other people*.

I wonder what Jack is doing. I wonder where he is, who he is with, who he is fucking, where he is working, if he's in the same job or is he doing something new.

I unblock him on Facebook, but he hasn't posted in a while.

Looking up from my laptop, I see him stood at the kitchen window, twisting his neck awkwardly as he tries to catch a glimpse of the sea. It is raining again. Since I last saw him he has grown astonishingly tall, too tall for this flat, and when he returns from the window he stands stooping in front of me, stupid and winsome, drooling slightly, his perennial bed hair wet, his blue eyes sparkling. After a pause, he begins to cough and choke, and he falls to his knees, then vomits seawater onto Bryan's carpet. In the gush of sick, small pebbles gleam.

He looks up at me and in a voice like it's coming down a bad line says: it's the colour of murder.

◎

No pressure, Bryan says.

Things move quickly. I find a place with two other women, recent graduates, younger than me but they seem okay. I tell myself this is just a temporary thing.

(We're all temporary things.)

I'm in Brighton now, still just off the Western Road, still close to the sea.

Maybe this is a good thing, Genni, my mother says.

Yes, I reply, sometimes change is not so bad.

I wonder where my mother's gone on holiday; I didn't think to ask. I haven't heard from her in a while.

A lot can change in a fortnight. In two days I go back to work.

◎

Suddenly the flat appalled me: its yellowness, its low ceilings, the fraying sofa and the peeling seal in the bathroom, the naff turquoise splashback tiles, all the damp and mould. All of it.

If you can get my deposit back quickly I can move at the end of the month, I say to Bryan, all businesslike, which surprises him, and he agrees, because he is a reasonable man. He stills wants to check the condition of things once but I persuade him not to. I've been a model tenant.

I make changes. I shall be positive. I shall get more exercise. I shall look for a new job. Let this be a new beginning. I go for *walks*. Apparently I am the only person on earth who did not know their phone could count their steps. Each day is a game: beat yesterday's count.

After a week of rain the sun comes out. The sea is a metal mirror, reflecting the sky. The lawns squelch only a little underfoot. The beach throngs.

I walk.

Sometimes you'll only notice that you're doing something once you've been doing it for a while.

My routes loop and widen, rise and swoop like cursive script. I listen to my old cassettes on the Walkman as I go. At first this felt like an absurd affectation, but I've taken to it. Yes: I am the Walkingman. I would look right at home, I think, with a chuckle, on one of the bar stools in the window of the Rescue Café.

But I'm counting the pennies. Walking is free.

I go back to work. The workload is still a nonsense, but my attitude has changed. My manager, a thin tall man with pencil eyebrows and a pencil moustache, seems impressed. I am efficient.

That training paid off, huh, he says to me, and I put him on the list, the one I keep inside my head.

I reach down into my Resilience sack and feel the heft of atrocious implements. They fit the hand. They are each a good weight.

I go out to Saltdean. I walk to Southwick. I crest the hill by the race track and look down onto the Whitehawk estate as the morning sun floods the valley. In the distance the sea ignites. Gulls swoop and call.

My manager asks if I'm sleeping okay.

Fine, I say.

He nods, looking off to the left.

On the promenade by the West Pier, a seagull shits on me. That means good luck.

All my routes, I see, studying the GPS patterns on my phone, which are mostly yellow and sometimes red and only sometimes green, pass through Wick Road. My calves have grown strong. I'm building up quite the head of steam.

Sometimes you'll only notice that you're doing something once you've been doing it for a while.

The lights are on. Scaffolding has gone up over the whole front of the building, and I wonder if Gerry's friend is back, walking around in the attic from which Gerry fell to his death. It can't be good news, dying in a stairwell. I should google this. Deaths in stairwells: does the spirit snag, and, in snagging, remain to haunt?

I would haunt you if I could, I think.

A silhouette appears in the window of the kitchen side of the kitchen-living room and I see what they're about to do before they do it, and I watch on with the satisfaction of someone witnessing precisely what they had foreseen. What they had written.

Perhaps I can, I think. Might the living haunt?

I am writing this and in writing it I make it happen.

From the street I watch the one who has displaced me. I wonder how much Bryan charges them, because I doubt he ever intended to exit the rental market. At length the silhouette resolves into a figure, then the figure into a person: a blur becomes legible. Stray dots connect.

Hello, mother.

Connections sing; they shine; a terrible sense is made. I see them through the fogged window of the Starbucks on the corner. I see her bags packed, more bags than even she would take on holiday.

The silhouette forces the sash window open. Then it stands there a moment, sighing contentedly, before leaning forward and looking out.

Ma

     ree

         an

I close my eyes and concentrate. I am a good student. I practiced hard. Now I apply myself.

Goodbye, mother.

I picture Gerry falling from the attic. I see my father stumble in the kitchen, then slowly fold, concertina-like, to the linoleum floor. Effect, meet Cause. See a distance collapse.

Up in that window the silhouette raises a hand to its temple, then sways, falls back. At the same time, in the same instance, the bulb that lights the window flares and then goes dark; and I can feel a headache coming on.

Then, some time afterwards, how long I couldn't say, my phone begins to vibrate, which shocks me out of this reverie, uncancelling time, bringing me back to myself and this soft floating madness.

I look at the screen and see my father's avatar: a FaceTime call.

All the things that cannot be, I think.

Yet *are*.

Company

i. PRESENCE

I am alone in the house, in the kitchen, running hot water into the sink. I'm not sure where you are—maybe visiting your father. I mix washing-up liquid in with the water and the water bubbles and foams. In the dead silence of the late afternoon, the noise of it running, splashing from plates and utensils, seems loud. I hum to myself, some pop song of which I have forgotten the lyrics and the name, though its melody is insistent.

Suddenly a figure moves behind me and I scream. A shadow shifts and disappears before my eyes can focus. But I feel it: company. In that instant I am not alone.

When I turn around, there is no one there. When I turn off the tap to listen for movement, the house is silent except for the mutter of the television on low in the living room. I try to remember leaving it on and cannot.

ii. ABSENCE

Sometimes I mute the television when I watch it. I like just looking at the images—sometimes the noise annoys me. Yawning, I wonder when you will be home. I hope your father is okay—you told me you didn't think he was getting the care he needed. He's lonely, you said.

The sudden ringing of the telephone startles me. I didn't know that I had fallen asleep.

Groggy, I walk out into the hallway to answer it, but the handset isn't on the base. I can hear it ringing upstairs. You're always leaving it lying around—sometimes the battery will die in the middle of a conversation.

It stops ringing when I reach the landing. It was in our bedroom. I stand there exhausted for a moment, and listen to the silence of the house. The calm of its emptiness. The dead afternoon. I wonder where you are—you said you would be back by four. Then I go into our bedroom—

—and you are lying on the bed, propped up against the headboard: I gasp. For a long moment I cannot understand how you could be there.

You are listening intensely, the phone pressed to your ear.

"Yes," you say. "I'll be right over."

You climb off the bed, take your coat from the seat, and look at me.

"It's my dad," you say, before hurrying downstairs. From the landing, I hear the front door close behind you. I sit down in the stairwell, in the empty house, and hum some pop song to myself.

I Told You Not to Go

Russell Carter died aged sixty-eight attempting to adjust his TV aerial during a thunderstorm. His wife, Pearl, watching gameshows while Russell read, had been on about the signal all evening until, drunk and muttering, Russell had gone out the back to the garage to get the ladder he needed for the job. It wasn't a big house, and he didn't mind heights. Didn't mind the pouring rain and too damn stupid to think of the thunder, which implied lightning, which implied a serious risk of death, and when the lightning struck it didn't strike twice but four, maybe five times, as if to make sure, and at the first strike of which Pearl seated in her armchair staring at the flickering box was shocked frigid and blanching by the sudden appearance of her husband's face within the screen. When she flicked the TV onto standby with the remote control and then, after a pause, back on again, there he remained, face bloated as a drowned man's floating in the rip and whorl of noise. Later she would wonder why he appeared like that and not burned to a crisp or some other state more appropriate to a lightning strike but in the moment she was too astonished by the fact of his appearing to wonder at the manner of it. All her life she'd believed in ghosts with not a shred of evidence, and now this.

Pearl told herself that if his face would just go away she would never complain about the signal again, she would make do with what they had, but by the time she had managed to cross the room from her chair to the socket to unplug the TV from the wall then plug it back in and switch it on again, which was what Paulie, their son, was always telling her to do, there he remained. It hadn't been twenty minutes since her husband had gone out in a cloud of belched profanities in search of the ladder she wouldn't have trusted to hold her drink and she had heard no scream, but with the shock of lightning, and in sudden certainty, she had understood. As if it made sense; as if, somehow, she had expected this. I told you not to go, she said, though in truth she had been grimly pleased that the stupid bastard was for once proving good to his word. I'll go, he had slurred, I'll go and fix it now, shall I? Shall I do that for you, so you can have your game show? Oh yes please, she had said, thinking even one as daft as Russell Carter wouldn't go. Oh I'll go. If my knees didn't hurt so much I'd come and look for you, she said to the empty room. She should call the police or an ambulance but tonight she knew that the emergency services would be up to their necks in it, so what was the use? He wasn't going anywhere. Hell, she thought, he's got all the time in the world.

Back on the sofa she waved the remote and jabbed the button several times before the screen lit up. His face had gone. I should ring Paulie, she thought to herself, or maybe said, she wasn't sure. But now the pain in her ankles and knees was worse and by the time she got to the phone in the hall she had to stand with her eyes closed clenching her teeth for a while waiting for it to subside. Then she lifted the phone to her ear and before she had even had the chance to dial the first digit of the six for Paulie their son she felt her blood run cold. Russell? she said, into the dead line. Russell is that you?

And she knew it was him, could hear his breathing, unmistakable, though the sound was quieter than his breathing had ever been in real life; he'd been a heavy breather for as long as she'd known him, which was a long time, too long to think on. Of all the things perhaps that had irked her most, his heavy breathing. Later, in the funeral parlour, when she and Paulie went to say goodbye, she would pause to listen and in the silence there think she could hear it still, the heavy breathing.

Russell? When he didn't reply she slammed the handset back down onto the cradle, as if a little violence might persuade the dumb instrument to work. Waited a moment, eyes closed, then picked it up again: heavy breathing. It was a while before she realised that there was no dial tone. She supposed the storm had seen to that as well. Wincing, Pearl crouched down to tug the cable from the socket. Then she clicked it in again and stood, wincing still. It's what Paulie would have done—she heard his patient voice: now have you turned it off and on again, like I always say to do? Yes I did, thought Pearl, yes I did, and heard herself sniffing at the imagined condescension.

Again close-eyed she waited for the pain to pass. It did not pass. Opening her eyes, she lifted the handset to her ear. No dial tone, just her husband's breathing. Oh Russell, she said, and hung up the phone.

In the months after the funeral things just got worse. Somehow the old man made it from the telephone to the mains supply. The mains hum which her husband had long told her he couldn't hear, must have been tinnitus, she should get her ears checked, if not her head, got even worse. Lights flickered on and off with malicious glee, if they'd come on at all. She knew he knew how she hated the dark. So you want to carry on the argument, Pearl said, watching the lamp at their bedside. Flash twice for yes or once for no. The bulb flashed twice. Could you not just let it rest? The bulb flashed once. If her knees didn't hurt quite so bad she might have laughed. You *rat*, said Pearl, and the bulb flashed twice, slowly, more like two Morse dashes now than single dots. Don't you take that tone with me, Russel Carter, she said, and this time there came no flash at all. After a moment's repose the bulb gave a flare, sputtered, fizzled, and died.

Pearl thought of the game show's lights, glowing wheels of fortune and doom, of risk and reward, and of the house that always wins.

After that he got in the plumbing. She knew it was him from the banging in the radiators. Funny, she thought, how dumb banging could convey a specific tone of voice. Bang bang bang. Won't you give it a rest? she said. Bang-bang. Jesus, just give it a rest. Then came a trill of quieter notes as she passed the radiator in the hall. The muffled petulance was unmistakable. In the living room she eased herself down into her seat only to groan in despair when she saw the power cable of the television lying limp like a dead thing on the floor. Had she not plugged it back in?

Regardless, the screen crackled on in mocking answer and there he was, floating in the noise, eyes white as boiled eggs. When the telephone rang out in the hall she knew with awful certainty that it was he who called. The cable hung loose from the wall limp like a second dead thing but still it rang impossibly. I'm lonely here, Pearl, my darling, he said, his voice made strange in death, as if it travelled now through a medium denser than air, heavy as water, the signal fading in and fading out, ebbing now and then flowing, ebbing now before flowing anew. Won't you join me? Say, won't a nice warm bath ease your joints a touch?

Yes, thought Pearl. Yes I think you're right. Might be the first time.

◎

Paulie their son found her the next day, at ease in water gone cold, a hair straightener plugged into the shaving socket by the cabinet floating limply like a third dead thing beside her in the tub.

Standing in the empty house, Paulie paused to listen, tuning in, felt the hairs on the back of his neck shiver erect, felt his balls tighten and his palms begin to sweat. It was a soft sound, the sound you might hear if all other sounds could cease, underlying the whole wide cacophonous chorus of the world. A susurration. Like someone's breathing, he thought, looking around, detecting something in the heavy silence that may or may not have been there. Like heavy breathing, he thought, or maybe said, he wasn't sure.

Paulie threw water from the kitchen sink over his face, tried to shake that feeling, tried to gather himself. He thought to call an ambulance though he knew it wouldn't be good for much, but when he lifted the handset to his ear there came no dial tone, no signal, no noise. Then the TV flicked on off its own bat.

At once there came a winning answer, followed by audience applause.

Lucida

I t's a large camera. It's heavy and modular, so the lens, film back and finder can all be changed. It has a certain presence smaller cameras lack: it takes up space. It gets in the way. You hold it by your waist or put it on a tripod and compose your picture on the focusing screen. When you press the button, the mirror clunks loudly as it swings out of the way. There's a kind of violence to it, and a finality. Then you crank the film on. The mechanism is a bit grungey now, so it takes a little effort, a little force, this shifting between moments. Better to put it on a tripod; most of my pictures are slightly out-of-focus because I do not have one. If you were to drop the camera on your foot, you would break a toe, but the camera would be fine. It's an old studio workhorse. It was built to last.

Hannah says, "But I didn't blink. Swear to God."

Even indoors there's something magical about the focusing screen, the camera's small rectangle of light nestled within its waist-level finder. Somehow things seem more real when they appear on it. The previous owner must have modified it somehow. There's a Fresnel lens, certainly, but there must be something else, though I'm damned if I know what it is. Either way, colours seem more colourful, as if the glass is stained. Edges have greater definition, greater acutance, as if somehow etched. It's like not knowing you needed glasses and then putting some glasses on for the first time. The gridlines frame the picture, transforming the empty golf course and the contours of the downs and the gorse trees in the distance into a mise-en-scéne, a backdrop, a landscape. The lenses are beautiful and the images of Hannah formed on the screen are so perfect it seems futile to commit them to film. The light is bright but the sky is overcast and the light diffused, so the shadows are soft. If I overexpose a little, everything will become gently luminous. I wish the glass of the focusing screen was really a glass plate and I could keep each image in that precious medium. It is the antithesis of lossy: it exceeds its subject, or somehow seems to; it contains a plenitude. Like in naff action films when some detective barks *enhance!* at the guy on the computer, who clicks a few buttons to enhance an image, once, twice, again and again, over and over, closer and closer, enhancing infinitely, as if the image always has more detail to yield. As if there is no hard limit of grain or noise to the things it might disclose. As if, even though it is a thing in the world, it contains more information than exists in the world: an impossible object. It makes the world seem thin.

"Honestly, I didn't blink."

Except this one thing.

"I'll show you. Anyway, I think it's your turn to sit for a portrait." Hannah's shivering. I realise that I am, too. "Or stand," she says, her boots squelching in the mud.

The camera has a Polaroid back and when you expose instant film you have to drag it out of the pack at an even speed, wait a certain amount of time, which varies depending on the temperature, and then peel the negative away from the backing once it has developed. You don't have to shake it. Sometimes the chemistry leaks a little bit. It can gunge up the rollers and if you're not careful the shot can get caught in the pack, and forcing it out will only tear it, resulting in gashes of colour and light across the picture, uneven and erratic development if it manages to develop much at all. The developing fluid is caustic. At first the print is moist and you have to wait for it to dry.

I hear the mirror clunking out of the way and the whisper-click of the shutter. Hannah pulls the shot out of the Polaroid back and waits. While she waits, she slides the dark slide back into its slot between the bellows and the back. The cable release dangles from the socket on the lens, moving with the breeze. Hannah shifts her weight from foot to foot, a little dance to keep warm. I know I didn't blink.

She peels the negative away from the print and frowns, shaking her head, baffled.

"Again?"

"Again."

"I don't understand."

In contrast to the image on the focusing screen, the photographs that the camera produces, whether instant prints, dark room prints or scans, always seem fainter, softer, their colours slightly washed out. I've tried with different types of film, colour negs and slides. I've tried with flatbed scans at home and with Flextight scans at some expense. There's always a pallor to skin tones. You don't look well. You look peaky. And in every portrait, in every picture containing faces, the eyes are closed.

At first you think it's a one-off and the sitter's just blinked, but we've tested this. In every frame, the eyes are closed.

When you take group shots with the camera on my phone, it shoots several frames, analyses them for closed eyes, then composites them together into an artificial moment in which no one was caught blinking. It's a kind of fiction, of course, a synthetic unity, but all photographs are a kind of fiction. I wonder if any of the digital backs you can get for this camera do such a thing. Probably not. But I imagine they would set you back the cost of a small car.

"One more time," says Hannah.

That forceful shifting between moments as she advances the frame. Then the mirror clunks out of the way, followed by the hiss-click of the shutter. I do not blink. My eyelids might be pinned back, fastened wide, and my eyes start to water in the autumn breeze.

I know I did not blink, but in the resulting photograph my eyes are closed, and I'm damned if I know how that could be, and I look even paler than I am in real life.

You can see the ghost of my figure on the negative, the bit you chuck away. The edges are smeared with glue, developing fluid, and colour dyes. Without a bath of fix, that figure will soon fade back into the darkness of the neg.

———

Sister

fter my sister died, in the appalling silence which filled our home, I made an effigy from the store of materials in her studio. I had never made anything before, never sung or played an instrument, never painted or drawn a thing in my life, but in that desolate winter I found myself imagining this figure in the empty spaces of our house, this odd likeness of my sister which was not my sister, and it seemed only natural to set about the task of making it. The flax fiber and plaster, the glue and the clay, segments of broomsticks and dowel rods I took from the cupboards in which she had kept her supplies: in the shadows there I found palettes scabbed with paint alongside bottles of coloured ink and stiff brushes, pots of glue, sharp knives and crêpe paper, tangled wigs and soldered jewellery, all kinds of fabric and card, charcoal sticks and knots of string, disassembled mannequins and wounded plastic figurines, a hoard of oddments and trinkets and tools, and that smell, which was the smell of all of these things in the cupboard and also, unmistakably, the scent of my sister working: for a moment—I do not know how long—it overwhelmed me, and I crouched there in silence for a while; I remember swaying with sudden dizziness when I stood up again, and nearly falling to the floor. In her bedroom, in the shuttered gloom, in the bottom drawer of her chest of drawers, I found a few items of clothing—socks, a crumpled blouse, a neckerchief—which I would tear into strips and stitch into some new garment for the model, fervently hoping all the while that my parents would not notice their disappearance from the drawer.

(The day before in the living room my mother had slapped me hard across the face, drawing blood from my cheek: I had gone into my sister's room and taken a book on sculpture down from one of her shelves. My mother had noticed the change immediately; I think, whenever she enters the room, she scans the arrangement of items for such subtle changes. My sister's room was a museum, a place of silent reverence where one might look but must not touch, and the precise effect of everything arranged as she had left that space was the delicate and terrible exhibit: to move one thing damaged it in its entirety, as if each object were the keystone. Unaltered, one could imagine my sister returning, seamlessly resuming the life she had left. When she struck me, my father did not speak, only glowered in his chair, and I knew then that he hated me. I felt the cut on my cheek and saw the blood on my fingertips. Nothing must change, she told me. I promised her I would put it back. And *make believe* that nothing has changed? At the thought of this my mother snarled, then turned away toward the mantelpiece, from where framed photographs of my sister watched the room. Later, when my parents were sleeping, I restored the book to its place on the shelf, and in the upstairs bathroom, by the moonlight shining through the window, examined the cut upon my cheek in the dusty glass of the mirror.)

I worked on the figure in my bedroom, in the attic of the house: I could well imagine the anger that would greet me if I used my sister's studio. I had, as I have said, never shown any aptitude or particular interest in art, but the work furnished me with purpose where I had felt listing and directionless. I had found something to concentrate upon, and which would, for hours at a time, distract me from my own anger and despair. I suppose I poured my grief into the work, though at the time I did not think of it this way, and the work absorbed me. I used my sister's tools to shape the clay and flax and wood, and would later dress the effigy in the new garment I had made. When my spirit flagged, when the work grew difficult and its finishing seemed beyond me, I would return to her bedroom, and take something, some possession of hers (a doll named Poupée, a white rock the shape of an ostrich's egg, a photograph which she had taken of me aged around seven years old, a nervous and diffident child, though I could not remember her taking it), and study it, feel its weight in my hand, its special heft, close my eyes and examine the idiosyncrasies of its shape with open palms and fingertips. Doing this, it seemed, released some energy pent up in the object or else inside myself, and I would return to my work on the sculpture revitalised, alive again to the possibilities of the clay, to the figure I knew was already present inside it, who I merely had to extract. Afterwards, I would of course return the object to the room, placing the rock that was not an egg back on the dresser or balancing the photograph of myself back against the candle on the dusty mantelpiece, hoping, again, that my mother would not notice any change in the arrangement of things.

The winter became a dismal spring of downpours and cold breezes, scarce sunshine seldom penetrating the clouds. The summer, albeit clammy, was no better; only the temperature improved, though even on the warmest days it was cold inside our house, a creaking building riddled with drafts: then suddenly it was autumn, as if the summer had never been. At length, after nine long months of work, of sketches and drafts and discarded attempts, I realised I had finished, although a certain dissatisfaction troubled me: the model fell short of what I had wanted, in some uncertain but vitally significant way, though I had reached the conclusion that there was nothing I could do now to bridge the gap between what I had made and what I had sought, nothing I could add to it that would not reduce it; and so it seemed there was nothing left for me to do with the figure except present it to my parents.

Our family dinners were silent affairs. I had not heard my father speak in a long time and indeed had sometimes wondered if his grief had rent his voice and made him mute. He and I sat at opposite ends of the long dinner table, my mother in the middle to my left, the empty space where my sister would have sat opposite her. My mother, in whispers shaded with irritation, directed proceedings: pass your father the salt, she would murmur, or hiss, though he had not made any motion to suggest he especially wanted the salt, and due to the length of the table I would have to leave my chair and carry the grinder to his side. Hold the fork in your left hand, Daniel, not your right. Please, eat with your mouth shut—I doubt your father wants to see you chewing. May I have the pepper, Jonathan?

After I had finished swallowing that mouthful of food, I glanced up, then looked at her, blinking, focusing, and she returned my gaze with a look of blank expectation. It was at this point I realised I could feel the dread in my gut. My mother was clearly waiting now: she knew I had something to say, and I knew then that I was committed to what I had decided, without fully understanding it, to do. I looked down at my plate, at the boiled vegetables I had listlessly moved around on the plate and hardly eaten.

"What is it, Daniel?" my mother asked.

Anxiety impeded speech. "I have something to show you," I said at last.

She held my gaze, then a moment later began to nod. "Very well," she said. "After dinner."

"Yes," I murmured. "Of course. Sorry." I do not know why I apologised.

"Daniel has something to show us, Jonathan," she said,

raising her voice abruptly, and my father nodded without looking up from his food.

I had begun to feel nauseous. The autumn wind rattled the windows of the room. Bits of stone, dislodged, could be heard falling in the chimney breast. I stared for a while with some intensity at the place where my sister would have sat, as if I might have divined there in her absence her opinion of what I was to do. As if that void might offer counsel. I tried, unsuccessfully, to calm myself. I tried to concentrate.

As I waited, I scratched the cut upon my face. That morning I had noticed that the scab which had formed over the cut, and begun to itch quite maddeningly, which I had now absentmindedly disturbed, had turned a sickly yellow colour, edged with green. It stung now, bleeding anew, but my nervousness and anticipation was ample distraction from any pain.

After dinner, we went upstairs, to my sister's study on the seventh floor, where she had worked when she was able. Though I had fashioned the model in the attic room where guests, when we had entertained guests, would have stayed, I had decided that the study was the appropriate room for the model's unveiling. In this place it would achieve a fullness of effect doubtless unavailable anywhere else. I had braced myself for some act of violence, for my mother's fury, for my father's weary distaste, but in the event nothing of the sort occurred.

As I laid my hand on the handle of the door, I glanced back at my parents, stood side by side without touching one another behind me. In the dim light of the landing my father, a tall man and a once-commanding presence, seemed reduced, hunched and tired, out of breath from the effort of climbing the stairs. Dust hanging in the air made me cough into my hand. I looked at my mother, and she nodded. Then I opened the door.

◎

It is three years now since I presented the model I had made to my parents, and three years since my sister resumed her life. She is a quiet, uncertain presence in the house; she seems to think a good deal before moving—the frightening spontaneity that had characterised her before her sickness is gone. At dinnertime she sits opposite my mother at the table, though she only moves her food around upon her plate and does not eat. She seldom speaks. She doesn't meet my gaze. I know my parents are hopeful that one day the faculty of speech will return to her in its entirety, but they know that she has been through a lot and that it cannot be forced. They are glad she is here, though I have begun to suspect that they, through some act of will, have forgotten that she died at all. As I say, she has resumed her life, all but seamlessly, but for her muteness and lack of appetite. And her smell has changed: she smells like the storeroom in which she still keeps her supplies, mingled with soap and talc and sweat, long settled dust and a certain dampness like washed clothes left too long in the machine. When she feels able, she works in her study. Sometimes I have entered the room and seen her simply sitting there in her chair, unmoving, as if waiting very quietly and very patiently for something to happen, and I know she has not heard me enter. Before her return, before the illness and its unsuccessful treatment had dulled her senses, she had always seemed to me almost supernaturally alert, more alive in herself than I had ever known myself to feel, more sharply present in the world, though now she gives the impression that she is moving through dense fog. I have seen her in her room, one of her books open on her lap, looking at the pages as if she has forgotten how to read.

We do not speak of her death. My mother does not allow it—she has never mentioned it, and I know the topic is proscribed. Perhaps she has forgotten entirely, perhaps she believes that if we do not speak of it, acknowledge it, permit its thought and expression, then it will cease to have been the case.

Several months after her return, my sister started painting again. I would watch her from the doorway and she would never give any indication that she knew that I was there. She paints her limbs or else the features of her face, delicate and exquisite work for which she does not seem to need the aid of any of her mirrors. Sometimes I have seen her re-stitching the stuffed fabric of her torso. I suppose I left the task unfinished, though I know I did as good a job as I could manage. Her seams are smoothed away. The awkward assemblage I fashioned is acquiring a kind of grace. I am writing this, now, in my attic room, to remind myself, so that my mother's will and forcefulness won't compel my own forgetting. In the mirror on my desk I can see the scar upon my cheek. It reminds me. Sometimes it itches, and numerous times in my sleep, filled with dread and agitation, I have scratched it anew and torn a fresh cut in the skin: in this way the injury persists. Somehow it comforts me. Downstairs I can hear my sister laughing with my mother, whose laughter is rather too forced for my liking, as if she is demonstrating that she can laugh and daring anyone who might overhear her so laughing to doubt the sincerity of her mirth. When my sister tries to speak, she lisps and spits, but with the help of speech therapists she is slowly learning how to shape words with her mouth once again.

She has never thanked me for what I did.

The night before I presented the model to my parents, I had a dream, and in that dream I learned what I was to do. The model had fallen short of the ideal I had pursued, but now I knew what I had to add to it, a simple thing that would not reduce it in that way that I had feared. From one of her sketchpads in her studio I tore an edge of paper, and with a piece of charcoal from the pot in the adjacent storage room, scrawled the letters of her name, in the clearest lines I could manage, upon it. Before dinner, after setting up the model of my sister in her studio, in the chair before the window, I opened its jaw and placed the piece of paper in its mouth.

I did not expect it to work. I did not expect my sister to return.

You know
What to Do

1.

On their third day in the new house he found the shelter.

It must be from the war, she said, agog, her hands on her hips, turning to survey the unexpected space as the beam of the camping torch bounced over the bare walls. She doubted this even as she said it. He was holding up his phone.

Bungaroosh, he murmured. Lime, flint, horsehair. Pebbles. Any old crap. This doesn't make sense.

She had joined him, squeezed through the narrow understairs cupboard and the unlikely second door at its back, in a state of some alarm, because his voice when he had called to her had seemed inflected with something not far away from panic. Then she had laughed in astonishment. He had had to force that second door, whereupon he had nearly sprawled down the steps into the darkness.

Which war? he said, suddenly noticing her, at which she laughed a laugh flawed with hesitation.

This wasn't—

No, he said.

—in any of the ads. Was it?

She felt as if she had stepped outside, or into a cave, open to the wind and prone to intermittent flooding. The air was thick with damp, and the stone floor was cold beneath her bare feet.

No.

Back in the living room she brought up the ads on her laptop. She examined the photographs and the 360-degree video walkthrough and the floor plans, which were not to scale. In one of the photographs, the cupboard door hung halfway open, a carelessness on behalf of whoever had taken it, but no amount of enlargement or lightening once she had downloaded the image would reveal anything more than shadows teeming with noise, become flatly grey with the altering. She saved the files to her Desktop, anyway.

Nothing, she said.

I know, he said.

Should we—she said.

No, he said.

She laughed again. Well, they can't put the price up now, can they, she said.

I guess they can't, he said, as they went back in, squeezing through the door behind the cupboard door.

Do you feel it, she said, looking at him.

Feel what? he asked.

I think you do, she said. It's why you don't want us to ask Jo.

Jo was, or had been, the seller. On the mantelpiece she had left a hardback A5 leatherette journal with gold trimmed edges, half of its cream pages filled with whimsical advice and information in a lovely cursive hand wrought in silver ink infused with glitter from a gel pen surely intended for birthday cards and not notes to the buyer with whom you had conducted aggressive negotiations, as well as a video on how to operate the gas fire, but nowhere had she mentioned the shelter, accessed through a small door concealed within the understairs cupboard, if a *shelter* was what it was, and already the manifest absurdity of such a thing had her doubting it. If he was right, if the walls were bungaroosh, then it had to be older.

Feel what, he said, annoyed.

It seems—she waved a hand, as if trying to catch the correct locution—as if we shouldn't tell them about it. She smiled, feeling like a child privy to a secret.

He bristled, though he didn't know why. He pursed his lips. For a good five minutes, the secret had been his.

It wasn't an Anderson shelter, corrugated iron sunk into the garden turf, cold and prone to flooding in the winter, and it certainly wasn't a Morrison shelter, to be constructed indoors like a wide-berthed coffin in which a couple might sleep, facts he had quickly ascertained via the consultation of an online hobbyists' forum a brief internet search had summoned from the depths, but standing in that bare space he found himself in little doubt that an air raid shelter was what it was. Somehow the space declared itself: anticipated disaster hung in the air like a cloud of invisible spores. An original cellar, perhaps, modified for the purpose. Or else dug in, added later—but how?

She wasn't so sure. Do you think the other houses have them? she asked.

I don't know, he said, still incredulous, amusement overwriting his shock. I wouldn't have thought so. But then I wouldn't have thought that this one would have it, either.

A rusted bakelite switch had fallen loose from the concrete wall to the left of the entrance; opposite, a squat wooden desk bore a speckled pelt of dust and damp. Beside this there was a cupboard built into the corner of the room, open, containing empty shelves. These elements gave the space an oddly stage set feel. He tapped the walls, listening to the resonance, pausing to frown as he rapped the plaster inside the cupboard, the only part of the space that bore plaster. Examining the light switch, he thought of barnacled wrecks come to rest in the lonely depths of the ocean. Perhaps it was the damp:

the wet air felt alive. It teemed. Somehow there appeared to be a draught. The house was close to the sea, close to the beach from which the pebbles in the walls must have come. The low ceiling brushed the top of his head. In what thin light seeped through the understair doors he could picture a child working at the bench. A child, he thought, with no idea why he was thinking this, privy to a secret.

Wow, he said, sounding distant.

He tapped the plaster within the cupboard again; it returned a slightly deeper sound.

She was squeezing back out through the door. She smiled when he turned to look at her, but the smile faltered when some kind of doubt—or, *something*—hovered in his eyes a moment.

I'm going to crack on with the books, she said, watching him.

They owned too many books. *Tsundoku*, she thought, the word popping into her head.

I wasn't even really sure that it was a door, he marveled.

He might, she thought, be speaking to himself.

I'll see you shortly, she said.

He glanced at her, flustered. Yes, he said. Of course.

2.

I was talking to Joyce, she said. Next door.

Joyce, he asked, looking down at his plate. When he ate he did so with an intensity of concentration that often amused her. He chewed his food carefully.

Next door. Number 20.

He nodded, chewing. A copy of *The Argus* was open on the table in front of him, but he wasn't reading it. Something about a footballer, benefits cheats, a missing person.

She doesn't have a shelter.

He looked at her sharply.

Or a cellar. Whatever it is.

Did you tell her we do?

What? No. Well—

She pulled a face. When the intensity of his scrutiny did not lessen, she continued:

No, we were just chatting. About the garden, really. We'll need a shed. I got to mentioning my parent's cellar somehow.

She looked at him.

That was *all*.

He nodded, chewing, looking down at his plate.

3.

Numbers 3, 31, and 35, on the other side of the road, and number 48 were also for sale; numbers 15 and 51 were up for let. The ads for numbers 40 and 52, long sold, still lingered in the cache.

She examined the photographs. 48 and 35 had 360 walkthroughs.

She examined the walkthroughs.

On 31, in one of the jpegs, an understairs cupboard was open. She saved it to the Desktop, then opened it into Photoshop.

Enhance! she thought.

But there was only shadow, teeming with noise.

She scrolled through pages of nothing, clicked through pop-out galleries of naught.

She went to *The Argus* website. The sad smile of a missing man, local to Hove, forty years old, a violin teacher, stared out from the screen. She wondered did such photographs look sad before their placement in the newsfeed—had the picture editors chosen that one particular image for that particular quality; or did they acquire it from the placement. The small miseries of local news. Someone killed at a roundabout. All the people sent to prison in Sussex this week. Something about a dispute at the waste recycling facility.

Then, just before giving up, she found number 20, lingered in the cache.

On the third of six photographs, an understairs cupboard, and the door hanging open.

She saved it to the Desktop, then opened it up.

Enhance!

In the wash of shadow, teeming with noise, there was something.

Enhance!

A Rorschach blot of a door behind the door. A door?

Perhaps, she said.

Huh? he said, entering the living room.

Nothing, she said, closing the laptop.

She looked up at him.

How're you feeling? she asked. He had kicked about, nervy pain in his legs, something like sciatica but not, stray signals of the nervous system, pain without source, all night long.

Not great, he said, rotating a hip one way and then back.

He stood at the window a moment, looking out into the street. Then he crossed the room and went back out into the hall.

From the dining table she heard him murmuring to himself. Then she heard him squeezing through the door inside the understairs cupboard.

She opened the laptop, closed the file in Photoshop, thought for a moment, then moved the files from the Desktop to the Documents folder. Then she opened the browser and deleted her history, deleted her cookies, and closed the laptop again.

She stood at the window, looking out into the street. A woman emerged from a parked car. She crouched down outside number 20 and seemed for a moment to be fiddling with something on the pavement.

Joyce, she said, thinking.

She wondered were there other things lingering in the cache.

4.

Packing for the move had not been ordinary packing, but archaeology. Every cranny contained something: remove that thing from its place and five others fell out. The flat had been tiny, low-ceilinged, a converted townhouse attic awash with light. She hadn't realised how densely packed-in they had become: distinct strata had become discernible in the compacting of their stuff. In the hall on their first viewing she had felt herself standing up straight as if for the first time. Now, their belongings in stacked and slumping boxes in the living room, it appeared that they had managed to fit more into that small one-bed, its kitchen a strip along its living room, than they could ever hope to fit into the house.

Those first few days she had enjoyed walking upstairs, stopping, and saying, Now I am upstairs, as she turned around 360 degrees on the landing. After this she would walk downstairs, sit on the second to last step, and say, Now I am downstairs. She wondered how long it would take for her wonder at this to fade.

And she wondered about the basement. She had decided to think of it as the basement, though she wondered if *basement* was an Americanism. She hadn't told him this: he was being distant, distracted, irritable. He was irritating her. Something had come over him. He wasn't sleeping. He wouldn't call it the *basement*. She could hear his disdain.

He was, she thought, spending too much time in the basement.

They had so much unpacking to do. He should have been excited, happy. Was that too much to ask?

Somehow she knew that he wouldn't want to use that

bonus space for storage. Thinking this, she felt the heat of that disdain. She could feel it in her cheeks. It wasn't a discussion they needed to have: the damp precluded it.

She stood at the cupboard door a moment, listening, and thought: what are you doing down there?

5.

Monday brought her return to work, the last of her annual leave used up. She had hoped to be further along with the unpacking. The boxes had begun to disgust her. An obscene proliferation of things, metastasised things. There seemed to be more now than they had started with.

The boxes gave the house a sense of transitoriness the flat, someone else's retirement income, had somehow never possessed.

Open one box and three more fell out.

He wasn't helping.

He kicked about in the night, stray signals, pain without source.

He had been great with the move. In something of a panic he had shifted most of their stuff in the car before the delivery guys had even started, and the week they had taken off had made the whole thing easier. The overlap of mortgage and rental tenancy had been fortunate. He had, she had thought, been excited. She was excited. But now they were in, something had changed in him. Perhaps he hadn't been excited, but anxious. The idea of ownership had made him uneasy, as if he had no right. He didn't seem in any hurry to get their things put away.

I'm going to take another week off, he said, looking up at the ceiling.

She turned on her side. You have leave left?

A week.

I'm jealous.

He stared up into the gloom.

I'll crack on with things, he said.

She nodded.

I wish I had a week left, she said.

He turned over; then, twisting, turned again.

6.

Tuesday evening and the house was quiet.

Hello? she called from the hallway.

I'll crack on with things.

No answer.

Work had depleted her. The first day back was always the worst. Routine allowed your body to adapt to the rigours of exploitation, discipline, constant self-surveillance; with time away you soon went slack, your body detrained. And then you returned to the emails you had missed. She kicked her shoes off, set her bag down beside the sofa his parents had given them, and then slumped into the armchair. She was thirsty. From this position she stared at the boxes.

Could there really be more?

She worked her phone from her pocket.

No messages. Perhaps he had gone for a run. It would have been the first time in a while.

In the kitchen she poured a glass of water. She drank it standing at the cupboard door, listening.

She put the emptied glass down on the side in the kitchen and then squeezed through the doors, understairs and then the underunderstairs.

Where the air was viscous with damp. A note of something else—bleach? White vinegar?

Under the beam of the torch she pictured a child at the table, working on something. A drawing or homework. The wood was clean. The pelt was gone.

Where are you? she said.

It was a relief to get back upstairs. She took her laptop from the table and sat down on the sofa.

She examined the jpegs in the Documents folder.

Joyce, she murmured.

Pardon? he said, suddenly before her in the centre of the room: she started.

She hadn't heard him enter the house or the living room. He wasn't there until he was and then when he was there unannounced his thereness shocked her.

Where were you? she asked.

In the basement, he said.

Really?

Yes, he said. I've been cleaning the walls.

She nodded at the boxes. What about these?

He smiled. Tomorrow, he said.

What you looking at? he asked.

She closed the laptop. Nothing, she said. Do we have any wine?

It's only Tuesday, he said, grinning. Well, I'm on holiday. It's Tuesday for you.

Fuck it. I want a drink. Join me?

Don't mind if I do.

7.

I'll crack on with things.

Any chance of a cuppa?

Next evening and the house responded to the question with the teeming silence of houses: something falling in the chimney breast, floorboards creaking in the stairwell untouched by any foot, canned laughter on the telly next door, a breeze registered but too weak to be consciously felt. The floorboards, the wooden stairwell, the white walls were like sound mirrors, reflecting her own presence back at her. For some reason it made her self-conscious.

The bathroom door was shut.

She listened for the toilet to flush but it did not.

He couldn't be running. He had done the 0 to 5k and then the less heralded 5k to 0.

She stood at the cupboard door, listening.

She made her own tea.

She drank it in bed, slumped, clothed, against the headboard, on top of the quilt.

With tremendous effort she sat up, undid her bra, sighed, sat back.

With her eyes closed she heard him enter the room. A soft tread—he'd always had a soft tread.

Where have you been? she said.

Downstairs, he said.

Downstairs.

Yeah. Tea? Then I went for a walk.

I'm okay, thanks. She nodded at the cup on the bedside, thinking: since when did you go for walks?

I met her next door, he said.

Her next door?

Whatsername. Joyce. Nice lady.

She nodded.

He looked at her.

I asked her, he said.

You asked her.

Directly, he said.

Okay.

Thought I was mad, he said. Sure you don't want a tea?

No.

She said her dad had had one. In the garden. But she didn't. Definitely. No doubts about it.

Okay, she said.

Is it?

Why wouldn't it be?

I don't know, he said. You just seemed—kind of bothered.

I seemed bothered. She sat up again.

He nodded.

It's pretty clean now, he said. Relatively speaking.

Okay, she said.

I think it's a good thing, he said.

We sell this place, we could get more than we bought it for.

She looked at him.

You want to sell?

Well, no, he said. But some day. It's got to add value.

Value, she said, nodding slowly.

Joyce said something weird, he said.

What's that?

She said Jo was desperate to sell.

Ha! Bullshit.

Seriously.

She could have fooled me.

Me too, he said, standing at the window, staring down into the street.

I saw her, he said. I think.

Who?

Jo.

You saw her?

At the end of the road. When I was walking. She was walking a dog, a greyhound or something. She'd stopped and was fiddling with something on the pavement.

What?

The cover for the stopcock. It was open.

She made a face.

Did you say hello?

No, he said.

Did she see you?

I think so, he said, turning away from the window, looking down at the floor.

8.

Jo had offered to arrange for some guys to sort out the shit in the attic, but they had persuaded her not to. They could shift it in their own time. Now, standing on a cross beam, looking at the shelving unit someone had for some reason constructed up here, and the bin bags and suitcases full of rubbish—a box containing the controller of a Nintendo Wii, circa 2006; a collection of adult colouring books, half coloured in; a bin bag of large slightly glossy men's shirts surely destined for one of the charity shops on the Portland Road, but waylaid; a lone Simply Red CD, similarly waylaid—she wished that they had taken Jo up on that offer. She hadn't realised how much stuff that woman had left.

Desperate to sell, she said aloud, in wonder. If only we had known.

Suddenly wearied by the thought of having to sort it all, she lowered herself into a careful crouch, then sat down on one of the chipboard panels, careful not to push her hand through a layer of fibreglass as she did so. It was cold in the loft; like the basement, it felt half outside, half in. Weird, she thought, to think that the house was topped and tailed with such spaces. As if you were never truly indoors. The wind ferreted in through the roof insulation. A bucket was jammed into one of the eaves at an angle, the inch of water it held the colour of rust.

If he was going to take up camp in the basement, she decided, maybe she could make the attic her own base of operations.

She sniffed, standing. Jo's rubbish bothered her. It was bad enough living surrounded by the accumulated stuff of their own lives.

I'll crack on with things.

Box Mountain had seemingly grown.

Earlier, she had said: I feel like we're living in someone

else's house.

To which he had not particularly reacted.

Any moment now she felt like the Owner might come home.

She prodded one of the bags with her toe, then gave it a kick. A cloud of dust escaped; then a cascade of photographs slid free. Red eyes, pale faces, sickly under direct flash. Some kind of party no one seemed to be enjoying.

She froze in shock as she picked them up: a sad smile stared out.

Her mouth felt suddenly dry.

9.

I found something, she said.

Me too, he said.

She stopped. What?

He held something up, pinched between index finger and thumb. It caught the light, the colour of whiskey, a chipped lump. It looked like it had been soft once but had subsequently hardened, gelatine become crystal.

Resin, he said. It was behind the desk. Stuck between its leg and the wall.

Huh.

She frowned, thinking.

What did you find? he asked.

Photographs.

She set them down on the table, fanned them out across the cloth.

Is there anything worse than other people's photographs? he asked.

Look, she said.

He looked, thinking. Maybe other people's dreams, he said.

Look.

I'm looking. What am I looking at?

She pointed to the sad smile and wondered was there really any sadness to it or had it accrued it from the newsfeed, like water flushed through old pipes taking the flavour of rust.

He picked it up, rotating it slightly, tilting his head.

Is this—

Yes, she said.

Jesus.

He extended his arm, to get it away from himself, but did not put it down.

She nodded, waiting, for what she didn't know.

Did the bin men come today?

What?

He put the photograph carefully down then went to the front door, opened it, stepped out.

Where are you—

Unfolding the crumpled *Argus* as he returned indoors.

He spread it out on the table, knocking over the few photographs that had remained in a pile.

That sad smile, gap-toothed and shy, staring back.

Resin, he said, turning it over in his hand.

10.

She dreamt of a child sat at a desk, deep in concentration, hunched over something.

A boy, privy to a secret.

The boy was drawing.

She did not want to startle him. In her dream, which possessed somehow the quality of being someone else's dream, it was very important not to startle the child. Something atrocious would happen if she startled him, yet she was drawn to the boy with all the terrible inexorability of dreams.

She remembered games of Grandma's Footsteps played in

Saunders Park, long ago.

She must not startle him. If she startled him, he would look at her, and—

What?

Now she was nearing him; now she was closer. Leaning forward onto the balls of her feet, she peered over his shoulder to see on the page a drawing of a violin, in the style of a child surely half the age of this boy: cack-handed heavy lines, a likeness tilting into incompetent abstraction, but not without charm.

From the balls of her feet to her toes; she was leaning; leaning—then starting inexorably to fall.

Then she fell awake, appalled, convinced momentarily that she was choking on clumps of dry, coarse hair.

11.

I'm going for a walk, she said. I need to get out. Wanna come?

Another time, he said, hesitating by the cupboard door.

She felt as though she had been underwater a long time. The late August evening was humid and close. It seemed a struggle to get the right amount of air into her lungs.

She walked down Milnthorpe Road, a terrace of cottages perpendicular to their own, and then crossed School Road in front of the black railings and red brick of the infant's school, then on a whim headed along towards Stoneham Park, from which shouts of laughter emerged from beneath a climbing frame, peculiarly isolated in the quiet evening as if recorded in separate sound booths and replayed in other rooms and other houses. Aldrington without traffic felt like the country-side. She could hear birdsong, and somewhere the barking of a dog. Voices reached her from open windows, insistent but indistinct. She walked through a patch of air spiced with the scent of cannabis, mellow and not unpleasant, though who was smoking it she could not see. It had been overcast all day but the light diffusing through the clouds had held a watery brightness that still clung to the buffed surfaces of parked cars, streetlamps, windows of houses behind which lace curtains had been drawn. Everything around her possessed a slightly muffled feel; she felt as if she had just awoken from a four-hour nap and would never quite shake off its residue. It felt misty but it wasn't. She sat on a bench by the corner of the play park and closed her eyes, leant back. The air was good. Thursday evening and the pubs would be filling up.

Traffic on the Portland Road; there was always traffic on the Portland Road, running east to west just shy of a mile up from the beach. The peace of Stoneham Park was gone, but she didn't mind. She looked in shop windows: flower shops dense with foliage, dark and half wild-looking after hours as if the end of the day's trading allowed the plants to withdraw from the curated postures of instagrammable display; shuttered bakeries; the cavernous Stoneham Pub, a creche for Hove children at the best of times, and where they had come for a drink after their first viewing of the house, just now starting to get noisy. Joggers in bright expensive shoes, plugged into a variety of wrist and arm-borne devices, picked their way along the pavements. The sight of them wore her out. That drink felt a long time ago: he had been excited then. She found herself peering into the interior of a shop selling second-hand vacuum cleaners, row upon row of them, positioned in the window like sad mannequins; then the window of a shop advertising musical instruments, sheet music, and related accessories.

For a moment she thought she heard the sound of a violin behind her. She froze, and glanced back; then, relaxing, noticed a window open in a flat above the music shop, through which the sound drifted on the slow breeze.

The tune was gathering pace: a trot become a canter.

The air felt wet; a mile from the sea and she felt the salt

of it sticking to her skin. Suddenly she was starting to feel cold, so turned on her heel, retracing her steps past the rows of vacuum cleaners like mannequins and windows of dark foliage and aggressive shouts of laughter from the pub, as the notes of the violin faded into the ambient murmur of the evening. Was the temperature really dropping so precipitously? She felt as though she had swum into a cold patch in a lake. The gentle breeze was finding strength. In contrast she felt suddenly tired, weakened by some delicate but fatal blow.

She was crossing their road again when she saw the shy mooch of the greyhound in the distance. The figure holding the leash was walking in the opposite direction, wiping something from one hand, but she recognised her at once.

Perhaps, she thought, Jo had come by to collect her post. But had she not moved to Lewes?

Outside their house the rusted cover of the stopcock was open, sticking up. She trod it down.

The key was stiff in the lock.

Hello? she called, and the house responded to the question with all the teeming silence of houses: something falling in the chimney breast, floorboards creaking in the stairwell untouched by any foot, canned laughter on the telly next door. The floorboards, the wooden stairwell, the white walls were like sound mirrors, reflecting her own presence back at her. It made her self-conscious.

All the post on the side by the front door was for Jo, or else addressed to the Owner or the Occupant, meaning Jo.

She stood at the door of the cupboard, listening.

Hello? she said, and leant back against the wall.

In the bedroom, looking down into the street, she wondered how long she would pretend to herself that perhaps he had gone out for a walk after all; or had popped to the shop.

Down below a car door opened; a moment later, Joyce emerged.

Then the door on the passenger side opened too, and a greyhound, stepping with careful elegance, made its way down onto the pavement.

Dry-mouthed, she let the curtain fall before she could see its owner follow it out into the street.

12.

Where was he?

She rang his phone but it clicked straight to voicemail.

Hi, it's me. You know what to do.

She tried again.

Hi, it's me. You know *what to do.*

A third time.

You *know what to do.*

Funny, she thought, how the inflection in a recorded voice might seem to change. By the third repetition he was starting to sound annoyed.

No such thing as repetition, she thought. Not in this world.

She took the camping torch from the shelf in the understairs cupboard, refusing for the moment to look towards the other door.

When she pressed the button the light came on feebly, flickered, then died. She shook it, which produced a slight pulse. Then, stepping out into the hall, she removed the batteries, swapped them around, then pressed the button a second time. The light came on.

She would add batteries to their shopping list. They had an app.

Hello? she called, stepping in.

The door at the end of the cupboard space was closed. There seemed to be a terrible finality to its closedness. The sight of it made her flinch, then fill with worry. She put her hand on it gently, then called his name.

A moment after this she put her ear to the door.

Violin music, drifting on the soft breeze.

She shook herself.

Come on, she said, pushing the door.

It resisted her.

A trot became a canter.

She pushed again, then swore.

Again.

What the—

She took a step back and then, tensing herself, shoved a shoulder into it, but while it shifted in its frame it did not give.

Okay, she said, turning around. She placed the lit torch on the shelf, pointing to the door.

What are you doing in there?

Her body obscured its light. She braced herself again, and this time slammed herself against the door, shoulder first, whereupon it gave suddenly, swung open, clattered the wall, and bounced back into her as she teetered on the edge of the steps, smacked hard by the damp chill.

For a moment she listened to the darkness, its teeming silence.

Torchlight bouncing over the walls, over the desk, the open cupboard.

Her eyes took a moment to adjust. The shelves of the cupboard had been removed from the wall and now lay on the ground; and the wall, she saw, had been half demolished. Rotten plaster littered the floor in front of it. It bore a large hole, perfectly black. Like a cut-out, she thought.

What are you doing? she murmured, stepping down into the room.

I'll crack on with things.

The desk was remarkably clean. At first, distracted by the damage inside the cupboard, her eyes did not register the copy of *The Argus* folded and lying on its surface. Beside it lay the lump of resin he had found. She unfolded the paper. Something about a footballer, benefits cheats, a dispute at the waste recycling facility in Woodingdean. Someone had been mutilating cats near the train station and the residents refused to believe it was a fox. There was a gallery of all the people who had been sent to prison in Sussex that month. A missing man.

The walls bore the circular traces of scrubbing. The room smelt strongly of bleach. She stared, baffled, at the hole in the plaster inside the cupboard inside the room beneath the cupboard under the stairs of their new house under its cold loft full of a stranger's belongings, torn, as if someone had punched their way through a paper screen.

Look.

She tried to steady the torch, but it flickered.

I'm looking.

Before it died she had time to see in its light behind the broken plaster another space.

Her stomach turned.

A narrow passage, leading down like the opening of a manhole; within, a metal ladder clung to the shadows.

She hurried back upstairs.

13.

Hi, it's me. You know what to do.

She paced the living room, tapping his name from the list.

Hi, it's me. You know—

She paced the hallway.

She found herself in the bedroom with no idea what had brought her here.

Hi, it's me.

She stood at the window, gazing down into the street.

Hi—

I would like to report a missing person, she said, rehearsing, repeating. Yes. I would like to report a missing person.

You know what to do.

I don't, she said. I don't think I ever have.

She looked at the photographs spread on the dining table and heard him, clear as voicemail played back:

What did you find?

Photographs.

Is there anything worse than other people's photographs?

Look.

Maybe other people's dreams.

Look.

I'm looking. What am I looking at?

The problem, she thought, looking at Jo's photographs, was that you were always somehow living through other people's dreams.

Hi, it's me.

I would like to report a missing person, she said.

Yes, she said.

Thank you.

Look.

I'm looking. What am I looking at?

She gave the operator their address.

Hi, he said. It's me.

She stood at the window, looking down into the street.

You know what to do.

Dollface

Raymond lived next door to my wife and I and sometimes he'd come over and we'd drink beers out on the
back patio. It didn't matter what the weather was like,
we always sat outside. He and I went a way back: we'd been
at primary school together, though we'd never been friends,
not in those days, and must have crossed paths only once or
twice after secondary school. But then a few years ago he and
his family happened to move into the house next to ours in
Mile Oak and, amused by the coincidence, we got to know
one another a little better over beers one night, which became
kind of a regular thing. My wife didn't like him. Raymond
had a wife too and a young daughter he liked to complain
about, and in fact he complained about the both of them a
good deal, his combined and ongoing complaint forming our
main topic of conversation, which was why my wife didn't
like him, because she didn't think it was very sensitive for
him to always be complaining about his daughter when we
ourselves had lost two babies, one at sixteen weeks and the
other the day after the birth. I tried to explain this to him once
but he didn't get it, which is why we'd always sit outside on
the patio, on old green camping chairs I was always meaning
to replace.

On this occasion, Raymond was complaining about his
sister-in-law, who so far as I knew my wife and I had never
met, because she had bought his daughter a present without

asking.

Well, a present's nice, I said. What's the problem?

The problem is the present itself and the fact that it isn't just a present. Not with Mylene. It's a present and it's some kind of a, I don't know. Some kind of a strategy. A device.

Okay, I said, and drank a swig of beer. In the summer I like to drink a nice chilled lager but in the winter I stick to ale. It was winter now. Raymond always sticks to lager, chilled or not, he wasn't particular, being as he was more interested in the ABV than the variety of hop.

What do you think it is she wants?

Oh, said Raymond, waving his hand. The usual. To drive a wedge. Between Mary and me, and between Sophie and me. The thing is, I knew her before I knew Mary, and she's never been, well…

He trailed off, muttering something under his breath. He was always swearing underneath his breath, which was another of my wife's given reasons for disliking him. He swore quite a lot over his breath, too.

Now he was staring at the patio, shaking his head.

So what was it? I asked.

What was what? said Raymond.

The present.

Oh, the present. That fucking thing. It's a doll.

He said the word 'doll' with considerable disgust. I nodded, wondering what could be so bad about a doll.

I hate dolls, said Raymond. Fucking dolls. Fucking Mylene.

Then he swore under his breath again, staring at the cracked patio, shaking his head.

◎

Maybe a week later he told me he might need my help with something.

That was unusual because usually all we did was drink

beer together out on the patio, but I said OK.

Thanks, said Raymond. Thanks.

I don't think I'd ever heard him say thank you before.

That bloody doll, he said. Bloody Mylene.

Shaking his head, he studied a crack in the patio.

Just tell me when, I said.

That bloody doll, said Raymond, nodding to himself.

Later that evening, after Raymond had left, my wife said to me: I don't know why you have to have him over all the time.

I nodded, looking up from my phone. We were sat on the sofa, in the glow of the television. Through the wall we could hear the TV in Raymond's living room. On the other side of the wall, he and Mary, or maybe just Mary, were watching the same programme.

Raymond and I go way back, I said. Same primary school and all.

My wife sniffed. Then she zapped the television off with the remote control and went up to bed.

I got up and went to turn it off properly, because the remote just puts it on standby, and when something's turned off I like it to actually be turned off and not just sleeping.

My mobile rang that night. It was three in the morning. It didn't actually ring because I keep it on silent but the screen lit up and filled the room with blue light, and I was awake anyway, as I often am. Tilting the screen down so as not to shine its cold light on my wife, who never has any trouble sleeping, I went out into the hall to answer.

When, said Raymond.

Pardon?

I'd started to wonder if I had been snoozing after all because I was as groggy as if I had just been jolted out of the deepest cycle of sleep. And the landing outside our bedroom had acquired a kind of dreamlike quality. Everything was normal, everything in its proper place, but somehow accentuated. I rubbed my eyes.

When.

Raymond, it's three in the morning.

You said to say when. I'm saying when. When when when. Okay?

I nodded, beginning to understand.

Can't this wait until the morning? I asked.

Nope. Sorry.

Now the banister and the stairwell and the little stained-glass window above the stairs down to the ground floor of the house had lost that odd accentuation. They were themselves again.

I've been drinking, said Raymond. Can you drive?

I counted the units in my head, considered the fact that I'd eaten and had finished X hours ago, and said Yes. Okay.

It was while saying 'Yes. Okay.' that I realised that what I should have said was 'Where?'

I went back into the bedroom and got dressed in the darkness. My wife turned over in her sleep.

Outside, Raymond was leaning against the car in our drive, holding a baby, cooing babyishly to it while it burbled back at him. He had a satchel over his shoulder. Backlit by the streetlamp, Raymond and baby and satchel formed a weird silhouette. It was such an odd sight it almost gave me a fright. Maybe the world hadn't quite lost that accentuation. I've always been a funny sleeper, and sometimes when I wake a little of the daft madness of dreams carries over into the day, like the sound of a television or an argument carrying through from the house next door. Not that it was day now, anyway. When I got closer I realised it wasn't a baby Raymond was holding.

Hi, I said.

Evening, said Raymond, though the evening had ended

hours ago. Look at this thing.

The orange light of the streetlamp gave the baby face a weird glow, but it was an ordinary doll, so far as I could tell. Nothing unusual about it. It had a slightly stubby nose, if you were to be critical, and maybe its big blue eyes were set a little far apart, but you had to really be looking for something to even think of that.

Well, I said. It's a doll.

Raymond was nodding. I'd often notice him nodding, when I'd not said anything. It was as if he was agreeing with something someone only he could hear had said. Sometimes it coincided with something I had said and I'd never be sure who he was agreeing with, with me or with the someone only he could hear.

It is that, he said. It is that. Let's drive.

Raymond gave directions like a satnav teeming with malware. He took us up the A27 and around the roundabouts where the A27 meets the A23, then back onto the A27 again and out east past the universities, before swinging us back towards town. The roads were mostly empty. It was eerie. I never really drive at that time of night. Who, outside of truckers, has anywhere to be going at that time of night? It made me wonder about the cars that we did pass. Where were they going?

Eventually, after several more circumlocutions, we reached Wild Park, which wasn't even really out of town but which might as well have been for all the time it took to get there.

Fucking Raymond, I thought.

He was clutching the doll in the passenger seat.

All I'd managed to get him to say about it was this:

Present from Mylene. It's a wedge. It's a fucking strategy. I know how that woman thinks. Oh, I know that woman. Mary doesn't know, or doesn't choose to, but I do. Christ, would you look at it?

And he held it up, reaching with one hand to flick on the

light in the roof of the car, which for a moment made it hard for me to see the road, but the road was empty.

Do you remember Mylene?

Before I could answer, he said:

We're here. Stop.

I stopped the car.

He took a torch out of the satchel.

Let's walk.

We walked.

Past the toilets, past the football pitches, into the woods.

It was dark in the woods.

Finally satisfied with the spot we'd found, Raymond crouched down. You squat like that, I thought, you'll fuck up your knees. It was a stupid thing to think.

Do you see the problem? said Raymond. He was staring at the doll as if he was hoping it would blink first. Daring it.

It didn't blink.

Not really, I said.

He tossed the doll down in front of him, onto the bracken, and sighed as if he was tired of dealing with people less intellectually capable than himself.

Mylene acts as though she doesn't know that I know what she's up to, but she does, he said.

I nodded, then stopped nodding when I realised it made it look as if I agreed. I didn't know if I agreed or not. Raymond often assumed you agreed with him, whether or not you actually did agree, and sometimes if you weren't careful you could get caught up in that assumption and become complicit in whatever it was he was on about. Mostly I just knew that I was tired.

And it was working, too, said Raymond.

What was working? I asked.

He looked at me sharply, as if I was playing dumb. I

blinked first. My eyelids were heavy.

Her plan, he said, looking down into the dirt.

I realised I was nodding again. Maybe it was like shivering: something you do to warm yourself up. I was shivering, too.

Wild Park is just a bit of woodland on the edge of the downs, on the outskirts of Brighton where the downland comes into town, bordered by the A27 to the north and Moulsecoomb and Hollingbury to the south. It isn't much, not really, though it is a nature reserve, to give it its due, but at four o'clock in the morning in the winter it can feel like quite a lot more, like a place befitting its name.

It got into my something, said Raymond, who hadn't said 'something'.

It got into what? I asked, looking up. Sorry.

He was nodding again, in that way he did. In the dark in the woods it wasn't so hard to imagine that maybe someone else had said something after all.

My head, he murmured. I've been dreaming about the fucking thing. And every time I walk into a room it's like, I don't know, there it is, looking at me. Leering at me. I go from one room into the next and it's there again as if it's fucking teleported. Except I can't quite remember if I had seen it in the room before, but I feel like I had. And it's only been getting worse. And Sophie, he said, trailing off.

I watched him for a moment. He was breathing weirdly.

What about Sophie? I asked.

Sophie loves it, he said. She loves it. She really does.

I looked down at the doll, at its stubby nose, at its big doll eyes set very slightly too far apart, and tried to see it as he seemed to see it. I couldn't do it.

Mylene knew, said Raymond. She knew.

I watched him. Then I looked at the doll again.

Raymond, I said. Why are we here?

He looked at me suddenly.

I need a witness, he said. To corroborate. The way things have been going lately, I've started doubting myself.

I realised I was rubbing my temple. I could feel a headache coming on. It was as if my tiredness had transmogrified, become a headache.

A witness for what?

It was beginning to annoy me, drawing him out.

So that I know it is dead, said Raymond.

He removed the satchel from his shoulder, the satchel that I'd forgotten he had with him.

As I watched he opened the satchel and brought out a box of matches, a small trowel, and then a can of deodorant. It was a black Lynx canister of some sort. In the dark I couldn't really see the satchel or the deodorant. In the dark it looked like he had removed the box of matches and the deodorant and the trowel from some secret pocket tucked away in the folds of the dark.

They might have been tucked away in the folds of the past, too: I remembered as kids once, a few of us, Raymond included, at this boy called Joe's house on Kimberley Road when his mother was out, arranging one of Joe's not-inexpensive Action Man figures and a load of toy soldiers in the corner of the patio in his garden. Joe had a load of bangers, which were illegal in England and which he'd brought back from a holiday in France, small little red explosives that looked like sticks of dynamite out of a cartoon. We carefully positioned them throughout the scene, then laid bits of kindling from the fireplace in the living room, bits of scrunched up newspaper, and a whole lot of matches all around. Then one of us—Joe, probably, but maybe Raymond—sprayed the whole tableau with deodorant. I had been the one holding the bucket of water, which to me meant that if we got into trouble later maybe I'd look like the responsible one. Now Raymond was holding the deodorant again but I didn't have the water.

In the dark the light of the fire when he lit it made my eyes hurt. Oddly accentuated, the doll burned. Its face began to melt. We watched it burn for a while.

We left the doll in the woods in a sad little grave that he dug with the trowel. Then we drove back home.

◎

The next day my wife didn't ask where I'd been. She gave the impression that she had no idea I'd even been anywhere, but I was pretty sure that she knew I'd been somewhere. She seemed more annoyed than usual that evening when Raymond came over for a beer.

We sat out on the patio, on the green camping chairs. They were getting tatty and old. I should buy some new ones, I thought.

For the first time ever, Raymond didn't say much. For the first time, I had to spur the conversation along.

Mary's pissed off, he said at last. She suspects something. Sophie's distraught.

I nodded as if I agreed.

They're staying with Mylene tonight.

Do they know?

No, but she suspects something. Mylene's got in her head. I spent all morning pretending to look for the fucking thing. It's surprisingly hard work, looking for something you bloody well know isn't there.

How're you feeling about it now? I asked.

He looked at me suddenly, then smiled. Much better, he said. So much better.

But later that night when he rang he wasn't feeling better anymore.

◎

It was 11 pm. My wife had gone to bed early for her, at 10, having scarcely said a word all evening, her face buried in the blue light of her phone. I'd found myself sitting in the living room, having another beer. The telly was on but I wasn't really watching it. I'd turned the volume down so low it was hard to tell if the sound was on at all.

I was thinking about the doll, about its eyes, set very slightly too far apart. My phone had dropped from the sofa to the carpet and I hadn't bothered to pick it up again. Then it began to glow suddenly with its own blue light and I saw that Raymond was calling.

Hi, I said.

He whispered something, his voice full of urgency, more a hiss than a whisper.

What? I said.

…come back, repeated Raymond.

They're back from Mylene's? I asked, sitting up, though I knew already that that was not what he had said.

No. The doll. It's back.

For the first time since we'd met I could hear fear in Raymond's voice.

But they're back too, he said. Came back this evening. And Sophie has the doll.

I took a sip of beer and tried to think about this. He had said the doll, not a doll.

Mylene replaced it? I asked.

No, for Christ sake, what I said. The doll is back. The one we—he whispered this—the one we disposed of.

That's impossible, I said. She must have bought a new one. They're hardly unique.

Even as I said this I don't think I really believed it. In the darkness of the living room, a few beers down, the clocks ticking to midnight, it wasn't too hard to believe that what Raymond was saying to me was true.

How do you know? I asked.

I just know.

Sure, I said. Sure. But is there anything particular—I mean, Raymond, you burnt the doll. We watched it melt. Then you buried it. I can corroborate this.

I know, it's impossible, but it's the same doll.

And is it melted?

Not at all.

Not at all, I said, nodding. My voice might have been the echo of Raymond's repeating down the line. For all I knew he was sat in the adjacent room, on the other side of the wall in front of me, but for now our voices were bouncing around through a network of satellites and computers, crossing absurd distances at absurd speeds, entertaining impossible notions.

How do you know? I said again.

The birthmark.

The doll has a birthmark?

Yep. I told you it was weird.

I was trying not to laugh.

Okay, I said. Have you seen any others? Do you know where Mylene bought it?

Mothercare, he said. I went and looked today.

Right, I said.

I was thinking maybe it was just that one and after Sophie reacted so badly I thought maybe I'd replace it. But when I went to the shop I didn't like the look of them. They're smart dolls.

Smart dolls? I said, baffled by the term.

Yeah, you hook them up to the WiFi and then you can talk to your kid through them. I bet she's been spying on us.

Smart dolls, I said, another echo repeating. The idea was new to me.

Anyway, said Raymond, those ones—I looked—those ones in the shop, they didn't have birthmarks.

Some kind of manufacturing defect, I thought, thinking I'd said it. For a moment I wasn't sure whether I'd said it or not.

I closed my eyes. I was rubbing my temple.

When I opened my eyes, the television was off, gone into some power saving mode, and I realised its screen had been the only light I'd had on, because I was sitting in shadows now.

I'll show you, said Raymond.

Tomorrow, I said.

No, I—

Tomorrow, I said, and ended the call. Then I powered the phone down and tossed it back onto the floor.

That night I slept on the sofa in the shadows of the living room and dreamt about the doll.

It was the same doll. He wasn't wrong. I could see that immediately. He showed me the birthmark. It didn't look like a manufacturing defect.

Jesus, I said, because there was nothing better to say. It was impossible and it was true. What do you say to that?

I can hardly bring myself to touch it, said Raymond. It's like it's contaminated. I'll see Sophie playing with it and it just turns my stomach. But then if you take it off her she just cries and cries.

What does Mary think?

She'd want me sectioned.

I nodded, shivering. It was cold out on the patio. The nights were getting even colder. Raymond had propped the doll up on the white table. It was a baby, of course, but of an age where it could hold itself up. It looked like it was holding itself up. In the dark it wasn't hard to mistake it for a real baby.

It had its slightly stubby nose. It seemed weird to me to give a doll a nose like that. Its eyes set slightly too far apart. Who had designed this thing? I thought. And its birthmark. Why the fuck did it have a birthmark?

Some of Raymond's fear was seeping into me. For him, the fear expressed itself as revulsion. For me it was a kind of attraction. There was something compelling about the doll. It made the things around it seem fainter, vaguer, less real. It seemed oddly accentuated. I wanted to touch it but I didn't want to touch it. I sat and peered at it, studying the texture of its bib and the plastic of its face and the synthetic hair glued into its head that, impossibly, wasn't melted anymore, and wanted to look at anything else and at the same time it was all I wanted to look at, the only thing.

What now? I said.

Raymond looked up. I realised he'd had his face in his hands. For a moment I thought he'd been crying but on second thoughts decided not.

Fire didn't work, he said, stroking his beard.

Usually he shaved but recently he hadn't been shaving. Looking at him I saw the exhaustion in his eyes. He looked like he'd been sleeping even worse than me.

I thought maybe I'd bury it.

We did that before.

But deeper.

Okay, I said.

I've got a better idea. You got your car keys?

I tried to calculate the units of alcohol I'd consumed, but the truth is I'm numerically dyslexic.

Yes, I said.

Carefully Raymond put the doll into his satchel. He did it with a kind of gentleness, like he was tucking it in for the night. Then we got in my car and drove to the beach. The night was cold and getting colder, and the wind was getting up.

There's a bronze statue of a donut or something that looks like a donut on the beach, a big green thing, two and a half metres wide, what's called a torus, to the west of the Palace Pier and to the east of the husk of the West Pier. Christ knows why. Public art. On the groyne there we stood looking at the waves. The lights of the working pier stained the black waves with their glow. In the winter in the dark with the cold and the rain the sea looked unforgiving. For a moment I thought Raymond was having second thoughts, then he turned and walked back down the groyne and skipped over the wall where it was low enough for him to jump down onto the beach, and I heard him land on the pebbles with a groan, cursing his knees.

Where are you going? I said, or maybe thought and didn't say. It was hard to hear even my own voice over the wind.

I walked over to the wall and looked down to see him gathering pebbles, and then I understood. He put the pebbles in his bag with the doll. Then he came back up on to the groyne and walked to its end and stood for a moment looking out at the churn of black waves.

I realised he had closed his eyes.

What if it comes back again? he said.

It won't, I said, and wondered if I believed that.

It did last time.

I nodded.

The night really was very cold, but it seemed inappropriate to try and hurry him along.

Raymond, I said.

He sighed and opened his eyes. Then he checked the buckles on the satchel.

How's your throw? he said, and I think I saw a smile on his face. In school I'd never been sporty like Raymond had been. That was probably the reason we'd never been friends back in those days. It gets boring getting beaten all the time.

He stepped back and took a deep breath. Then, frowning, he took a few more steps, giving himself a run up. Then he ran, stopping suddenly at the seaward wall, and for a second I was certain he was about to tumble over it, but instead he launched the bag high, high up into the dark.

He had a good throw. I didn't hear it splash.

I'm going to need a new bag, said Raymond.

Yep, I replied, thinking it would probably just wash up on the beach in the morning.

Oh, fuck, he said, halting in dismay.

What? I said.

What now? I thought. Jesus it is cold, I thought.

My keys were in the bag.

He started patting his pockets. Then he closed his eyes.

Piss.

What?

I think my phone was also in it.

We walked back to my car, parked up on Black Lion Street on the other side of the promenade and the Kings Road. We sat in the car for a while and then I drove us home.

The next day, I don't know why, I called in sick to work and, leaving my car in the drive, got a bus into town. I got off at the stop on North Street, then headed south down East Street, and it was only once I'd reached the beach that I realised what I was doing.

I'd been thinking about the doll, about its stubby nose, its large staring eyes set too far apart, and the fact that dolls came chipped these days, hooked up to the internet, and I'd been thinking about this Mylene.

Did I expect to find the satchel? I don't know. It would be an absurd thing to say, of course, that I expected to find it, but through those last few weeks absurdities had rather begun to accumulate.

The beach might have been a different beach. It was the daytime now, of course, but the wind had gone, and the sea was flat, and the world felt peculiarly airless. It wasn't hard to imagine some fucker with a Jesus complex trying to walk on it, the sea was that flat. And with the aforementioned accumulating absurdities they'd probably succeed. But it was so cold that you wouldn't want to fail.

I was giving up on the bag, pretending to myself that I hadn't come down here for that, that I'd just wanted some air, nothing unreasonable, when I saw a kid struggling with something on the pebbles. He was maybe seven. I looked around but there were no adults in sight.

I think immediately I knew it was the bag.

Hey, I said, approaching him. Hey.

He glanced up with a look that said he was doing something he shouldn't have been doing.

For a moment I didn't know what to say. He stared at me, and for a moment I thought he was going to try and leg it.

That's my bag, I said, and when I moved forward, ready for a tug-of-war over the satchel, a forty-year-old man ready to grapple with a seven-year-old child, he scrambled to his feet and scurried away.

I watched him leave the beach, disappearing up onto the promenade, kicking up pebbles in his wake. Then I looked down at the bag.

Huh, I said.

There was no doubt.

I crouched down. My eyes widened and I recoiled when I touched it, as if every thread of its fabric coursed with diabolical electricity.

It wasn't wet.

The boy had unclipped one of the buckles but the other was still secure. I unclipped it and opened the impossibly dry top flap, revealing the zip over the main impossibly dry compartment. Under the flap but not in the main compartment there were a few small pockets for pens and things. Opening one of these, I found Raymond's house keys, and in the other I found his phone. The battery was in the red, in a power saving mode, but it wasn't dead. There were several missed calls from Mylene.

Fucking Mylene, I thought, in Raymond's voice.

In the main compartment, under some pebbles, I found the doll, which was also dry.

I dropped the bag back onto the pebbles and stood up straight. I realised I could hear myself breathing heavily, breathing weirdly. I was trying and failing to think. For a moment I felt short of breath and like a wave of black panic was about to swell out of the calm of my mind, sweeping everything away, but it didn't.

I crouched down again and removed the house keys and the mobile phone from the front pockets of the bag. I fiddled with the phone until I managed to power it off. I looked around for a moment, checking that there was no one nearby to see me, and then running forward I hurled each of them, the house keys and the phone, out to sea.

I'd never had a good throw before, but that was a good one.

When I couldn't find my car where I'd thought I'd parked it up on Black Lion Street, I walked up to Western Road and took a number 1A bus back home.

The house was empty. For a moment its weird airless emptiness surprised me, until I remembered that my wife was at work. I should open some windows, I thought, but didn't.

Instead I went out on to the patio and, standing up on tiptoes, peered over the fence into Raymond's garden. I looked up at the windows of his house. The curtains of the rear extension were drawn and the curtains in the windows of the back bedroom above it were also drawn. The other window on that floor was the bathroom window and that window was frosted for privacy, and was closed.

With the satchel over my shoulder I looked down at the doll's head poking through the pebbles in the main compartment. Then I slung it up and over the fence, into the garden next door.

Fucking Mylene, I thought, in Raymond's voice.

Raymond didn't come over for a beer that evening or the next, and he didn't ring. The curtains at the back of the house remained drawn and the curtains round the front stayed drawn too. Whenever he watched television he'd have the television on pretty loud, because he was a little deaf, and we'd be able to hear it through the living room wall. Sometimes we'd hear him swearing through that wall. But for the next few nights we wouldn't hear either, TV or swearing, at all.

On the Wednesday, sitting out on the patio on my own, working my way through a bottle of Doombar, I remembered the satchel. Standing up from the camping chair, I went over to the fence, and going on tiptoes stood to peer over into Raymond's garden.

The satchel was gone.

Returning to the chair, I went to sit back down but the damn thing collapsed underneath me, causing me to swear and spill beer. Swearing some more, under my breath and over my breath, I went and took the other chair, which I thought of as Raymond's chair, from the shed. Then after testing the stability of the chair I sat back down and drank what remained of the beer.

◎

Someone was knocking at the door. My wife was out for Sunday lunch with a friend and for a moment I'd assumed she'd forgotten her key and had come back without it, but when I looked down from the stairwell the figure I saw through the translucent glass of the door was shorter than my wife, who's pretty tall for a woman, and slimmer.

That morning I'd heard movements in the living room next door. I'd stopped to listen, wondering if it was Raymond, but I didn't hear any swearing so had decided it was his wife. Then, later, I'd heard two voices arguing, women's voices, Raymond's wife Mary and another voice I couldn't place. Then the door had slammed.

At that point I'd gone upstairs to take a pee. After a few moments I heard the knocking at the door, and after a small delay I realised it was our door that they were knocking at and not Raymond and Mary's door next door.

I think even then I knew who it was.

I recognised the shape of her through the translucent glass of the door.

Mylene, I said, squinting against the bright diffuse daylight.

Startled, her expression broke out into a smile.

Well isn't it a small fucking world, she said.

What do you want?

Aren't you going to invite me in? she said, staring up at me with big blue eyes set very slightly too far apart. Put the kettle on?

No, I said. I don't think I am. What do you want?

My sister told me the neighbour might know where her useless husband is. I didn't realise the neighbour was you.

I nodded as if I agreed.

I've no idea, I said.

Mylene was leaning against the wall, looking at me sort of sideways, clearly amused by the whole situation.

Okay, she said, suddenly annoyed by what I assumed was her failure to elicit a reaction from me. Well, if you see him, say I need to talk to him.

She turned away. I watched her walk down the drive. At the gate, she turned back, smiling again.

About what? I asked.

Tell him I'm pregnant, she said, and started to laugh.

Fucking Raymond, I thought, suddenly nauseous with what I can only describe as jealousy, and shut the door. It shook in the frame. When I opened it again, Mylene was gone.

The next evening when I took a beer from the box in the utility room and went out to the shed the chairs were gone, the broken one and the one that wasn't broken. Coming out of the shed, I saw my wife stood in the doorway, watching me.

A woman called round earlier, she said.

Oh, I said.

She had the wrong address, she said.

Right, I said.

My wife thought for a moment.

I kind of recognised her, she said.

Uh huh, I said.

I realised I was nodding, but not at anything she had said, so I made myself stop.

Suddenly my wife smiled.

What's happened to the chairs? I asked.

Oh, I chucked them out, said my wife. One of them was broken.

She shivered.

And they were starting to rot. Honestly, did the smell not bother you at all?

Other Houses

There are some memories so exact in their detail you would bet your life on their being true. For example: the time I pushed my sister into the pond in Queen's Park, one autumn morning out with our father after the rain had stopped. That October it had been hard to imagine it ever ceasing to fall. It's the kind of memory that's a bodily thing: my feet remember, my eyes remember; my arms recall the ripple of goose pimples in the autumn air. Closing my eyes, I can see the dew still ablaze in the grass, and the path we followed, curving round the pond, a plate of dark water in the stillness. I remember the glare of the light and the haze, and the tears in my eyes, and my sister shivering, sodden and in shock, and my father comforting her. I remember how far removed I felt from them in that moment, as if, standing not ten feet away, the execution of that sudden act of cruelty had placed them beyond some impenetrable screen. I must have been ten years old, Rebecca six. I remember my hand on her shoulder and the soaking filth of her hooded top, and the guilt tingling in my palm as the dampness passed from the fabric to my fingertips. I remember the excitement and shame of the shove, of its sudden and unpremeditated violence. I can still feel it in my fingertips, like the tactile memory of an electric shock. Years later, to my bewilderment, they told me Rebecca had slipped: it had nothing to do with me—I was a way back down the path. Perhaps I had wanted to push her. Maybe I had fantasised about doing so. Either way, for years I had tended an ever-burning shame. I could place it out of mind for as long as I liked, but at some point I would always turn around and find it there, burning still. I had felt the redness of it in my face and ears and the rise of acid sickness in my throat, and I had never questioned my guilt: it was a fact in the world, as inarguable as a building or a photograph, and when I brought it up, the first time I can remember ever bringing it up, Rebecca shook her head, half frowning, seeming to grimace at the memory, and then our father agreed, looking at me momentarily, irritated, from the newspaper open across his lap. It shakes your sense of things, this sort of abrupt revision of your life.

For example: previous tenants of the house my father had moved into after our mother had died knocked through walls and built new walls where no walls had ever stood, seemingly without much thought, giving the building a somehow whimsical structure. For a time the basement had been separated and rented out, the old stairwell sealed off, then the man who had lived there before us had reunited the lower and upper maisonettes, but never quite along the old lines. As a consequence the house never really added up. Specifically: I remember the small staircase that lead nowhere, from the understairs cupboard in the basement. I would wager my life—my memories, my sanity—that that cupboard in my father's house contained a stairwell leading nowhere at all. I remember how it had fascinated me: I imagined ghost rooms, ghost floors, ghost extensions of the familiar home, intersecting with the known building on stranger axes. Then my father did a lot of work on the place. There were always strange men around in paint-splattered overalls, drinking tea and sanding things, hammering things, drilling through and painting or repainting things, as their portable radio, encrusted with dust and paint, played tinny chatter and pop songs. Something about the building seemed to inspire such modifications, as if it was never quite right, never quite made sense, but was always on the cusp of doing so—if you only changed this one small thing. And there was always that one small thing. Somehow the building always seemed to feel as if it were falling down. I think I had assumed that the staircase had been taken out, then replaced with something more sensible. I hadn't ventured down into the basement in years. I had not thought about the allure that cupboard had exerted over me as a child for a long time. Then one day, visiting Dad the day after he had returned home from hospital following a fall, after having thought about it not once in countless years, I remembered the staircase that had led nowhere and the whole structure of invisible extensions I had imagined ghosting out of the building, and which you might have seen on a clear day, when the light was right and your mood was calm and your looking undistracted by the buzzing busy business of the day, when the world seemed settled into a kind of repose, or which on other occasions you might have glimpsed in passing (all things are glimpsed in passing, I think to myself, are only glimpsed in passing) out of the corner of your eye. And I smiled in that reverie and said to my father: Dad, do you remember the stairwell that led nowhere at all? and he looked at me through that fog of irritated confusion that had become his predominant mood and said No. No, I don't know what you're talking about, in a familiar tone of voice that served to end that particular line of conversation. When I left him, I wasn't ready to go home, and so decided to go for a drive. Heading out of Brighton, I rang Rebecca, and her voice filled the car through the Bluetooth connection.

Just saw Dad, I told her.

Good, she said. How is he?

Tired. A bit irritable.

I'll see him on Saturday, Rebecca said. David and I can drive over after we've dropped the boys off at BYC.

For a moment I watched the rain run along the windscreen, my focus receding from the road. It was dark except for the tungsten of the streetlamps and the glow of the dashboard and my phone stuck awkwardly in the coffee holder. The snake of cats' eyes on the tarmac vanishing beneath the vehicle, curving with the contours of the invisible downs. I felt the passage of other vehicles and the lives they contained as soft vibrations passing through the steering wheel, into my hands. Into my fingertips. Then I said: Rebecca?

Yes?

Do you remember the staircase in Dad's house, the one downstairs?

The staircase?

Yes, in the cupboard.

The staircase in the cupboard? No.

She paused, then said: Where did it go, Narnia?

I frowned. Okay, don't worry.

Okay.

Speak to you soon.

Yes, speak to you soon.

Bye.

Goodbye.

Bye.

As I drove on through the night, watching the cats' eyes disappear and the small stretch of visible road twist and curve in the weak illumination of the headlights, the sudden sense that I was driving much too fast seized me, tightening my chest, catching my breath in my throat. Then the sensation flipped, and it wasn't that I was moving at all but rather that the road was speeding under me, the darkness rushing over me, the glowing of the dashboard become a confusion of light. Gasping, I slowed the vehicle, and when a service station appeared, shining neon green and yellow against the darkness, I pulled into the car park to stop the car and gather myself. The way that the cats' eyes had captivated me—I don't think I had accelerated rashly, but rather that my focus had shifted from the road, and in the night and my sudden confusion I had lost my grip on things, had lost my purchase on the world.

ii.

Something in Rebecca's tone when I had asked her about the old staircase had terminated that particular line of conversation. She had always resembled our father in that regard: if she didn't want to talk about something, we wouldn't be talking about it, simple as that: it was out of bounds, whatever it was, though why it had to be so I could never say. Somehow she had always borne a little of our father's authority, and it was an authority founded on mystery: there always seemed to be something crucial that I did not know.

Dad got worse. When you started to think he couldn't get worse, when it seemed like everything that he once had owned had already been taken from him, he still got worse: it seemed there was always more to be taken. His decline had begun as an inconvenience, become an annoyance, then escalated into an outrage, a scandal. There were appointments, visits to the doctor, to the hospital, visits at home from the social worker and the meals-on-wheels people and a woman named Joanne who came by twice a week to pick up groceries and tidy and pass the time of day. For a while he entertained the benign delusion that he and Joanne were to marry, believing my scepticism to be a disapproval stemming from the view, which I did not hold, that it was unfair on our mother. As if she could have cared. Aren't you going to congratulate me? he asked once, laughing. I don't know if he ever discussed this with Joanne—she never mentioned it to me.

In the winter he grew suddenly worse. It was like someone

was reeling him in, inch by inch, and then, overcome with impatience, had snapped on the line. A second stroke had left his face slightly lopsided, lending him an unintentionally quizzical expression. A constant itchiness of the skin foretold worse news to come. He grew stiffer and less mobile. He fell again and returned to hospital. Then, soon afterwards, after much careful but insistent persuasion, we moved him into a home, Gracewell's, where he could get the care he needed, and receive visits from Rebecca and I and from old friends he would struggle to recognise. After I drove him to the home on that first day, his mood one of cantankerous resignation, after settling him in, I stood in his old living room and cried. I knew that I had not 'settled him in'. I had never seen someone look so unsettled in my life.

The thought of Rebecca coming round and finding me there and finding me crying shook me out of it. Weeping wasn't something she did: that time by the pond might have been the last time I had seen her cry. Emotion, really, wasn't something she did, or liked to show, or to see shown. It was as if there was a kind of uncleanliness to it, an unseemliness. It was always inappropriate. Except in the blandest of forms, it was always out of bounds.

I wiped my eyes and blew my nose with some tissues from the box on the dining room table. A pile of newspapers, magazines, all three months out-of-date at least. Bills, bank statements, a copy of *Watchtower*. My father's reading glasses. A tobacco knife. Coins: Euros, English pennies, an English pound. A copy of one of his books, translated into Dutch, John Hague's characteristic watercolour and ink work a dreamlike spread of pastels and pitch shadows; Hague, my father's decades-long collaborator, who had died two years before. A photograph of Rebecca's boys, Jack and Harry, in school uniform, against a marbled backdrop. An SLR camera, with one frame unshot, which I picked up, and began to turn over in my hands. I wondered when Dad had last picked it up, when he had last raised its viewfinder to his eye.

I turned around and looked at the dining room, then through into the living room, already hunting for the scene I would frame, as if to even hold the thing placed you in a certain relation to your surroundings. Hold a knife and the world becomes an array of things to be cut, hold a hammer and everything starts to look like a nail. Pick up a camera and the world begins to arrange itself around you. Piles of tat become a mise-en-scène. In the living room, on the television, women danced in some music video, muted and made eerie by the silence, but I couldn't remember turning it on. I raised the camera to my eye. Looked at the TV, at the dancing women, all quite faultlessly beautiful, who in their faultlessness and muteness now assumed an odd malevolence. Looked at the pile of magazines. Looked at the photograph of Rebecca's boys through the meagre viewfinder and wondered how that photograph would look, photographed in its turn. Then turning I saw myself in the large mirror opposite the dining room table, raised the camera to my eye again, and pressed the shutter. Click. A weak flash bounced back from the surface of the glass. It brought the gloom into focus. I stood there still, empty-headed, stalled, as if I had been caught by the flash, ensnared in its light.

A moment later—maybe an eon later, a small eternity—I removed the camera from my eye and looked at it, turned it over in my hands, wondered where Dad had gotten it and where he'd shot the other frames. He would have bought it, I assumed, for one of his holidays. He liked to go abroad. Throughout my childhood we had only ever gone on camping holidays in Cornwall, Devon, Dorset, sometimes Wales. He never liked to go very far: he said travel disrupted his writing. But after Rebecca and I had finally left home, he had taken to going a little farther afield. He went to France and drove down into Spain through the Pyrenees. He went to Belgium and Germany. He went to Marrakesh. He would send me postcards with no messages beyond *Dad x* from each place he visited, accompanied by a small sketch of some local detail in his unmistakable hand, an expressive scratching of fountain pen ink, both chaotic and precise in its line. He knew I worried. I kept them all.

I went through into the kitchen. For a while I stood there looking at the garden through the window, the eucalyptus tree a blur through condensation, February an impressionist smear of coloured forms, browns and greys. It was raining. Since the start of January it had always been raining, a constant drizzle that softened the edges of things. It made the world feel like a television channel not quite tuned in, the signal of things edged with shimmering noise. The dampness insinuated its way into your bones. I had had a sort of a cough for who knew how long, something short of a cough, a tickling in the throat. Sniffles. I was always on the verge of getting ill. I stood there looking at the window, at it and not through it, not knowing what to do. Then I began to wash up the few dishes in the sink. After that I tidied up the living room. In the stillness I felt a tension in the house: as if at any moment Dad might return. Surely he was due. If I closed my eyes I could picture him through the translucent glass of the front door, coming down the path, his figure growing larger and clearer as he neared. I could hear the crunch of his feet on the gravel, the jangling of his keys as he approached the door, the sounds of a muffled cough and muttered words, a sniff, a sucking of air through teeth. Exact memories prefiguring future moments that were not to be. The house haunted by someone who was not yet dead. A ghost of the living. Can the living haunt? I opened my eyes and the silence shocked me. It was a total silence, as mute as the television. You couldn't imagine anyone ever talking in that house again.

At four o'clock, shivering, I took my handbag, took my coat down from the banister, put it on, put on my boots again, and left. I double-locked the door behind me. From the drive

I saw that I had left the television on, but after hesitating did not return indoors to switch it off. Women dancing in a muted video. I couldn't imagine Dad watching music videos. He would be upstairs, in his office, writing and drawing. But it looked like someone was in. As if he was just sitting in his chair.

As I drove out of Brighton, joining the rush hour traffic on the A27, intending to meet a friend in Lewes, I remembered the staircase leading nowhere. I should have looked for it. Even then I knew that in some way I did not believe what my father and my sister had said. But nor I did not think that they were lying to me. In that silence where my Dad had been I could well imagine stumbling upon it there, ordinary and unassuming, as real as anything had any right to be. I found myself in an uneasy mood, distracted and restless. Instead of meeting my friend, I circled back at a roundabout, taking the bypass back towards town. At home when I put my handbag down on the dining room table, sighing loudly, running my hands through my hair, the bag toppled and the camera fell out, falling from the table to the floor. I stared down at it for a moment, puzzled. I couldn't remember putting it in my bag.

Then I picked it up, turned it over in my hands, and raised the viewfinder to my eye.

iii.

When did you first know sadness? Is it possible to recall such a moment, or does it dissolve in the medium of your life upon entry before spreading out until it permeates it all? Is it possible to reach back, through memory, and mark the point before which there was no sadness in your life and after which it was there? Not the distress of something you had—the bottle, the breast—being taken away from you. Not anger at something you could not understand. Sadness is more insidious than that. It creeps into the cracks of things. It slips itself into your memories of happier times, such that you grow to doubt if you were ever happy at all. Was it not all a sham, and the sadness—the Sadness: let's afford it the dignity of a proper name—now merely your realisation of that fact? In this way it corrupts even the good things. By means of some bad magic, it detaches from its causes and becomes an autonomous entity, a Thing that rules your life. People give it different names or pictures, as if in the naming or picturing of the Thing they might exercise some control: Melancholia, Depression, Sadness, Anhedonia; black dogs, sad clowns, grey rain. Each term captures something of it and lets other parts go. In many respects, as a child, I had no reason to be sad: we were well cared for, my sister and I, and dearly loved by our father; after his first book became successful, far more successful than he or his publisher had anticipated, our father became a wealthy man. Our material needs were met. Our mother died when I was five, Rebecca not yet one, and it was a strange, gentle death, a fading away, but that was not the first grief in my life. When did I first know sadness? Rorschach, of course. That stupid dog.

I was four years old when Rorschach, as my father had named him, disappeared.

I remember Rorschach far more vividly than I remember my mother. He was a collie crossed with Christ knew what, anxious and ingratiating, desperate for affection, a stray my father had adopted from the RSCPA kennels on the A23 just outside of Brighton. I was immensely proud of him and took great care of him. I would brush his coat and lay out his food and watch television snuggled up next to him on the carpet in front of the sofa. He was my friend.

We would walk up around the hill fort, north of Brighton, parking on the side of Ditchling Road, my father with Rebecca in a sling, her face poking over his shoulder, wide-eyed and red-nosed in the cold, under a woolly hat, as Rorschach ran off among the gorse. Dad would throw a tennis ball for him along the path through the woods and he would bound after it, disappearing into the bushes and only returning much later on, sometimes with the ball, other times without. Once I remember Dad throwing a stick for him to chase into the dew pond, and in my memory I can see him leaping into the water, shattering the reflection of the blood orange sky the evening had stained upon its surface. As the shadows deepened we sat on the bench by the trig point and counted until the sun went down, Rorschach curled up at my father's feet; other times my father sat me on the concrete column, where men had once positioned a theodolite in order to map the land, a process my father explained to me though I was far too young to understand, and Rorschach would leap up, trying to reach me, which I found hilarious. On clear days sometimes we would see the Isle of Wight in the distance. My father would point it out, and promise to take me there, although he never did. This was, I think, before Rebecca was old enough to come between my father and me. It was before I pushed her into the pond. It was before our mother died, although even then she hardly figures in my memories.

Are these memories too vivid? In my mind they possess an etched clarity, the colours of that world as rich as stained glass: the sunset, the gathering shadows, the yellow petals of the gorse, the rows of which in recollection loom like some vast labyrinth on the downs. I had dreams, after Rorschach disappeared, of that labyrinth. In those dreams I could hear him howling. I ran through the labyrinth, the avenues among the gorse trees enclosed in a way in which they were not enclosed in waking life, searching for him, but though I could hear him there I could not find him. Once I saw him looking back, but when I reached the spot where he had stood he was gone, and only further branching avenues of gorse would meet me. I had the dreams well into adolescence; I have had them once or twice as an adult, though in these versions I am alone and cannot hear the howling of my dog.

Rorschach vanished. He was out in the garden on his own, as he often was, and had started barking furiously, so I went out to find him. By the time I got to the steps that led down to the patio and beyond it the lawn the barking had ceased. The garden was empty. I could still hear his barking in my head: furious, in agony. That sound would echo in me for a long time. Puzzled, I called for him. I heard my father come into the kitchen behind me.

What is it?

Rorschach, I said.

Worzak, my father said, imitating the way I mispronounced his name.

Where is he? he asked, stepping ahead of me, looking down the steps. Rorschach?

He called a second time. Usually you would never need to call his name more than once: he always responded with such excitement, delighted that someone wanted to see him, and come leaping out from wherever it was he had gone. But this time he did not come leaping. My father called his name a third time. A fourth. Strange, he said.

I think I started to cry.

Later on my father and I called round at our neighbours, asking if they had seen my dog. Nobody had. My father made posters which we put up on lampposts and telephone poles. Wherever I went, I was looking for him. We never found him. Rorschach did not return.

It must have been a few months after Rorschach's disappearance that my father first started putting him into the stories he told me as he tucked me into bed at night. Before long Rorschach became a recurring character in his children's books. Worzak. He would, in time, become one of the most popular. That stupid, lovely dog. My dog. In time he belonged to everyone.

My memories of Rorschach, as I have said, are more vivid than my memories of my mother. I know how terrible this sounds. Only much later on would I begin to realise why. I have since, for the first time in years, read through some of the Rorschach books, illustrated in John Hague's indelible scratchy ink and watercolour style. Sometimes I wonder if my memories are of the dog as I had known him or of the character in those books. No doubt they are the combination of the two, though where the one part begins and the other ends I could not say.

iv.

Dad died in April, on the 23rd, two months and three days after moving into Gracewell's. Even after that slow decline, that piecemeal dismantlement, grief shocked me beyond any shock I had known: my world keeled, tossed suddenly on violent waves. I experienced a kind of nausea, a churning sea-sickness on dry land. What had seemed steady and durable was exposed as only a temporary stillness, a passing form, a frail raft. And underneath the world black water, waiting to swallow it all.

My sister and I did not speak for a long time. On frequent occasions over the course of our relationship, since child-hood, I would wonder if I had offended her, but even in childhood I had learned not to ask. To wait out her silences. As a child, Rebecca had long seemed like the older one. Older, wiser, more mysterious, always in possession of some piece of knowledge only she and my father were privy to and which I was judged for not possessing, or which I could not be trusted to possess.

She did not say much to me at the funeral. It was held in St Michael and All Angels Church, a church in Clifton Hill I doubt Dad had ever stepped foot inside in his life; Rebecca arranged everything. I was happy to let her. She gave a speech, the detail of which I cannot recall, but I didn't speak. I had no voice. Grief, it seemed, had pulled my tongue out at the root. I studied the stained-glass scenes of the windows, archangels and a triptych of episodes from Christ's life, opulent colours dull on a dull day, and the stone arch in the chancel, and the stone columns, bearing carved foliage. The priest spoke in tones so soft it was easy not to listen, but I found it blandly comforting. Brief passages would drift into clarity before ebbing back into the sonorous flow: "For I am convinced that neither death nor life," I heard, briefly tuning in, "neither angels nor demons, neither the present nor the future, nor any powers, neither height nor depth, nor anything else in all creation, will be able to separate us..." His voice might have reached my ears from another room, through locked doors and fortified walls. I was seated at the back, next to Joanne; a last-minute impulse had driven me from the front. I knew Rebecca would be angry, but I didn't care. As the priest spoke, I noticed for the first time quite how beautiful the woman who had helped look after my father through the last eighteen months of his life really was. She had long hair, black and thick, falling in curls. She was in her early fifties, and looked her age, and looked well for her age, ten years older than I was and not half as tired. As I thought this, I felt the depth of my exhaustion again. I felt used-up. The last few months had depleted me.

After the service, after thanking the well-wishers, neighbours, and friends of my father I hardly knew, for coming, as we walked out of the church, exchanging small talk about God knows what, Joanne turned to me quite suddenly, almost but not quite smiling, and took my elbow, glancing around to check that no one would overhear what she was about to say. Then she said it: You know, I've never mentioned this to you, but your father proposed to me. A year ago.

I stopped. I felt suddenly removed from things, at a slant to the quiet road and the blank day and the cold. The cold and the blank day and the quiet road withdrew, and I was in some odd pocket of the world. Momentary alarm crossed Joanne's face, so I jerked myself forward, back into the proper course of things. I felt the wind on the back of my neck, still edged with winter. The air still smelled like December air, I thought. It's been December a very long time.

The funny thing is, Joanne continued, laughing, trying to resume where she had left off before the interruption of my reaction, I almost said yes. I thought about it. I really did care about him. I wasn't sure if I was playing along. I think I might have been serious, you know.

I laughed, or tried to laugh. How sweet, I said, smiling.

The priest's words, the few I remembered, replayed in my thoughts: neither the present nor the future, nor any powers, neither height nor depth, nor anything else in all creation, will be able to separate us.

Three days after the funeral, I found Dad's little old camera on the mantelpiece in my living room, and after a moment's fumbling worked out how to remove the wound film from its back. Little and old, true, but it was in excellent nick. Its black body, bearing the Nikon name above the lens mount, was strong, I noticed; it was very well built.

I had spent those days indoors, not knowing what to do with myself, not wanting to do anything, and for all the world it seemed as if the walls of my flat had started to inch inwards from the periphery of my vision. Outside the weather hadn't changed, an oppressive greyness into which it was impossible to imagine the spring erupting, the colour of things as faint as the detail of someone else's dream. The sky felt close, like the dome of a snow globe low over the town, the outside world a small and distant thing. When my mood is low I find it very easy to stay indoors. It isn't hard to get trapped, stuck, stalled. I had booked two weeks off work, with the funeral on the fourth of the fourteen days, not knowing what I would do with myself but knowing I could not face going to the office and sitting at a desk; I hadn't taken time off in a long time, anyway: I was due the leave. I drank coffee and tried to read and didn't get dressed or even out of bed in the mornings. I watched television but found even the simplest of plots difficult to follow. I hardly cooked. I thought about my father. I dreamt about him. Good dreams, in which he had never grown ill, but when I awoke into the world in which he had died those good dreams in retrospect acquired the tenor of nightmares. Waking up I would find myself in shock, as if each time I awoke the bad news was new again, each time the first time I had received it. In that same movement the gap between the world of those dreams in which my father lived, vigorous and big-hearted, in good humour, as large and strange as he had seemed to me as a child, and the world as it was seemed small, as if nothing substantial separated the two. Neither the present nor the future, I thought, nor any powers. I turned the camera over in my hands. I peered at the film canister as if the surface of the thing might offer up some intimation of its contents. Of the world it contained, or the fragments of a world. As I held it then it struck me as the most mysterious of things. I finally had a reason to go outside.

v.

Boots had an option offering turnaround within the hour. I dropped the roll of film off there with the teenager at the counter, paid, took the receipt, slipping it into my purse, and went back outside. So I had sixty minutes to kill. The drab overcast skies of the previous few days had given way to the first pleasant hours of spring. It wasn't warm, but the sun was out, and walking through town with its rays on my back I believed I could at least feel the approach of the coming warmer months. And not before time: I realised how the cold and drear had been getting to me. Perhaps it was time for a holiday? I imagined going to some of the places my father had gone. I could drink in the bars and cafés where he had sat writing in his notebooks, go for walks in the places he had wandered, and send him postcards that he would never receive. Perhaps I would even take some photographs with his camera. It was a nice idea. I knew I didn't have the energy: the previous few months had drained me dry. But walking through town in the cool spring sunshine I could at least imagine feeling like I might be up for something like that soon, and imagining doing so was a pleasure itself. Not now, maybe not this month or next, but soon. A fog was lifting. Spears of light had penetrated the gloom.

I took a balcony seat in a cafe overlooking Kensington Gardens, and watched pedestrians walk along the narrow road below, past little shops selling jewellery and clothes and vinyl records, shoes and ointments and remedies. After finishing my coffee, I looked at my watch, and was surprised that the hour had passed so quickly. I yawned. I was tired, I realised. I might have been dreaming. It was time to get the photographs, small prints on gloss paper and a CD of scans. Pursing my lips, I wondered what to do after that. I didn't want to go back to my little flat, didn't want to become stuck again. *No,* I thought, and startled myself by saying it aloud, as if someone else had uttered what I myself had only thought.

After paying the bill at the counter, I decided I would take the pictures to Dad's house, where I could look at them on the table in the dining room. I wouldn't open them before then. I hadn't been back since I had found the camera; I wondered if music videos still played to the empty living room. Clouds passed across the sun as I walked down to London Road. I should have brought a cardigan: it was chilly in the shade.

Dad's house, when I arrived, seemed shockingly quiet, as if someone had muted the sound of the building with a casual flick of a remote control. There was something unnatural about it, something inorganic. As if silence might bear qualities: a metallic silence, a cold silence, somehow extra-terrestrial, airless but laden with a strange density. Entering the living room, I saw that the television was not on. It wasn't on standby, either, its little red light glowing, which meant that it hadn't turned itself off to save energy: Rebecca had been here. Of course she had. I had no doubt that she would tell me off for having left it on, entertaining the empty room.

Whatever, I said to the empty room, and I sounded more like a petulant teenager than a forty-year-old.

Thinking of my sister, I felt a sudden lurch of sadness. I hadn't spoken to her since the funeral, and even then only very briefly. That wasn't my fault, but all the same the terse chill of our interactions that day began to upset me then, in my father's living room, though such concerns hadn't breached the walls of my grief that day in church; perhaps they had stood waiting at the door all along. I found myself taking a seat in my father's favoured basket chair as I thought about Rebecca. I wondered where she was. I wondered what she was doing then, at that exact moment in time. I wondered how she was feeling. As I have said, she was never one to broadcast her emotions, whether those of delight or dismay. She had been a taciturn, clever girl who had grown into a quietly judgemental woman. If her manner was the product of some great repression, unconscious or otherwise, then no symptoms of that effort ever seemed to trouble the calm surface of her personality. Ripples, perhaps, but no more, no waves. Her bond with our father had been private and intense, as if they were partisans in some opaque conspiracy. As I slumped into the chair, the grief for my father become grief for my sister, that grief now turned a third time, sinuous and wrenching, becoming grief for the relationship Rebecca and I might have enjoyed had our lives turned out otherwise. In my head it all traced back to that incident in Queen's Park. I remembered the still water of the pond, the unmoving reeds, the cold autumn air. Something had changed that day, and I realised then that I believed this whether or not my father and sister were correct in saying that it had never happened at all. Things do not need to happen to take effect. False memories have their own heft and force. But even then, in my heart of hearts, in my bones, in my gut, I did not believe that memory to be false.

I looked up, and realised I had been crying. I stood to my feet and went to take a tissue from the table in the dining room. Blowing my nose, I looked down and saw my handbag on the floor by the sofa, and remembered what I had come here to do. I put the tissue in the paper basket in the corner of the room, then took the pack of photographs from my bag.

The pictures came in a white envelope adorned with the blue Boots logo. I realised as I turned it over in my hands that I hadn't seen such packets in years. Dad had boxes of them, stowed away in the attic, Fuji packs and Kodak packs and packs from other brands, family photographs and the products of his own amateur photographic obsessions all commingled, stray prints and strips of negatives fallen loose in the stacks, the kind of chaotic family archive without index that all families of the late twentieth century possess, but I hadn't looked at these since the funeral, nor for years before. Holding that physical envelope, turning it over in my hands, it seemed like an artefact from another time, an earlier period of the world, and smiling to myself I supposed that it was. When I opened it, that smile first stiffened and then began to fade. It was replaced first by puzzlement, and then by shock.

People, many people, some of whom I vaguely recognised, others who were total strangers, in formal attire, milled around with glasses of wine and champagne in the grounds of some grand building. An event was being held. The strangeness of these images was already dawning on me, though it had yet to fasten onto any detail. It looked, I realised, as I continued flicking through, like a wedding in a film. There was something not quite real about the sunny day, the smiling people, the grand environs. I began to wonder when and where these pictures had been taken. It could have been a year ago; it could have been twenty years ago. People were dancing. There were members of the estate staff bearing trays of canapés and champagne. There were children I did not recognise running around a dance floor, careering after one another across the lawns of the estate. The sequence of the pictures seemed to disobey the proper chronology of a wedding day. Time was all mixed-up: late evening was followed by what could have been midday. As my confusion deepened, I tried to focus on the phones people were holding as a way to date the pictures, but to no avail: no one seemed to have one. Yet the pictures did not seem so old.

In the middle of the thirty-six exposures, and not at the end of the roll where it should have been located in the sequence, was the photograph I myself had taken in my father's dining room. The flash detonating in the dirty mirror. I turned from the printed picture to the strips of negatives to confirm its position in the order: perhaps someone at Boots had shuffled the deck. But no: it seemed to occupy the mid-point of the film roll. As I wondered how that frame could possibly have pictures from the wedding either side of it, something else struck me as stranger still: narrowing my eyes, I realised I could not see my own figure in the glass. The flash was not so bright that the room was obscured: I could see the dining table in front of which I had stood as I took the picture, the framed school portrait of Rebecca hanging on the wall above it, but in the place where I had stood I was nowhere to be seen.

Was my memory so faulty? I was sure I remembered precisely my position as I had taken the photo. I had stood in front of the table, facing the mirror. I had seen myself in the reflection and had shot directly ahead, a self-portrait obscured by

flash but not so totally transformed by it that my body might
have become transparent to the camera's indiscriminate gaze.
And yet there it was: there I was not. I moved on to the next
picture, and felt again as I had felt talking to Joanne outside
the church: removed suddenly from the course of things, in
some odd pocket of the world.

For now there she was, beautiful, smiling, in a white dress,
the bride of this strange wedding: Joanne, my father's carer.

No, I said aloud.

I went on to the next picture. Shock made me drop the
photographs.

No.

My father, the groom. My father kissing his bride. Joanne
cutting the cake while my father watched on with a smile.

He looked well. He could have been sixty, a healthy sixty.
He looked better than I could ever remember him looking. He
looked happy.

I stood up suddenly, not knowing what else to do, staring
down at the photographs now spread across the sofa, unassuming objects that now seemed to pulse with some demonic
charge, hoping that the intensity of my gaze might erase the
images from their thin substrate.

How could such a thing be?

I remembered what she had said to me outside the church,
word for word:

I almost said yes.

Almost.

Could she have lied?

I left the living room and stood for a moment, unsure what
to do, where to put myself, how to proceed, stalled, in the
silent hallway. Then I went into the kitchen, moving jerkily, as
if each individual faltering movement now required careful
deliberation. I poured a glass of water from the tap above the
sink. If moments before the photographs had seemed unreal,
a film set wedding, smiling cast in roles gathered in the

performance of a fiction, now it was my turn to feel false and impalpable.

The cold water helped. I poured a second and downed that too. Then I went back into the living room.

The photographs had not disappeared, as I had hoped they would. Frowning, I fumbled through my pockets for my phone, then remembered that it was in my handbag. Like a puppet jerked on wires I went to the bag, opened it, and rifled through. When I didn't find it immediately I raised it up, flipped it upside down, and emptied the contents onto the floor.

I picked the handset up, unlocked the screen, and scrolled quickly through my contacts list to the letter J.

By the time she finally answered I thought the call was about to switch to answerphone. For a brief moment I thought her voice was a recording telling me to leave a message after the beep.

Joanne? I said. Joanne?

Yes. Hello. How are you doing?

The normality of her tone almost knocked me sideways.

I'm... okay, I said. I had a question.

I was rushing ahead. I must have sounded strange.

Yes? What is it? Is everything okay?

Yes, everything's—everything's fine, thanks. I just had a question.

I closed my eyes.

What is it, honey?

After the funeral, you said something to me.

Right.

About a proposal. You said my father proposed to you.

She laughed. Oh, yes, she said. Yes, he did.

And you said you didn't accept.

Well, I thought about it...

But you didn't accept?

No, of course not, that would have been... why do you ask?

No reason, I said. I was just thinking about it. Thank you. So you never got married.

She laughed. I think we would have told you about it.

Of course. Okay. Thank you. Thank you.

Are you okay?

Yes, fine. Thanks. That was all. Bye now. Goodbye.

Are you—

Bye...

I put the phone in my pocket. I opened my eyes. The photographs had not moved from the sofa.

I sat back down and began to gather them up. I held them by the corners, not to avoid leaving fingerprints on the surface of the prints but because handling them seemed to carry some obscure risk, as if they might scald or shock or poison me. As if they were contaminated. Returned neatly to a pile, arranged in a sequence that made as much logical sense as the weird order of the individual frames on the six strips of colour negative film, I put them back into the pack, resealed the flap, put the pack into my bag and zipped it up. Then I shunted the bag with my foot into the space down by the sofa. I didn't want to see it. I could look at them again later and try to find some plausible reason for the obtuse fact of their existence while in a better frame of mind. Slumping back into the sofa, I closed my eyes.

Jesus, I said.

Somewhere a dog barked. A lorry rattled by outside.

Opening my eyes, I saw that the television was on. I frowned. I couldn't remember turning it on. An advert played, its frenzied attention-seeking vitiated by silence. I couldn't work out what it was trying to sell me. Whatever. I closed my eyes again.

A dog barked.

I recognised that bark.

I opened my eyes again and tried to listen out for a third bark, but none came. Standing to my feet, I realised that the sound felt as though it had come from somewhere within the house rather than the street outside. Feeling distant, somehow removed from myself and out of plumb with my surroundings, I smiled. It had sounded like Rorschach. Of course. Worzac. That silly dog.

I went to the window and peered outside. Since I had arrived at the house it had started to rain. It was a light rain now, a drizzle hazing the world of cars and houses and distant pedestrians, but something told me it would grow heavy soon. I wondered whether to go home. I didn't fancy walking in the rain. It occurred to me that I could stay the night here if I wanted to. There were still beds in our old bedrooms. Or I could sleep in my father's bed. I could stay the night and maybe I would feel better tomorrow. No doubt I would open the envelope of photographs from Boots and find images from my father's last holiday. As the rain began to pour and the little light in the sky outside began to fade, as that sense of my removal from the world grew slowly greater and as the languor of my mood became increasingly dreamlike, touched with a faint nausea, I decided that sleep would help me shake it off. I would stay the night. I would shake it off.

A dog barked.

I remembered talking to my sister through the Bluetooth connection in my car several months before.

Tired. Quite irritable.

I'll see him on Sunday. David and I can drive over after we've dropped the boys off at the club.

Rebecca?

Yes?

Do you remember the staircase in Dad's house, the one downstairs?

The staircase?

Yes, in the understairs cupboard.

The staircase in the cupboard? No.

Where did it go, Narnia?

Okay, don't worry.

Okay.

Speak to you soon.

Yes, speak to you soon.

Bye.

Goodbye.

Goodbye.

I found myself drifting out into the hallway. A bizarre calmness had settled over me. I smiled as I passed the photographs of Rebecca that lined the ground floor hall and for the first time in my life found myself wondering why they were all of Rebecca and none were of me. Strange, I thought, the things you never question. But the thought was too distant to be bothersome. I stopped at the top of the stairs, my hand lightly holding the banister, and closed my eyes. As I stood there I became aware of how exhausted I felt, how utterly depleted, my legs heavy, arms heavy, my head a dead weight upon my shoulders. I stood swaying. I was losing my purchase on the world. I knew that then, but it didn't bother me this time: it seemed no bad thing. The stairwell and the banister and the pictures of Rebecca began to recede around me. The house began to recede. I felt myself again in that odd pocket of the world. It was a gentle thing: it was not unpleasant. As if the world might ebb away. It was like falling asleep, after a long day, with your eyes open. You feel the first intimation of dreams. Things begin to detach from their proper place. The world begins to loosen up. The hard edges of bricks and banisters, floorboards and doorways, hinges and handles become smooth, become softer; the world becomes softer, less certain, more quietly suggestive. It becomes something that might respond to the unspoken questions of the heart.

I realised I was walking down the stairs. I was at the bottom of the stairwell now, my hand still on the banister.

The understairs cupboard door was open.

A dog barked.

vi.

I had lost my purchase on the world; I had lost my purchase on myself. In slow-motion freefall I realised I had forgotten my own name. It was not unpleasant. I felt unburdened, loosed from some hard point to which the accumulating events of my life had fastened me.

Worzak. Here, boy.

Inside the cupboard, a stairwell. The uncarpeted steps led upwards beyond the spot where I knew a hard brick wall had once stood; they led upwards, I saw, to a landing, bathed in diffuse light, that I recognised even as I saw it for the first time.

Rorschach came bounding with all the energy of a young pup, slipping here and there on the floorboards as he careered downstairs, his nails scratching the wood. He leapt up at me and as I caught him began to lick my hands. I realised I was laughing. He barked in response.

Worzak, I said, what on earth are you doing here?

I fell to my knees under the weight of his enthusiasm. I stroked him. His coat was immaculate. He wore no collar. He licked my hands, tail pounding the step. That enthusiasm. The smell of him. He barked again. I held him close to me, breathing him in.

Worzak, I said. You silly dog.

He barked again and clambered off my lap. He leapt up four of the steps and turned back to face me, barking once more. Then he skipped up another few steps and turned back again, imploring me to follow him. He tilted his head, quizzical.

Holding the banister, I pulled myself to my feet. I brushed my creased skirt smooth. Laughing still, weeping without self-consciousness or shame, I followed him, watching the happy wag of his tail as he passed up onto the landing and out of sight.

At the top of the stairs I stopped and closed my eyes. I understood. I think I understood. I took a deep breath and wondered whether when I opened my eyes I would find myself in my father's bed. I would have stayed the night. Morning would be at the window, soft light through white clouds, the parked cars and distant strangers, a cyclist going down the hill, a milk float trundling to a stop and a woman walking a dog that was not my dog, all softly luminous, a world of soft shadows and diffused light and muffled voices heard as if through the walls of terraced houses, through closed windows and latched doors.

But when I opened my eyes I remained on that strange landing: a place in a building that I recognised though I had never seen it before. The paint flaking from the scuffed skirting board. The walls painted the same grey as in the other rooms of the house I knew; the same uncarpeted floorboards, the same tatty rugs of autumnal hues, and the same creaking banister. Photographs of Rebecca unsmiling and reserved hung in black frames along the wall; I reached to straighten one that had fallen askew. In all of the pictures she seemed to retain some secret measure of herself, yielding only a thin exterior to the scrutiny of the lens. Then I stopped and looked back, to doublecheck. The steps led down to the basement where the shadows lay like a roiling fog. The understairs cupboard was a cupboard no more.

In the distance, through that stairwell, I heard the buzzing of a doorbell, and after a moment of no thinking realised it was the doorbell to this house. I didn't mind. Let them ring. The sound had the insistence of the faintest memory: the echo of a doorbell, recalled in dreams. It hailed you but it didn't matter if you answered. They could come back later or not at all. Why would I mind? They could try the telephone. They could push a note through the letterbox. I didn't mind.

Behind me, Worzak barked. I turned around and continued along the landing, my hand on the banister. He had disappeared into one of the rooms. A game: I would find my dog.

Instead I found my sister; she was seated on an old green sofa I faintly recognised but could not place, in a room that might have been a living room were the living room I had known for almost the entirety of my life not been located in another part of the house. I tried to think whereabouts I was: I had come down into the basement, then gone up another stairwell through what had once been an understairs cupboard, and was now—where? How many steps had I ascended? Had it not begun to corkscrew like the stairwell of a lighthouse as I had made my way to the top? Already I couldn't remember. The more I thought about it, the less sense it made. The house did not add up: within its walls, two plus two equalled five, or nine, or nine thousand and five. And so it was easier not to think. Looking at my sister sitting there, on a green sofa I had not seen since God knew when, except in some of the old photographs my father had kept in his study, I decided not to think: I had spent my life trying to understand, and where had it got me? Maybe the problem was precisely that I was always trying to understand. Maybe the problem was precisely that understanding always came too soon.

Rebecca, I said.

Rorschach was sat on the floor in front of her; Rebecca was leaning forward, stroking his head.

Hello, she replied.

A distant thought, like something tugging at me gently along a long thread: she was angry. She was furious I was here. I was not supposed to be here. I was trespassing. I had done something unspeakably wrong.

Well, she said. I suppose it was only a matter of time. I did try my best, though.

She looked up at me.

There was a blankness in her gaze, I saw then, an

uncertainty not of doubt but of a million possibilities suspended, a cloud of probabilities and no single option any
more persuasively real than any other. It was as if I could
see her thinking, cycling through these options, assessing
each, computing each, as if I could see the mechanisms at
play within the black boxes of her eyes. The hard edges of
bricks and banisters, floorboards and doorways, hinges and
handles had become smooth, become softer, the sum of infinite calculations, infinite options, infinite bets; the world had
become softer, less certain, more quietly suggestible: morning
at the window, soft light through white clouds, parked cars
and distant strangers, a cyclist going down the hill, a milk
float trundling to a stop and a woman walking a dog stopped
sniffing the foot of a streetlamp, all softly luminous, a world
of soft shadows and diffused light and muffled voices heard
as if through the walls of terraced houses, through closed
windows and latched doors and shuttered hearts. The world
was a receiver losing its signal, declining into noise. No signal
now, only noise, only interference. A cloud of possibilities,
each suspended on the cusp of their realisation. All this in
the blankness of her gaze.

How are you doing? she asked, and the ordinariness of her
tone of voice shocked me, and the shock was like the crack
and rumble of distant thunder in the sky.

Why don't you sit down?

Rorschach was looking at me, head tilted again in that
quizzical way. There was a rocking chair in the corner of
the room, I noticed now. I had seen it before: it had belonged
to my grandmother, my father's mother, a long time ago. I
had last seen it in photographs: I couldn't recall if I could remember seeing it or if what I recalled was seeing it in those
photographs. But sitting down, my body remembered the
feel of the polished wood against my thighs, my buttocks,
the wood of the chair's arms beneath my own arms and its
slats against my back: a bodily memory, as if objects leave

a negative imprint on your flesh, and now pressed together again the contours of each ease back into their proper place. I gripped the handles of the chair until my knuckles went white, then released them, and watched the colour return. I gripped the handles until my knuckles went white again, and then released.

Do you know where we are?

I didn't reply.

She pursed her lips. Rorschach trotted over and began nosing at my shoes.

It would help, said my sister, if I knew how much you know.

Was she telling me off?

I don't know anything, I said.

Ok. She began to nod, frowning; then the frown disappeared, but the nodding continued.

I asked you if you remembered the stairwell in the cupboard, I said.

Her nodding stopped.

You said you didn't.

Well, she said, weighing her words, I lied. I'm sorry.

It's okay.

I've been feeling so strange recently, I said. Not quite myself. Not quite real. Have you ever had that?

The look she gave me suggested I was mad to think that she had ever felt otherwise.

Since Dad died, I continued. Since before. I don't know.

As I spoke I began to feel as if I were overhearing my own voice, as if I had tapped a telephone and was quietly listening into the tinny murmur of familiar voices on the line, made strange by their travel across unfathomable distance.

I'm so tired. I laughed. I guess I've not been sleeping very well.

I looked up. I looked at my sister.

Where are we, Rebecca?

Don't you know?

She pursed her lips again, eyes narrowed, trying to suss me out. Did she think I was lying?

No. I don't know. I feel like I do, but I don't. I don't think I do.

There are places where the world grows thin, she said. Dad calls them the soft places. Where stable things become uncertain. It's an uncertainty one can exploit, if one needs to. But not without consequence.

What do you mean?

There is a cost. A certain price in stability to be paid. Dad found this place after mum died. Or perhaps he made it, in his grief—it's hard to say.

I nodded, as if I understood. Rorschach had fallen asleep at my foot. I rocked gently in the chair, as if this were a normal sororal conversation.

Someone called a name. My name. Rebecca looked up.

Sugar, she said, standing and walking quickly to the door of the room. Was Joanne here with you?

No.

Rorschach looked up at her. His tail beat the floor once.

Was there a wedding? I asked.

Rebecca looked back. She was thinking. She didn't reply.

From out on the landing I heard her call Joanne's name. I heard her feet on the rugs and the creaking floorboards beneath; I heard her heading down the stairs.

I sat back in the chair and closed my eyes.

You need to go.

I opened my eyes. I hadn't heard Rebecca return, but she was seated on the sofa opposite me again.

You need to go, she repeated. It isn't safe for you to be here.

I nodded. I don't want to.

It doesn't matter if you want to. Come on.

She stood up and moved toward me with purpose. I gazed

up at her. That blank look in her eyes. The calculation of infinite probabilities, the realisation of each a branching and re-branching of gnarled, snarling fates: of lives and lifelines and unexpected destinies.

Doesn't seem to be doing you any harm.

You don't know what you're talking about.

I felt her hand on my shoulder. I looked at her hand, frowning. Her grip began to tighten.

Stop that, I said. You owe it to me.

She leant down, placed her mouth near my ear, and said: Listen to me. You do not understand what you are dealing with. The longer you stay here the worse it will get. It's already happening. I can see it in you. Do you understand me?

I laughed. No, I said. No, I don't think that I do.

Rorschach, waking, looked up at Rebecca.

Come on. Get up. We're moving.

She reached under my arms with her hands and tried to lift me. I didn't resist, but I didn't try to make it easy for her, either. I was so profoundly tired. I wasn't sure I had the strength to move, whether she wanted me to or not. But Rebecca was stronger than I would have known.

You owe me an explanation, I said, as she manoeuvred me out of that second living room and onto the secret landing. The chair continued rocking in the empty room.

Narnia, I thought.

I'll explain later.

I pushed her away. No. You explain now.

She closed her eyes, dug into her temples with her fingers, leaving the crescent imprints of her fingernails in the skin; I saw the muscles in her jaw clench and unclench, clench and unclench.

Dad… came here sometime after mum died. He calls it the soft places.

Are there others?

Everywhere. He retreated here. That's what matters.

Ok.

Then there was… an accident. You would have to ask him. A long time ago.

I laughed again. Can't exactly do that.

She glanced at me, then looked away. There was an accident. One of us drowned. Nearly. He brought us here.

I pushed you into the pond, I said, beginning to understand.

No. Perhaps. In some versions. One of us nearly drowned. Or actually drowned. It doesn't matter now: here, we nearly drowned. He brought us here, afterwards.

I pushed you.

Did you?

I remember. I remember.

Perhaps. Or perhaps I pushed you. It doesn't matter. He brought us here.

How long were we here?

Months. He… I suppose he fixed us. Made us better again. Whichever one of us it was. At least that's what he thought he had done.

Do you remember?

No.

I remember.

So you keep telling me.

Rebecca closed her eyes. There was the cost, she continued. There was a bill to be paid.

A certain price in stability, I said. That's what you said.

I have spent my life, said Rebecca, opening her eyes, I have spent my life trying to hold things together. And now.

She looked at me and smiled sadly. Now it's coming apart.

I realised I was nodding, as if I understood. Perhaps if I pretended to understand, understanding would come: if I acted as though I believed, belief would come.

Rorschach, I said.

Rorschach was the first. Or the first successful attempt. At least to some degree. The first was... somewhat botched.

I glanced up, looked down the landing. Rorschach had trotted over to the doorway leading back down into the basement and the house as I had known it. Something had piqued his attention. He barked and looked back at us.

I wondered about the first attempt. If Rorschach was the second, Rebecca or I were the third. And the first?

And Dad? I said, burying that thought. Is Dad here too? Like Rorschach. Fucking Rorschach. Christ.

I started to laugh again, and then to cry again, and before long I couldn't tell one from the other.

Christ.

Rebecca was looking at me, thinking.

Well? I said, suddenly impatient, suddenly angry at her, at our father, at all of them, for all of it, for everything: all the years of secrecy and deceit, all the times I had found myself on the outside of their little world, which was also my world, the only world that I had, peering in, simultaneously within and without. I remembered what she had said, and the memory might have echoed on the landing for all I could tell: I have spent my life, my life, holding things together. And now. Now it's all coming apart.

Answer me, I murmured. Answer me.

In a manner of speaking.

Oh for fuck's sake. Is he here? Can I see him? Or do I have to stand here and just listen to your evasions?

Rorschach barked again.

Something shifted in Rebecca's eyes: a renewed steeliness. She did not like to be sworn at. I knew that. I knew she thought me petulant—she always had. But a little swearing, a little petulance—was it not in order? Was it not the time and place? It seemed to me to be very much in order, very much the time and place.

No, Rebecca said at last. No. As I said. You have to go. It

isn't safe. The longer you remain here, the worse it gets.

Her hand on my hip, manoeuvring me. I pushed her away. Don't. Don't you dare.

Rorschach barked again. Exasperated, he barked once more, then scrambled forward without us, running down the stairs.

Panicking, Rebecca hurried after him. She swore. She never swore. Come with me, she said. Come on.

I made to go with her, hurrying to the end of the landing, where I stopped as she clattered downstairs, calling for Rorschach. At the same time I heard someone else call a name. My name. It was Joanne. She had returned.

A few steps down, I paused and listened closely. I could hear the murmur of voices. Straining, I tried to be silent, but the beating of my heart was loud and my breathing was heavy.

What are these, Rebecca? I heard her say. What the actual hell are these?

Had I left the photographs out? I tried to remember. Had I not put them back in the packet and then put the packet in my bag, and pushed the bag with my foot down beside the sofa? I couldn't recall. Had I left them spread out across the pillows? Had Joanne seen them from the window? I thought of the way I had handled them, only holding the edges, as if they might scald or poison me; I thought of that poison leaking out, spreading, seeping into things, contaminating the world with rank absurdity.

My sister was speaking. Her voice was low and insistent and I couldn't make out her words.

Your sister rang me, I heard Joanne say, much louder, half-hysterical, half-laughing. That's why I came here. Is she here? I just had the weirdest feeling...

Rebecca raised her voice. No, she said. Joanne—

I heard her footsteps on the other stairs. She was down in the basement. She called a name. My name. Are you here?

she yelled.

Rorschach was barking, excited. I heard him scramble down the stairs behind her. I heard her muttering to herself.

Joanne—

Her face appeared in the door of the cupboard below, curious, confused, peering round. She noticed the steps leading upwards and started to frown.

Joanne, I said.

Hi, she said, and her tone of voice was so ordinary I almost laughed. Well I've never seen these stairs before, she said. Wasn't this bricked over?

She gripped the handle of the banister and took a step up. She didn't seem to trust the banister: it creaked badly with her weight. She seemed to be testing the steps, unsure she could trust them. She had some of the photographs in her hand. She held them up to me.

Can you explain these? she asked.

You told me he proposed to you.

She laughed, taking the steps one at a time, as if she thought they might give way were she to move too quickly. Rorschach appeared at the foot of the stairwell, tail wagging, followed quickly by Rebecca.

I have spent my life, my life, holding things together.

Yes, but I didn't accept. I didn't—Jesus...

Joanne, it isn't safe up there, said Rebecca. Come back down.

It's strange, said Joanne, I don't remember this staircase. Was it always here? Surely...

She was addressing me purposefully, pointedly ignoring Rebecca.

Joanne.

She started laughing as she reached the top of the stairs, stepping up onto the landing. Rorschach scrambled up behind her, slipped past her legs, and leapt up at me. Then he barked.

Joanne? I asked, beginning to worry: she had stopped stock still on the landing. Though she was facing me, her gaze was fixed a way behind me. I realised then that I could not bring myself to turn around. Whatever was there, Rorschach had seen it too: he barked a second time, and then was quiet.

Joanne started to frown.

Who is that? she asked, slowing raising a hand to point.

Rorschach was the first, Rebecca had said. Or the first successful attempt. At least to some degree.

My breathing had become shallow. A strange dread began to twist in my stomach, in my gut. Rebecca emerged from behind Joanne, exasperation in her expression giving way to dismay as her gaze fell upon the thing behind me. Rorschach barked again.

And now. Now it's all coming apart.

Hello, Rachel, said my mother, her voice creaking in the silence that had filled that unlikely landing.

I remembered that voice, remembered that smell, felt her cool hand gently grip my shoulder, and in that moment, after everything, I finally lost my purchase on the world.

Publication History

"New To it All" is original to this collection.
"Like a Zip" is original to this collection.
"Hand-Me-Down" is original to this collection.
"Holes" is original to this collection.
"I Would Haunt You if I Could" is original to this collection.
"Company" is original to this collection.
"I Told You Not to Go" is original to this collection.
"You Know What to Do" is original to this collection.

"Dollface" was first published in *Shadows & Tall Trees, Vol. 8*, edited by Michael Kelly (Undertow Publications) 2020.
"Out of the Blue" was first published in *Black Static* #64, 2018.
"The Turn" was first published in *Black Static* #74, 2020.
"Lucida" was first published in *Oculus Sinister*, edited by CM Muller (Chthonic Matter Press) 2020.
"Sister" was first published in *Black Static* #31, 2012.
"Other Houses" was first published in *Black Static* #71, 2019.

Acknowledgements

With thanks to Michael Kelly, Carolyn Macdonell-Kelly, and Courtney Kelly. This collection is immeasurably better for their work on it, and I am so grateful and pleased to have joined Undertow's list. Additional thanks to Andy Cox, at TTA Press, for publishing several of these pieces in *Black Static* over the years.

About the Author

Seán Padraic Birnie is a writer and photographer from Brighton. He holds a B.A. from Manchester Metropolitan University in English Literature and Creative Writing, and an M.A. in Photography from the University of Brighton, where he works as a Technical Demonstrator on the photography courses. His short fiction has appeared in venues such as *Black Static*, *BFS Horizons*, *Litro*, and *Shadows & Tall Trees*, and his writing on photography has appeared in scholarly journals and artists' books. For more info, see: seanbirnie.com.

CPSIA information can be obtained
at www.ICGtesting.com
Printed in the USA
LVHW031727280421
685863LV00007B/1250